Grimm's Fairy Tales

DOVER · THRIFT · EDITIONS

Grimm's Fairy Tales

JACOB AND WILHELM GRIMM

Translated by
Margaret Hunt

DOVER PUBLICATIONS, INC.
Mineola, New York

DOVER THRIFT EDITIONS

GENERAL EDITOR: MARY CAROLYN WALDREP

EDITOR OF THIS VOLUME: ALICE GLEASON

Bibliographical Note

This Dover edition, first published in 2007, is an unabridged republication of forty-three stories from *Grimm's Household Tales, with the Author's Notes,* published by G. Bell and Sons, London, in 1884.

Library of Congress Cataloging-in-Publication Data

Kinder- und Hausmärchen. English. Selections

Grimm's fairy tales / Jacob and Wilhelm Grimm ; translated by Margaret Hunt.
p. cm. — (Dover thrift editions)

"This Dover edition, first published in 2007, is an unabridged republication of forty-three stories from Grimm's household tales, with the author's notes, published by G. Bell and Sons, London, in 1884."

ISBN-13: 978-0-486-45656-0

ISBN-10: 0-486-45656-0

1. Fairy tales—Germany. I. Grimm, Jacob, 1785–1863. II. Grimm, Wilhelm, 1786–1859. III. Hunt, Alfred William, Mrs., 1831–1912. IV. Title.

GR166.K53213 2007

398.20943—dc22

2007005341

Manufactured in the United States by Courier Corporation

45656002

www.doverpublications.com

Publisher's Note

Two impoverished lads find a magical key that brings them untold riches . . .

Their early life echoed one of their own stories. Young Jacob and Wilhelm Grimm were the sons of a widow in reduced circumstances, and the key was a teacher's library, filled with centuries'-old books that inspired the brothers' lifelong passion for folktales.

Now ranking behind only Shakespeare and the Bible in sales, *Grimm's Fairy Tales* (originally titled *Children's and Household Tales*) was originally published for adults, with scholarly footnotes, in 1812. The brothers had collected stories from various oral sources, primarily women, and saw their book as a patriotic effort, aimed at defending German folklore in the Napoleonic era. These age-old tales at first retained the harsh details of medieval life—abandoned orphans, abject poverty and draconian punishments. Then, as the market for European children's literature developed, the Grimms tempered and gentled their narratives, replacing the footnotes with illustrations, while keeping the lessons of manners and virtue intact.

But the stories in this book are infinitely richer than folklore or morality tales. Translated into more than 160 languages, they have been adapted by Disney, Japanese theme parks, and almost every medium from opera to advertising. With ease, they leapfrog over cultural barriers, providing comfort, encouragement, stimulation and *satisfaction* to children and adults from Siberia to Tierra del Fuego. After all, how can anyone, child or adult, *not* cheer at the end of "The Wolf and the Seven Little Kids" when the young goats emerge from the sleeping wolf's belly and fill it with big stones? Don't we all smile when the duck carries Hänsel and Grethel, one at a time, across the river? And doesn't the taut suspense of "The Robber Bridegroom" rival any edge-of-the-chair thriller, as the miller's daughter escapes, then entraps, her murderous fiancé? Today, the Grimm brothers' stories live on in children's hearts and minds, their appeal undiminished after nearly two hundred years.

Contents

Grimm's Fairy Tales

THE FROG-KING, OR IRON HENRY

IN OLD times when wishing still helped one, there lived a king whose daughters were all beautiful, but the youngest was so beautiful that the sun itself, which has seen so much, was astonished whenever it shone in her face. Close by the King's castle lay a great dark forest, and under an old lime-tree in the forest was a well, and when the day was very warm, the King's child went out into the forest and sat down by the side of the cool fountain, and when she was dull she took a golden ball, and threw it up on high and caught it, and this ball was her favorite plaything.

Now it so happened that on one occasion the princess's golden ball did not fall into the little hand which she was holding up for it, but on to the ground beyond, and rolled straight into the water. The King's daughter followed it with her eyes, but it vanished, and the well was deep, so deep that the bottom could not be seen. On this she began to cry, and cried louder and louder, and could not be comforted. And as she thus lamented some one said to her, "What ails thee, King's daughter? Thou weepest so that even a stone would show pity." She looked round to the side from whence the voice came, and saw a frog stretching forth its thick, ugly head from the water. "Ah! old water-splasher, is it thou?" said she; "I am weeping for my golden ball, which has fallen into the well."

"Be quiet, and do not weep," answered the frog, "I can help thee, but what wilt thou give me if I bring thy plaything up again?" "Whatever thou wilt have, dear frog," said she—"my clothes, my pearls and jewels, and even the golden crown which I am wearing."

The frog answered, "I do not care for thy clothes, thy pearls and jewels, or thy golden crown, but if thou wilt love me and let me be thy companion and play-fellow, and sit by thee at thy little table, and eat off thy little golden plate, and drink out of thy little cup, and sleep in thy little bed—if thou wilt promise me this I will go down below, and bring thee thy golden ball up again."

"Oh, yes," said she, "I promise thee all thou wishest, if thou wilt but bring me my ball back again." She, however, thought, "How the silly frog does talk! He lives in the water with the other frogs, and croaks, and can be no companion to any human being!"

But the frog when he had received this promise, put his head into the water and sank down, and in a short time came swimming up again with the ball in his mouth, and threw it on the grass. The King's daughter was delighted to see her pretty plaything once more, and picked it up, and ran away with it. "Wait, wait," said the frog. "Take me with thee. I can't run as thou canst." But what did it avail him to scream his croak, croak, after her, as loudly as he could? She did not listen to it, but ran home and soon forgot the poor frog, who was forced to go back into his well again.

The next day when she had seated herself at table with the King and all the courtiers, and was eating from her little golden plate, something came creeping splish splash, splish splash, up the marble staircase, and when it had got to the top, it knocked at the door and cried, "Princess, youngest princess, open the door for me." She ran to see who was outside, but when she opened the door, there sat the frog in front of it. Then she slammed the door to, in great haste, sat down to dinner again, and was quite frightened. The King saw plainly that her heart was beating violently, and said, "My child, what art thou so afraid of? Is there perchance a giant outside who wants to carry thee away?" "Ah, no," replied she. "It is no giant, but a disgusting frog."

"What does the frog want with thee?" "Ah, dear father, yesterday as I was in the forest sitting by the well, playing, my golden ball fell into the water. And because I cried so the frog brought it out again for me, and because he insisted so on it, I promised him he should be my companion, but I never thought he would be able to come out of his water! And now he is outside there, and wants to come in to me."

In the meantime it knocked a second time, and cried,

"Princess! youngest princess!
Open the door for me!
Dost thou not know what thou saidst to me
Yesterday by the cool waters of the fountain?
Princess, youngest princess!
Open the door for me!"

Then said the King, "That which thou hast promised must thou perform. Go and let him in." She went and opened the door, and the frog hopped in and followed her, step by step, to her chair. There he sat and cried, "Lift me up beside thee." She delayed, until at last the King commanded her to do it. When the frog was once on the chair he wanted to be on the table, and when he was on the table he said, "Now, push thy little golden plate nearer to me that we may eat together." She did this, but it was easy to see that she did not do it willingly. The frog enjoyed what he ate, but almost every mouthful she took choked her. At length he said, "I have eaten and am satisfied; now I am tired, carry me into thy little room and make thy little silken bed ready, and we will both lie down and go to sleep."

The King's daughter began to cry, for she was afraid of the cold frog which she did not like to touch, and which was now to sleep in her pretty, clean little bed. But the King grew angry and said, "He who helped thee when thou wert in trouble ought not afterwards to be despised by thee." So she took hold of the frog with two fingers, carried him upstairs, and put him in a corner. But when she was in bed he crept to her and said, "I am tired, I want to sleep as well as thou, lift me up or I will tell thy father." Then she was terribly angry, and took him up and threw him with all her might against the wall. "Now, thou wilt be quiet, odious frog," said she. But when he fell down he was no frog but a King's son with beautiful kind eyes. He by her father's will was now her dear companion and husband. Then he told her how he had been bewitched by a wicked witch, and how no one could have delivered him from the well but herself, and that to-morrow they would go together into his kingdom. Then they went to sleep, and next morning when the sun awoke them, a carriage came driving up with eight white horses, which had white ostrich feathers on their heads, and were harnessed with golden chains, and behind stood the young King's servant Faithful Henry. Faithful Henry had been so unhappy when his master was changed into a frog, that he had caused three iron bands to be laid round his heart, lest it should burst with grief and sadness. The carriage was to conduct the young King into his kingdom. Faithful Henry helped them both in, and placed himself behind again, and was full of joy because of this deliverance. And when they had driven a part of the way the King's son heard a cracking behind him as if something had broken. So he turned round and cried, "Henry, the carriage is breaking."

"No, master, it is not the carriage. It is a band from my heart, which was put there in my great pain when you were a frog and imprisoned in the well." Again and once again while they were on their way something cracked, and each time the King's son thought the carriage was breaking; but it was only the bands which were springing from the heart of faithful Henry because his master was set free and was happy.

CAT AND MOUSE IN PARTNERSHIP

A CERTAIN cat had made the acquaintance of a mouse, and had said so much to her about the great love and friendship she felt for her, that at length the mouse agreed that they should live and keep house together. "But we must make a provision for winter, or else we shall suffer from hunger," said the cat, "and you, little mouse, cannot venture everywhere, or you will be caught in a trap some day." The good advice was followed, and a pot of fat was bought, but they did not know where to put it. At length, after much consideration, the cat said, "I know no place where it will be better stored up than in the church, for no one dares take anything away from there. We will set it beneath the altar, and not touch it until we are really in need of it." So the pot was placed in safety, but it was not long before the cat had a great longing for it, and said to the mouse, "I want to tell you something, little mouse; my cousin has brought a little son into the world, and has asked me to be godmother; he is white with brown spots, and I am to hold him at the christening. Let me go out to-day, and you look after the house by yourself." "Yes, yes," answered the mouse, "by all means go, and if you get anything very good, think of me, I should like a drop of sweet red christening wine too." All this, however, was untrue; the cat had no cousin, and had not been asked to be godmother. She went straight to the church, stole to the pot of fat, began to lick at it, and licked the top of the fat off. Then she took a walk upon the roofs of the town, looked out for opportunities, and then stretched herself in the sun, and licked her lips whenever she thought of the pot of fat, and not until it was evening did she return home. "Well, here you are again," said the mouse, "no doubt you have had a merry day." "All went off well," answered the cat. "What name did they give the child?" "Top off!" said the cat quite coolly. "Top off!" cried the mouse, "that is a very odd and uncommon name, is it a usual one in your family?" "What does it signify," said the cat, "it is no worse than Crumb-stealer, as your god-children are called."

Before long the cat was seized by another fit of longing. She said to the mouse, "You must do me a favour, and once more manage the house for a day alone. I am again asked to be godmother, and, as the child has a white ring round its neck, I cannot refuse." The good mouse consented, but the cat crept behind the town walls to the church, and devoured half the pot of fat. "Nothing ever seems so good as what one keeps to oneself," said she, and was quite satisfied with her day's work. When she went home the mouse inquired, "And what was this child christened?" "Half-done," answered the cat. "Half-done! What are you saying? I never heard the name in my life, I'll wager anything it is not in the calendar!"

The cat's mouth soon began to water for some more licking. "All good things go in threes," said she, "I am asked to stand godmother again. The child is quite black, only it has white paws, but with that exception, it has not a single white hair on its whole body; this only happens once every few years, you will let me go, won't you?" "Top-off! Half-done!" answered the mouse, "they are such odd names, they make me very thoughtful." "You sit at home," said the cat, "in your dark-grey fur coat and long tail, and are filled with fancies, that's because you do not go out in the daytime." During the cat's absence the mouse cleaned the house, and put it in order, but the greedy cat entirely emptied the pot of fat. "When everything is eaten up one has some peace," said she to herself, and well filled and fat she did not return home till night. The mouse at once asked what name had been given to the third child. "It will not please you more than the others," said the cat. "He is called All-gone." "All-gone," cried the mouse, "that is the most suspicious name of all! I have never seen it in print. All-gone; what can that mean?" and she shook her head, curled herself up, and lay down to sleep.

From this time forth no one invited the cat to be godmother, but when the winter had come and there was no longer anything to be found outside, the mouse thought of their provision, and said, "Come, cat, we will go to our pot of fat which we have stored up for ourselves—we shall enjoy that." "Yes," answered the cat, "you will enjoy it as much as you would enjoy sticking that dainty tongue of yours out of the window." They set out on their way, but when they arrived, the pot of fat certainly was still in its place, but it was empty. "Alas!" said the mouse, "now I see what has happened, now it comes to light! You a true friend! You have devoured all when you were standing godmother. First top off, then half done, then—" "Will you hold your tongue," cried the cat, "one word more, and I will eat you too." "All gone" was already on the poor mouse's lips; scarcely had she spoken it before the cat sprang on her, seized her, and swallowed her down. Verily, that is the way of the world.

THE STORY OF THE YOUTH WHO WENT FORTH TO LEARN WHAT FEAR WAS

A CERTAIN father had two sons, the elder of whom was sharp and sensible, and could do everything, but the younger was stupid and could neither learn nor understand anything, and when people saw him they said, "There's a fellow who will give his father some trouble!" When anything had to be done, it was always the elder who was forced to do it; but if his father bade him fetch anything when it was late, or in the night-time, and the way led through the churchyard, or any other dismal place, he answered "Oh, no, father, I'll not go there, it makes me shudder!" for he was afraid. Or when stories were told by the fire at night which made the flesh creep, the listeners often said, "Oh, it makes us shudder!" The younger sat in a corner and listened with the rest of them, and could not imagine what they could mean. "They are always saying, 'It makes me shudder, it makes me shudder!' It does not make me shudder," thought he. "That, too, must be an art of which I understand nothing."

Now it came to pass that his father said to him one day, "Hearken to me, thou fellow in the corner there, thou art growing tall and strong, and thou too must learn something by which thou canst earn thy living. Look how thy brother works, but thou dost not even earn thy salt." "Well, father," he replied, "I am quite willing to learn something—indeed, if it could but be managed, I should like to learn how to shudder. I don't understand that at all yet." The elder brother smiled when he heard that, and thought to himself, "Good God, what a blockhead that brother of mine is! He will never be good for anything as long as he lives. He who wants to be a sickle must bend himself betimes."

The father sighed, and answered him, "Thou shalt soon learn what it is to shudder, but thou wilt not earn thy living by that."

Soon after this the sexton came to the house on a visit, and the father bewailed his trouble, and told him how his younger son was so backward in every respect that he knew nothing and learnt nothing. "Just think," said he, "when I asked him how he was going to earn his bread, he actually wanted to learn to shudder." "If that be all," replied the sexton, "he can learn that with me. Send him to me, and I will soon polish him." The father was glad to do it, for he thought, "It will train the boy a little." The sexton therefore took him into his house, and he had to ring the bell. After a day or two, the sexton awoke him at midnight, and bade him arise and go up into the church tower and ring the bell. "Thou shalt soon learn what shuddering is," thought he, and secretly went there before him; and when the boy was at the top of the tower and turned round, and was just going to take hold of the bell rope, he saw a white figure standing on the stairs opposite to the sounding hole. "Who is there?" cried he, but the figure made no reply, and did not move or stir. "Give an answer," cried the boy, "or take thy self off, thou hast no business here at night."

The sexton, however, remained standing motionless that the boy might think he was a ghost. The boy cried a second time, "What dost thou want here?—speak if thou art an honest fellow, or I will throw thee down the steps!" The sexton thought, "he can't intend to be as bad as his words," uttered no sound and stood as if he were made of stone. Then the boy called to him for the third time, and as that was also to no purpose, he ran against him and pushed the ghost down the stairs, so that it fell down ten steps and remained lying there in a corner. Thereupon he rang the bell, went home, and without saying a word went to bed, and fell asleep. The sexton's wife waited a long time for her husband, but he did not come back. At length she became uneasy, and wakened the boy, and asked, "Dost thou not know where my husband is? He climbed up the tower before thou didst." "No, I don't know," replied the boy, "but some one was standing by the sounding hole on the other side of the steps, and as he would neither give an answer nor go away, I took him for a scoundrel, and threw him downstairs, just go there and you will see if it was he. I should be sorry if it were." The woman ran away and found her husband, who was lying moaning in the corner, and had broken his leg.

She carried him down, and then with loud screams she hastened to the boy's father. "Your boy," cried she, "has been the cause of a great misfortune! He has thrown my husband down the steps and made him break his leg. Take the good-for-nothing fellow away from our house." The father was terrified, and ran thither and scolded the boy. "What wicked tricks are these?" said he, "the devil must have put this into thy head." "Father," he replied, "do listen to me. I am quite innocent. He was standing there by night like one who is intending to do some evil. I did not know who it was, and I entreated him three times either to speak or to go away." "Ah," said the father, "I have nothing but unhappiness with you. Go out of my sight. I will see thee no more."

"Yes, father, right willingly, wait only until it is day. Then will I go forth and learn how to shudder, and then I shall, at any rate, understand one art which will support me." "Learn what thou wilt," spake the father, "it is all the same to me. Here are fifty thalers for thee. Take these and go into the wide world, and tell no one from whence thou comest, and who is thy father, for I have reason to be ashamed of thee." "Yes, father, it shall be as you will. If you desire nothing more than that, I can easily keep it in mind."

When day dawned, therefore, the boy put his fifty thalers into his pocket, and went forth on the great highway, and continually said to himself, "If I could but shudder! If I could but shudder!" Then a man approached who heard this conversation which the youth was holding with himself, and when they had walked a little farther to where they could see the gallows, the man said to him, "Look, there is the tree where seven men have married the ropemaker's daughter, and are now learning how to fly. Sit down below it, and wait till night comes, and thou wilt soon learn how to shudder." "If that is all that is wanted," answered the youth, "it is easily done; but if I learn how to shudder as quickly as that, thou shalt have my fifty thalers. Just come back to me early in the morning." Then the youth went to the gallows, sat down below it, and waited till evening came. And as he was cold, he lighted himself a fire, but at midnight the wind blew so sharply that in spite of his fire, he could not get warm. And as the wind knocked the hanged men against each other, and they moved backwards and forwards, he thought to himself, "Thou shiverest below by the fire, but how those up above must freeze and suffer!" And as he felt pity for them, he raised the ladder, and climbed up, unbound one of them after the other, and brought down all seven. Then he stirred the fire, blew it, and set them all round it to warm themselves. But they sat there and did not stir, and the fire caught their clothes. So he said, "Take care, or I will hang you up again." The dead men, however, did not hear, but were quite silent, and let their rags go on burning. On this he grew angry, and said, "If you will not take care, I cannot help you, I will not be burnt with you," and he hung them up again each in his turn. Then he sat down by his fire and fell asleep, and the next morning the man came to him and wanted to have the fifty thalers, and said, "Well, dost thou know how to shudder?" "No," answered he, "how was I to get to know? Those fellows up there did not open their mouths, and were so stupid that they let the few old rags which they had on their bodies get burnt." Then the man saw that he would not carry away the fifty thalers that day, and went away saying, "One of this kind has never come in my way before."

The youth likewise went his way, and once more began to mutter to himself, "Ah, if I could but shudder! Ah, if I could but shudder!" A waggoner who was striding behind him heard that and asked, "Who art thou?" "I know not," answered the youth. Then the waggoner asked, "From whence comest thou?" "I know not." "Who is thy father?" "That I may not tell thee." "What is it that thou art always muttering between thy teeth." "Ah," replied the youth, "I do so wish I could shudder, but no one can teach me how to do it." "Give up thy foolish chatter," said the waggoner. "Come, go with me, I will see about a place for thee." The youth went with the waggoner, and in the evening they arrived at an inn where they wished to pass the night. Then at the entrance of the room the youth again said quite loudly, "If I could but shudder! If I could but shudder!" The host who heard that, laughed and said, "If that is your desire, there ought to be a good opportunity for you here." "Ah, be silent," said the hostess, "so many inquisitive persons have already lost their lives, it would be a pity and a shame if such beautiful eyes as these should never see the daylight again."

But the youth said, "However difficult it may be, I will learn it, and for this purpose indeed have I journeyed forth." He let the host have no rest, until the latter told him, that not far from thence stood a haunted castle where any one could very easily learn what shuddering was, if he would but watch in it for three nights. The King had promised that he who would venture should have his daughter to wife, and she was the most beautiful maiden the sun shone on. Great treasures likewise lay in the castle, which were guarded by evil spirits, and these treasures would then be freed, and would make a poor man rich enough. Already many men had gone into the castle, but as yet none had come out again. Then the youth went next morning to the King, and said, if he were allowed he would watch three nights in the that enchanted castle. The King looked at him, and as the youth pleased him, he said, "Thou mayest ask for three things to take into the castle with thee, but they must be things without life." Then he answered, "Then I ask for a fire, a turning lathe, and a cutting-board with the knife." The King had these things carried into the castle for him during the day. When night was drawing near, the youth went up and made himself a bright fire in one of the rooms, placed the cutting-board and knife beside it, and seated himself by the turning-lathe. "Ah, if I could but shudder!" said he, "but I shall not learn it here either." Towards midnight he was about to poke his fire, and as he was blowing it, something cried suddenly from one corner, "Au, miau!

how cold we are!" "You simpletons!" cried he, "what are you crying about? If you are cold, come and take a seat by the fire and warm yourselves." And when he had said that, two great black cats came with one tremendous leap and sat down on each side of him, and looked savagely at him with their fiery eyes. After a short time, when they had warmed themselves, they said, "Comrade, shall we have a game at cards?" "Why not?" he replied, "but just show me your paws." Then they stretched out their claws. "Oh," said he, "what long nails you have! Wait, I must first cut them for you." Thereupon he seized them by the throats, put them on the cutting-board and screwed their feet fast. "I have looked at your fingers," said he, "and my fancy for card-playing has gone," and he struck them dead and threw them out into the water. But when he had made away with these two, and was about to sit down again by his fire, out from every hole and corner came black cats and black dogs with red-hot chains, and more and more of them came until he could no longer stir, and they yelled horribly, and got on his fire, pulled it to pieces, and tried to put it out. He watched them for a while quietly, but at last when they were going too far, he seized his cutting-knife, and cried, "Away with ye, vermin," and began to cut them down. Part of them ran away, the others he killed, and threw out into the fish-pond. When he came back he blew up the embers of his fire again and warmed himself. And as he thus sat, his eyes would keep open no longer, and he felt a desire to sleep. Then he looked round and saw a great bed in the corner. "That is the very thing for me," said he, and got into it. When he was just going to shut his eyes, however, the bed began to move of its own accord, and went over the whole of the castle. "That's right," said he, "but go faster." Then the bed rolled on as if six horses were harnessed to it, up and down, over thresholds and steps, but suddenly hop, hop, it turned over upside down, and lay on him like a mountain. But he threw quilts and pillows up in the air, got out and said, "Now any one who likes, may drive," and lay down by his fire, and slept till it was day. In the morning the King came, and when he saw him lying there on the ground, he thought the evil spirits had killed him and he was dead. Then said he, "After all it is a pity,—he is a handsome man." The youth heard it, got up, and said, "It has not come to that yet." Then the King was astonished, but very glad, and asked how he had fared. "Very well indeed," answered he; "one night is past, the two others will get over likewise." Then he went to the innkeeper, who opened his eyes very wide, and said, "I never expected to see thee alive again! Hast thou learnt how to shudder yet?" "No," said he, "it is all in vain. If some one would but tell me!"

The second night he again went up into the old castle, sat down by the fire, and once more began his old song, "If I could but shudder." When midnight came, an uproar and noise of tumbling about was heard; at first it was low, but it grew louder and louder. Then it was quiet for awhile, and at length with a loud scream, half a man came down the chimney and fell before him. "Hollo!" cried he, "another half belongs to this. This is too little!" Then the uproar began again, there was a roaring and howling, and the other half fell down likewise. "Wait," said he, "I will just blow up the fire a little for thee." When he had done that and looked round again, the two pieces were joined together, and a frightful man was sitting in his place. "That is no part of our bargain," said the youth, "the bench is mine." The man wanted to push him away; the youth, however, would not allow that, but thrust him off with all his strength, and seated himself again in his own place. Then still more men fell down, one after the other; they brought nine dead men's legs and two skulls, and set them up and played at nine-pins with them. The youth also wanted to play and said "Hark you, can I join you?" "Yes, if thou hast any money." "Money enough," replied he, "but your balls are not quite round." Then he took the skulls and put them in the lathe and turned them till they were round. "There, now, they will roll better!" said he. "Hurrah! Now it goes merrily!" He played with them and lost some of his money, but when it struck twelve, everything vanished from his sight. He lay down and quietly fell asleep. Next morning the King came to enquire after him. "How has it fared with thee this time?" asked he. "I have been playing at nine-pins," he answered, "and have lost a couple of farthings." "Hast thou not shuddered then?" "Eh, what?" said he, "I have made merry. If I did but know what it was to shudder!"

The third night he sat down again on his bench and said quite sadly, "If I could but shudder." When it grew late, six tall men came in and brought a coffin. Then said he, "Ha, ha, that is certainly my little cousin, who only died a few days ago," and he beckoned with his finger, and cried "Come, little cousin, come." They placed the coffin on the ground, but he went to it and took the lid off, and a dead man lay therein. He felt his face, but it was cold as ice. "Stop," said he, "I will warm thee a little," and went to the fire and warmed his hand and laid it on the dead man's face, but he remained cold. Then he took him out, and sat down by the fire and laid him on his breast and rubbed his arms that the blood might circulate again. As this also did no good, he thought to himself "When two people lie in bed together, they warm each other," and carried him to the bed, covered him over and lay down by him. After a short time the dead man became warm too, and began to move. Then said the youth, "See, little cousin, have I not warmed thee?" The dead man, however, got up and cried, "Now will I strangle thee."

"What!" said he, "is that the way thou thankest me? Thou shalt at once go into thy coffin again," and he took him up, threw him into it, and shut the lid. Then came the six men and carried him away again. "I cannot manage to shudder," said he. "I shall never learn it here as long as I live."

Then a man entered who was taller than all others, and looked terrible. He was old, however, and had a long white beard. "Thou wretch," cried he, "thou shalt soon learn what it is to shudder, for thou shalt die." "Not so fast," replied the youth. "If I am to die, I shall have to have a say in it." "I will soon seize thee," said the fiend. "Softly, softly, do not talk so big. I am as strong as thou art, and perhaps even stronger." "We shall see," said the old man. "If thou art stronger, I will let thee go—come, we will try." Then he led him by dark passages to a smith's forge, took an axe, and with one blow struck an anvil into the ground. "I can do that better still," said the youth, and went to the other anvil. The old man placed himself near and wanted to look on, and his white beard hung down. Then the youth seized the axe, split the anvil with one blow, and struck the old man's beard in with it. "Now I have thee," said the youth. "Now it is thou who wilt have to die." Then he seized an iron bar and beat the old man till he moaned and entreated him to stop, and he would give him great riches. The youth drew out the axe and let him go. The old man led him back into the castle, and in a cellar showed him three chests full of gold. "Of these," said he, "one part is for the poor, the other for the king, the third is thine." In the meantime it struck twelve, and the spirit disappeared; the youth, therefore, was left in darkness. "I shall still be able to find my way out," said he, and felt about, found the way into the room, and slept there by his fire. Next morning the King came and said "Now thou must have learnt what shuddering is?" "No," he answered; "what can it be? My dead cousin was here, and a bearded man came and showed me a great deal of money down below, but no one told me what it was to shudder." "Then," said the King, "thou hast delivered the castle, and shalt marry my daughter." "That is all very well," said he, "but still I do not know what it is to shudder!"

Then the gold was brought up and the wedding celebrated; but howsoever much the young King loved his wife, and however happy he was, he still said always "If I could but shudder—if I could but shudder." And at last she was angry at this. Her waiting-maid said, "I will find a cure for him; he shall soon learn what it is to shudder." She went out to the stream which flowed through the garden, and had a whole bucketful of gudgeons brought to her. At night when the young King was sleeping, his wife was to draw the clothes off him and empty the bucketful of cold water with the gudgeons in it over him, so that the little fishes would sprawl about him. When this was done, he woke up and cried "Oh, what makes me shudder so?—what makes me shudder so, dear wife? Ah! now I know what it is to shudder!"

THE WOLF AND THE SEVEN LITTLE KIDS

THERE WAS once on a time an old goat who had seven little kids, and loved them with all the love of a mother for her children. One day she wanted to go into the forest and fetch some food. So she called all seven to her and said, "Dear children, I have to go into the forest, be on your guard against the wolf; if he come in, he will devour you all—skin, hair, and all. The wretch often disguises himself, but you will know him at once by his rough voice and his black feet." The kids said, "Dear mother, we will take good care of ourselves; you may go away without any anxiety." Then the old one bleated, and went on her way with an easy mind.

It was not long before some one knocked at the house-door and called, "Open the door, dear children; your mother is here, and has brought something back with her for each of you." But the little kids knew that it was the wolf, by the rough voice; "We will not open the door," cried they, "thou art not our mother. She has a soft, pleasant voice, but thy voice is rough; thou art the wolf!" Then the wolf went away to a shopkeeper and bought himself a great lump of chalk, ate this and made his voice soft with it. The he came back, knocked at the door of the house, and cried, "Open the door, dear children, your mother is here and has brought something back with her for each of you." But the wolf had laid his black paws against the window, and the children saw them and cried, "We will not open the door, our mother has not black feet like thee; thou art the wolf!" Then the wolf ran to a baker and said, "I have hurt my feet, rub some dough over them for me." And when the baker had rubbed his feet over, he ran to the miller and said, "Strew some white meal over my feet for me." The miller thought to himself, "The wolf wants to deceive some one," and refused; but the wolf said, "If thou wilt not do it, I will devour thee." Then the miller was afraid, and made his paws white for him. Truly men are like that.

So now the wretch went for the third time to the house-door, knocked at it and said, "Open the door for me, children, your dear little mother has come home, and has brought every one of you something back from the forest with her." The little kids cried, "First show us thy paws that we may know if thou art our dear little mother." Then he put his paws in through the window, and when the kids saw that they were white, they believed that all he said was true, and opened the door. But who should come in but the wolf! They were terrified and wanted to hide themselves. One sprang under the table, the second into the bed, the third into the stove, the fourth into the kitchen, the fifth into the cupboard, the sixth under the washing-bowl, and the seventh into the clock-case. But the wolf found them all, and used no great ceremony; one after the other he swallowed them down his throat. The youngest, in the clock-case, was the only one he did not find. When the wolf had satisfied his appetite he took himself off, laid himself down under a tree in the green meadow outside, and began to sleep. Soon afterwards the old goat came home again from the forest. Ah! what a sight she saw there! The house-door stood wide open. The table, chairs, and benches were thrown down, the washing-bowl lay broken to pieces, and the quilts and pillows were pulled off the bed. She sought her children, but they were nowhere to be found. She called them one after another by name, but no one answered. At last, when she came to the youngest, a soft voice cried, "Dear mother, I am in the clock-case." She took the kid out, and it told her that the wolf had come and had eaten all the others. Then you may imagine how she wept over her poor children.

At length in her grief she went out, and the youngest kid ran with her. When they came to the meadow, there lay the wolf by the tree and snored so loud that the branches shook. She looked at him on every side and saw that something was moving and struggling in his gorged body. "Ah, heavens," said she, "is it possible that my poor children whom he has swallowed down for his supper, can be still alive?" Then the kid had to run home and fetch scissors, and a needle and thread, and the goat cut open the monster's stomach, and hardly had she make one cut, than one little kid thrust its head out, and when she cut farther, all six sprang out one after another, and were all still alive, and had suffered no injury whatever, for in his greediness the monster had swallowed them down whole. What rejoicing there was! Then they embraced their dear mother, and jumped like a tailor at his wedding. The mother, however, said, "Now go and look for some big stones, and we will fill the wicked beast's stomach with them while he is still asleep." Then the seven kids dragged the stones thither with all speed, and put as many of them into his stomach as they could get in;

and the mother sewed him up again in the greatest haste, so that he was not aware of anything and never once stirred.

When the wolf at length had had his sleep out, he got on his legs, and as the stones in his stomach made him very thirsty, he wanted to go to a well to drink. But when he began to walk and to move about, the stones in his stomach knocked against each other and rattled. Then cried he,

"What rumbles and tumbles
Against my poor bones?
I thought 'twas six kids,
But it's naught but big stones."

And when he got to the well and stooped over the water and was just about to drink, the heavy stones made him fall in and there was no help, but he had to drown miserably. When the seven kids saw that, they came running to the spot and cried aloud, "The wolf is dead! The wolf is dead!" and danced for joy round about the well with their mother.

FAITHFUL JOHN

THERE WAS once on a time an old king who was ill, and thought to himself, "I am lying on what must be my death-bed." Then said he, "Tell Faithful John to come to me." Faithful John was his favourite servant, and was so called, because he had for his whole life long been so true to him. When therefore he came beside the bed, the King said to him, "Most faithful John, I feel my end approaching, and have no anxiety except about my son. He is still of tender age, and cannot always know how to guide himself. If thou dost not promise me to teach him everything that he ought to know, and to be his foster-father, I cannot close my eyes in peace." Then answered Faithful John, "I will not forsake him, and will serve him with fidelity, even if it should cost me my life." On this, the old King said, "Now I die in comfort and peace." Then he added, "After my death, thou shalt show him the whole castle: all the chambers, halls, and vaults, and all the treasures which lie therein, but the last chamber in the long gallery, in which is the picture of the princess of the Golden Dwelling, shalt thou not show. If he sees that picture, he will fall violently in love with her, and will drop down in a swoon, and go through great danger for her sake, therefore thou must preserve him from that." And when Faithful John had once more given his promise to the old King about this, the King said no more, but laid his head on his pillow, and died.

When the old King had been carried to his grave, Faithful John told the young King all that he had promised his father on his deathbed, and said, "This will I assuredly perform, and will be faithful to thee as I have been faithful to him, even if it should cost me my life." When the mourning was over, Faithful John said to him, "It is now time that thou shouldst see thine inheritance. I will show thee thy father's palace." Then he took him about everywhere, up and down, and let him see all the riches, and the magnificent apartments, only there was one room which he did not open, that in which hung the dangerous picture. The picture was, however, so placed that when the door was opened you looked straight on it, and it was so admirably painted that it seemed to breathe and live, and there was nothing more charming or more beautiful in the whole world. The young king however plainly remarked that Faithful John always walked past this one door, and said, "Why dost thou never open this one for me?" "There is something within it," he replied, "which would terrify thee." But the King answered, "I have seen all the palace, and I will know what is in this room also," and he went and tried to break open the door by force. Then Faithful John held him back and said, "I promised thy father before his death that thou shouldst not see that which is in this chamber, it might bring the greatest misfortune on thee and on me." "Ah, no," replied the young King, "if I do not go in, it will be my certain destruction. I should have no rest day or night until I had seen it with my own eyes. I shall not leave the place now until thou hast unlocked the door."

Then Faithful John saw that there was no help for it now, and with a heavy heart and many sighs, sought out the key from the great bunch. When he had opened the door, he went in first, and thought by standing before him he could hide the portrait so that the King should not see it in front of him, but what availed that? The King stood on tip-toe and saw it over his shoulder. And when he saw the portrait of the maiden, which was so magnificent and shone with gold and precious stones, he fell fainting on the ground. Faithful John took him up, carried him to his bed, and sorrowfully thought, "The misfortune has befallen us, Lord God, what will be the end of it?" Then he strengthened him with wine, until he came to himself again. The first words the King said were, "Ah, the beautiful portrait! whose it it?" "That is the princess of the Golden Dwelling," answered Faithful John. Then the King continued, "My love for her is so great, that if all the leaves on all the trees were tongues, they could not declare it. I will give my life to win her. Thou art my most Faithful John, thou must help me."

The faithful servant considered within himself for a long time how to set about the matter, for it was difficult even to obtain a sight of the King's daughter. At length he thought of a way, and said to the King, "Everything which she has about her is of gold—tables, chairs, dishes, glasses, bowls, and household furniture. Among thy treasures are five tons of gold; let one of the goldsmiths of the Kingdom work these up into all manner of vessels and utensils, into all kinds of birds, wild beasts and strange animals, such as may please her, and we will go there with them and try our luck."

The King ordered all the goldsmiths to be brought to him, and they had to work night and day until at last the most splendid things were prepared. When everything was stowed on board a ship, Faithful John put on the dress of a merchant, and the King was forced to do the same in order to make himself quite unrecognizable. Then they sailed across the sea, and sailed on until they came to the town wherein dwelt the princess of the Golden Dwelling.

Faithful John bade the King stay behind on the ship, and wait for him. "Perhaps I shall bring the princess with me," said he, "therefore see that everything is in order; have the golden vessels set out and the whole ship decorated." Then he gathered together in his apron all kinds of gold things, went on shore and walked straight to the royal palace. When he entered the courtyard of the palace, a beautiful girl was standing there by the well with two golden buckets in her hand, drawing water with them. And when she was just turning round to carry away the sparkling water she saw the stranger, and asked who he was. So he answered, "I am a merchant," and opened his apron, and let her look in. Then she cried, "Oh, what beautiful gold things!" and put her pails down and looked at the golden wares one after the other. Then said the girl, "The princess must see these, she has such great pleasure in golden things, that she will buy all you have." She took him by the hand and led him upstairs, for she was the waiting-maid. When the King's daughter saw the wares, she was quite delighted and said, "They are so beautifully worked, that I will buy them all of thee." But Faithful John said, "I am only the servant of a rich merchant. The things I have here are not to be compared with those my master has in his ship. They are the most beautiful and valuable things that have ever been made in gold." She wanted to have everything brought to her there, but he said, "There are so many of them that it would take a great many days to do that, and so many rooms would be required to exhibit them, that your house is not big enough." Then her curiosity and longing were still more excited, until at last she said, "Conduct me to the ship, I will go there myself, and behold the treasures of thine master."

On this Faithful John was quite delighted, and led her to the ship, and when the King saw her, he perceived that her beauty was even greater than the picture had represented it to be, and thought no other than that his heart would burst in twain. Then she got into the ship, and the King led her within. Faithful John, however, remained behind with the pilot, and ordered the ship to be pushed off, saying, "Set all sail, till it fly like a bird in air." Within, however, the King showed her the golden vessels, every one of them, also the wild beasts and strange animals. Many hours went by whilst she was seeing everything, and in her delight she did not observe that the ship was sailing away. After she had looked at the last, she thanked the merchant and wanted to go home, but when she came to the side of the ship, she saw that it was on the deep sea far from land, and hurrying onwards with all sail set. "Ah," cried she in her alarm, "I am betrayed! I am carried away and have fallen into the power of a merchant—I would die rather!" The King, however, seized her hand, and said, "I am not a merchant. I am a king, and of no meaner origin than thou art, and if I have carried thee away with subtlety, that has come to pass because of my exceeding great love for thee. The first time that I looked on thy portrait, I fell fainting to the ground." When the princess of the Golden Dwelling heard that, she was comforted, and her heart was inclined unto him, so that she willingly consented to be his wife.

It happened, however, while they were sailing onwards over the deep sea, that Faithful John, who was sitting on the fore part of the vessel, making music, saw three ravens in the air, which came flying towards them. On this he stopped playing and listened to what they were saying to each other, for that he well understood. One cried, "Oh, there he is carrying home the princess of the Golden Dwelling." "Yes," replied the second, "but he has not got her yet." Said the third, "But he has got her, she is sitting beside him in the ship." Then the first began again, and cried, "What good will that do him? When they reach land a chestnut horse will leap forward to meet him, and the prince will want to mount it, but if he does that, it will run away with him, and rise up into the air with him, and he will never see his maiden more." Spake the second, "But is there no escape?"

"Oh, yes, if any one else gets on it swiftly, and takes out the pistol which must be in its holster, and shoots the horse dead with it, the young King is saved. But who knows that? And whosoever does know it, and tells it to him, will be turned to stone from the toe to the knee." Then said the second, "I know more than that; even if the horse be killed, the young King will still not keep his bride. When they go into the castle together, a wrought bridal garment will be lying there in a dish, and looking as if it were woven of gold and silver; it is, however, nothing but sulphur and pitch, and if he put it on, it will burn him to the very bone and marrow." Said the third, "Is there no escape at all?"

"Oh, yes," replied the second, "if any one with gloves on seizes the garment and throws it into the fire and burns it, the young King will be saved. "But what avails that?" Whosoever knows it and tells it to him, half his body will become stone from the knee to the heart."

Then said the third, "I know still more; even if the bridal garment be burnt, the young King will still not have his bride. After the wedding, when the dancing begins and the young Queen is dancing, she will suddenly turn pale and fall down as if dead, and if some one does not lift her up and draw three drops of blood from her right breast and spit them out again, she will die. But if any one who knows that were to declare it, he would become stone from the crown of his head to the sole of his foot." When the ravens had spoken of this together, they flew onwards, and Faithful John had well understood everything, but from that time forth he became quiet and sad, for if he concealed what he had heard from his master, the latter would be unfortunate, and if he discovered it to him, he himself must sacrifice his life. At length, however, he said to himself, "I will save my master, even if it bring destruction on myself."

When therefore they came to shore, all happened as had been foretold by the ravens, and a magnificent chestnut horse sprang forward. "Good," said the King, "he shall carry me to my palace," and was about to mount it when Faithful John got before him, jumped quickly on it, drew the pistol out of the holster, and shot the horse. Then the other attendants of the King, who after all were not very fond of Faithful John, cried, "How shameful to kill the beautiful animal, that was to have carried the King to his palace." But the King said, "Hold your peace and leave him alone, he is my most faithful John, who knows what may be the good of that!" They went into the palace, and in the hall there stood a dish, and therein lay the bridal garment looking no otherwise than as if it were made of gold and silver. The young king went towards it and was about to take hold of it, but Faithful John pushed him away, seized it with gloves on, carried it quickly to the fire and burnt it. The other attendants again began to murmur, and said, "Behold, now he is even burning the King's bridal garment!" But the young King said, "Who knows what good he may have done, leave him alone, he is my most faithful John."

And now the wedding was solemnized: the dance began, and the bride also took part in it; then Faithful John was watchful and looked into her face, and suddenly she turned pale and fell to the ground as if she were dead. On this he ran hastily to her, lifted her up and bore her into a chamber—then he laid her down, and knelt and sucked the three drops of blood from her right breast, and spat them out. Immediately she breathed again and recovered herself, but the young King had seen this, and being ignorant why Faithful John had done it, was angry and cried, "Throw him into a dungeon." Next morning Faithful John was condemned, and led to the gallows, and when he stood on high, and was about to be executed, he said, "Every one who has to die is permitted before his end to make one last speech; may I too claim the right?" "Yes," answered the King, "it shall be granted unto thee." Then said Faithful John, "I am unjustly condemned, and have always been true to thee," and related how he had hearkened to the conversation of the ravens when on the sea, and how he had been obliged to do all these things in order to save his master. Then cried the King, "Oh, my most Faithful John. Pardon, pardon—bring him down." But as Faithful John spoke the last word he had fallen down lifeless and become a stone.

Thereupon the King and the Queen suffered great anguish, and the King said, "Ah, how ill I have requited great fidelity!" and ordered the stone figure to be taken up and placed in his bedroom beside his bed. And as often as he looked on it he wept and said, "Ah, if I could bring thee to life again, my most faithful John." Some time passed and the Queen bore twins, two sons who grew fast and were her delight. Once when the Queen was at church and the two children were sitting playing beside their father, the latter full of grief again looked at the stone figure, sighed and said, "Ah, if I could but bring thee to life again, my most faithful John." Then the stone began to speak and said, "Thou canst bring me to life again if thou wilt use for that purpose what is dearest to thee." Then cried the King, "I will give everything I have in the world for thee." The stone continued, "If thou wilt will cut off the heads of thy two children with thine own hand, and sprinkle me with their blood, I shall be restored to life."

The King was terrified when he heard that he himself must kill his dearest children, but he thought of faithful John's great fidelity, and how he had died for him, drew his sword, and with his own hand cut off the children's heads. And when he had smeared the stone with their blood, life returned to it, and Faithful John stood once more safe and healthy before him. He said to the King, "Thy truth shall not go unrewarded," and took the heads of the children, put them on again, and rubbed the wounds with their blood, on which they became whole again immediately, and jumped about, and went on playing as if nothing had happened. Then the King was full of joy, and when he saw the Queen coming he hid Faithful John and the two children in a great cupboard. When she entered, he said to her, "Hast thou been praying in the church?" "Yes," answered she, "but I have constantly been thinking of Faithful John and what misfortune has befallen him through us." Then said he, "Dear wife, we can give him his life again, but it will cost us our two little sons, whom we must sacrifice." The Queen turned pale, and her heart was full of terror, but she said, "We owe it to him, for his great fidelity." Then the King was rejoiced that she thought as he had thought, and went and opened the cupboard, and brought forth Faithful John and the children, and said, "God be praised, he is delivered, and we have our little sons again also," and told her how everything had occurred. Then they dwelt together in much happiness until their death.

THE TWELVE BROTHERS

THERE WERE once on a time a king and a queen who lived happily together and had twelve children, but they were all boys. Then said the King to his wife, "If the thirteenth child which thou art about to bring into the world, is a girl, the twelve boys shall die, in order that her possessions may be great, and that the kingdom may fall to her alone." He caused likewise twelve coffins to be made, which were already filled with shavings, and in each lay the little pillow for the dead, and he had them taken into a locked-up room, and then he gave the Queen the key of it, and bade her not to speak of this to any one.

The mother, however, now sat and lamented all day long, until the youngest son, who was always with her, and whom she had named Benjamin, from the Bible, said to her, "Dear mother, why art thou so sad?"

"Dearest child," she answered, "I may not tell thee." But he let her have no rest until she went and unlocked the room, and showed him the twelve coffins ready filled with shavings. Then she said, "My dearest Benjamin, thy father has had these coffins made for thee and for thy eleven brothers, for if I bring a little girl into the world, you are all to be killed and buried in them." And as she wept while she was saying this, the son comforted her and said, "Weep not, dear mother, we will save ourselves, and go hence." But she said, "Go forth into the forest with thy eleven brothers, and let one sit constantly on the highest tree which can be found, and keep watch, looking towards the tower here in the castle. If I give birth to a little son, I will put up a white flag, and then you may venture to come back, but if I bear a daughter, I will hoist a red flag, and then fly hence as quickly as you are able, and may the good God protect you. And every night I will rise up and pray for you—in winter that you may be able to warm yourself at a fire, and in summer that you may not faint away in the heat."

After she had blessed her sons therefore, they went forth into the forest. They each kept watch in turn, and sat on the highest oak and looked towards the tower. When eleven days had passed and the turn came to Benjamin, he saw that a flag was being raised. It was, however, not the white, but the blood-red flag which announced that they were all to die. When the brothers heard that, they were very angry and said, "Are we all to suffer death for the sake of a girl? We swear that we will avenge ourselves!—wheresoever we find a girl, her red blood shall flow."

Thereupon they went deeper into the forest, and in the midst of it, where it was the darkest, they found a little bewitched hut, which was standing empty. Then said they, "Here we will dwell, and thou Benjamin, who art the youngest and weakest, thou shalt stay at home and keep house, we others will go out and get food." Then they went into the forest and shot hares, wild deer, birds and pigeons, and whatsoever there was to eat; this they took to Benjamin, who had to dress it for them in order that they might appease their hunger. They lived together ten years in the little hut, and the time did not appear long to them.

The little daughter which their mother the Queen had given birth to, was now grown up; she was good of heart, and fair of face, and had a golden star on her forehead. Once, when it was the great washing, she saw twelve men's shirts among the things, and asked her mother, "To whom do these twelve shirts belong, for they are far too small for father?" Then the Queen answered with a heavy heart, "Dear child, these belong to thy twelve brothers." Said the maiden, "Where are my twelve brothers, I have never yet heard of them?" She replied, "God knows where they are, they are wandering about the world." Then she took the maiden and opened the chamber for her, and showed her the twelve coffins with the shavings, and pillows for the head. "These coffins," said she, "were destined for thy brothers, but they went away secretly before thou wert born," and she related to her how everything had happened; then said the maiden, "Dear mother, weep not, I will go and seek my brothers."

So she took the twelve shirts and went forth, and straight into the great forest. She walked the whole day, and in the evening she came to the bewitched hut. Then she entered it and found a young boy, who asked, "From whence comest thou, and whither art thou bound?" and was astonished that she was so beautiful, and wore royal garments, and had a star on her forehead. And she answered, "I am a king's daughter, and am seeking my twelve brothers, and I will walk as far as the sky is blue until I find them." She likewise showed him the twelve shirts which belonged to them. Then Benjamin saw that she was his sister, and said, "I am Benjamin, thy youngest brother." And she began to weep for joy, and Benjamin wept also, and they kissed and embraced each other with the greatest love. But after this he said, "Dear sister, there is still one difficulty. We have agreed that every maiden whom we meet shall die, because we have been obliged to leave our kingdom on account of a girl." Then said she, "I will willingly die, if by so doing I can deliver my twelve brothers."

"No," answered he, "thou shalt not die, seat thyself beneath this tub until our eleven brothers come, and then I will soon come to an agreement with them."

She did so, and when it was night the others came from hunting, and their dinner was ready. And as they were sitting at table, and eating, they asked, "What news is there?" Said Benjamin, "Don't you know anything?" "No," they answered. He continued, "You have been in the forest and I have stayed at home, and yet I know more than you do." "Tell us then," they cried. He answered, "But promise me that the first maiden who meets us shall not be killed." "Yes," they all cried, "she shall have mercy, only do tell us."

Then said he, "Our sister is here," and he lifted up the tub, and the King's daughter came forth in her royal garments with the golden star on her forehead, and she was beautiful, delicate and fair. Then they were all rejoiced, and fell on her neck, and kissed and loved her with all their hearts.

Now she stayed at home with Benjamin and helped him with the work. The eleven went into the forest and caught game, and deer, and birds, and wood-pigeons that they might have food, and the little sister and Benjamin took care to make it ready for them. She sought for the wood for cooking and herbs for vegetables, and put the pans on the fire so that the dinner was always ready when the eleven came. She likewise kept order in the little house, and put beautifully white clean coverings on the little beds, and the brothers were always contented and lived in great harmony with her.

Once on a time the two at home had prepared a beautiful entertainment, and when they were all together, they sat down and ate and drank and were full of gladness. There was, however, a little garden belonging to the bewitched house wherein stood twelve lily flowers, which are likewise called students.* She wished to give her brothers pleasure, and plucked the twelve flowers, and thought she would present each brother with one while at dinner. But at the self-same

---

***Studenten-Nelken,* or *Studenten-Lilien,* are a species of small pinks, and are so called because they are much worn by the students of various universities, in the button-hole of their coats. They are sometimes called *Federnelken* (Feather-pink, or "sop in the wine"). The brothers Grimm themselves, in the notes to "De drei Vügelkens," speak of this flower as the narcissus.—Tr.

moment that she plucked the flowers the twelve brothers were changed into twelve ravens, and flew away over the forest, and the house and garden vanished likewise. And now the poor maiden was alone in the wild forest, and when she looked around, an old woman was standing near her who said, "My child, what hast thou done? Why didst thou not leave the twelve white flowers growing? They were thy brothers, who are now for evermore changed into ravens." The maiden said, weeping, "Is there no way of delivering them?"

"No," said the woman, "there is but one in the whole world, and that is so hard that thou wilt not deliver them by it, for thou must be dumb for seven years, and mayst not speak or laugh, and if thou speakest one single word, and only an hour of the seven years is wanting, all is in vain, and thy brothers will be killed by the one word."

Then said the maiden in her heart, "I know with certainty that I shall set my brothers free," and went and sought a high tree and seated herself in it and span, and neither spoke nor laughed. Now it so happened that a king was hunting in the forest, who had a great greyhound which ran to the tree on which the maiden was sitting, and sprang about it, whining, and barking at her. Then the King came by and saw the beautiful King's daughter with the golden star on her brow, and was so charmed with her beauty that he called to ask her if she would be his wife. She made no answer, but nodded a little with her head. So he climbed up the tree himself, carried her down, placed her on his horse, and bore her home. Then the wedding was solemnized with great magnificence and rejoicing, but the bride neither spoke nor smiled. When they had lived happily together for a few years, the King's mother, who was a wicked woman, began to slander the young Queen, and said to the King, "This is a common beggar girl whom thou hast brought back with thee. Who knows what impious tricks she practises secretly! Even if she be dumb, and not able to speak, she still might laugh for once; but those who do not laugh have bad consciences." At first the King would not believe it, but the old woman urged this so long, and accused her of so many evil things, that at last the King let himself be persuaded and sentenced her to death.

And now a great fire was lighted in the courtyard in which she was to be burnt, and the King stood above at the window and looked on with tearful eyes, because he still loved her so much. And when she was bound fast to the stake, and the fire was licking at her clothes with its red tongue, the last instant of the seven years expired. Then a whirring sound was heard in the air, and twelve ravens came flying towards the place, and sank downwards, and when they touched the earth they were her twelve brothers, whom she had delivered. They tore the fire asunder, extinguished the flames, set their dear sister free, and kissed and embraced her. And now as she dared to open her mouth and speak, she told the King why she had been dumb, and had never laughed. The King rejoiced when he heard that she was innocent, and they all lived in great unity until their death. The wicked step-mother was taken before the judge, and put into a barrel filled with boiling oil and venomous snakes, and died an evil death.

BROTHER AND SISTER

LITTLE BROTHER took his little sister by the hand and said, "Since our mother died we have had no happiness; our step-mother beats us every day, and if we come near her she kicks us away with her foot. Our meals are the hard crusts of bread that are left over; and the little dog under the table is better off, for she often throws it a nice bit. May Heaven pity us. If our mother only knew! Come, we will go forth together into the wide world."

They walked the whole day over meadows, fields, and stony places; and when it rained the little sister said, "Heaven and our hearts are weeping together." In the evening they came to a large forest, and they were so weary with sorrow and hunger and the long walk, that they lay down in a hollow tree and fell asleep.

The next day when they awoke, the sun was already high in the sky, and shone down hot into the tree. Then the brother said, "Sister, I am thirsty; if I knew of a little brook I would go and just take a drink; I think I hear one running." The brother got up and took the little sister by the hand, and they set off to find the brook.

But the wicked step-mother was a witch, and had seen how the two children had gone away, and had crept after them privily, as witches do creep, and had bewitched all the brooks in the forest.

Now when they found a little brook leaping brightly over the stones, the brother was going to drink out of it, but the sister heard how it said as it ran, "Who drinks of me will be a tiger; who drinks of me will be a tiger." Then the sister cried, "Pray, dear brother, do not drink, or you will become a wild beast, and tear me to pieces." The brother did not drink, although he was so thirsty, but said, "I will wait for the next spring."

When they came to the next brook the sister heard this also say, "Who drinks of me will be a wolf; who drinks of me will be a wolf." Then the sister cried out, "Pray, dear brother, do not drink, or you will become a wolf, and devour me." The brother did not drink, and said,

"I will wait until we come to the next spring, but then I must drink, say what you like; for my thirst is too great."

And when they came to the third brook the sister heard how it said as it ran, "Who drinks of me will be a roebuck; who drinks of me will be a roebuck." The sister said, "Oh, I pray you, dear brother, do not drink, or you will become a roebuck, and run away from me." But the brother had knelt down at once by the brook, and had bent down and drunk some of the water, and as soon as the first drops touched his lips he lay there a young roebuck.

And now the sister wept over her poor bewitched brother, and the little roe wept also, and sat sorrowfully near to her. But at last the girl said, "Be quiet, dear little roe, I will never, never leave you."

Then she untied her golden garter and put it round the roebuck's neck, and she plucked rushes and wove them into a soft cord. With this she tied the little beast and led it on, and she walked deeper and deeper into the forest.

And when they had gone a very long way they came at last to a little house, and the girl looked in; and as it was empty, she thought, "We can stay here and live." Then she sought for leaves and moss to make a soft bed for the roe; and every morning she went out and gathered roots and berries and nuts for herself, and brought tender grass for the roe, who ate out of her hand, and was content and played round about her. In the evening, when the sister was tired, and had said her prayer, she laid her head upon the roebuck's back: that was her pillow, and she slept softly on it. And if only the brother had had his human form it would have been a delightful life.

For some time they were alone like this in the wilderness. But it happened that the King of the country held a great hunt in the forest. Then the blasts of the horns, the barking of dogs, and the merry shouts of the huntsmen rang through the trees, and the roebuck heard all, and was only too anxious to be there. "Oh," said he, to his sister, "let me be off to the hunt, I cannot bear it any longer;" and he begged so much that at last she agreed. "But," said she to him, "come back to me in the evening; I must shut my door for fear of the rough huntsmen, so knock and say, 'My little sister, let me in!' that I may know you; and if you do not say that, I shall not open the door." Then the young roebuck sprang away; so happy was he and so merry in the open air.

The King and the huntsmen saw the pretty creature, and started after him, but they could not catch him, and when they thought that they surely had him, away he sprang through the bushes and could not be seen. When it was dark he ran to the cottage, knocked, and said, "My little sister, let me in." Then the door was opened for him, and he jumped in, and rested himself the whole night through upon his soft bed.

The next day the hunt went on afresh, and when the roebuck again heard the bugle-horn, and the ho! ho! of the huntsmen, he had no peace, but said, "Sister, let me out, I must be off." His sister opened the door for him, and said, "But you must be here again in the evening and say your pass-word."

When the King and his huntsmen again saw the young roebuck with the golden collar, they all chased him, but he was too quick and nimble for them. This went on for the whole day, but at last by the evening the huntsmen had surrounded him, and one of them wounded him a little in the foot, so that he limped and ran slowly. Then a hunter crept after him to the cottage and heard how he said, "My little sister, let me in," and saw that the door was opened for him, and was shut again at once. The huntsman took notice of it all, and went to the King and told him what he had seen and heard. Then the King said, "To-morrow we will hunt once more."

The little sister, however, was dreadfully frightened when she saw that her fawn was hurt. She washed the blood off him, laid herbs on the wound, and said, "Go to your bed, dear roe, that you may get well again." But the wound was so slight that the roebuck, next morning, did not feel it any more. And when he again heard the sport outside, he said, "I cannot bear it, I must be there; they shall not find it so easy to catch me." The sister cried, and said, "This time they will kill you, and here am I alone in the forest and forsaken by all the world. I will not let you out." "Then you will have me die of grief," answered the roe; "when I hear the bugle-horns I feel as if I must jump out of my skin." Then the sister could not do otherwise, but opened the door for him with a heavy heart, and the roebuck, full of health and joy, bounded into the forest.

When the King saw him, he said to his huntsmen, "Now chase him all day long till night-fall, but take care that no one does him any harm."

As soon as the sun had set, the King said to the huntsmen, "Now come and show me the cottage in the wood"; and when he was at the door, he knocked and called out, "Dear little sister, let me in." Then the door opened, and the King walked in, and there stood a maiden more lovely than any he had ever seen. The maiden was frightened when she saw, not her little roe, but a man come in who wore a golden crown upon his head. But the King looked kindly at her, stretched out his hand, and said, "Will you go with me to my palace and be my dear wife?" "Yes, indeed," answered the maiden, "but the little roe must go with me, I cannot leave him." The King said, "It shall stay with you as long as you live, and shall want nothing." Just then he came running in, and the sister again tied him with the cord of rushes, took it in her own hand, and went away with the King from the cottage.

The King took the lovely maiden upon his horse and carried her to his palace, where the wedding was held with great pomp. She was now the Queen, and they lived for a long time happily together; the roebuck was tended and cherished, and ran about in the palace-garden.

But the wicked step-mother, because of whom the children had gone out into the world, thought all the time that the sister had been torn to pieces by the wild beasts in the wood, and that the brother had been shot for a roebuck by the huntsmen. Now when she heard that they were so happy, and so well off, envy and hatred rose in her heart and left her no peace, and she thought of nothing but how she could bring them again to misfortune. Her own daughter, who was as ugly as night, and had only one eye, grumbled at her and said, "A Queen! that ought to have been my luck." "Only be quiet," answered the old woman, and comforted her by saying, "when the time comes I shall be ready."

As time went on, the Queen had a pretty little boy, and it happened that the King was out hunting; so the old witch took the form of the chamber-maid, went into the room where the Queen lay, and said to her, "Come, the bath is ready; it will do you good, and give you fresh strength; make haste before it gets cold."

The daughter also was close by; so they carried the weakly Queen into the bath-room, and put her into the bath; then they shut the door and ran away. But in the bath-room they had made a fire of such deadly heat that the beautiful young Queen was soon suffocated.

When this was done the old woman took her daughter, put a night-cap on her head, and laid her in bed in place of the Queen. She gave her too the shape and the look of the Queen, only she could not make good the lost eye. But in order that the King might not see it, she was to lie on the side on which she had no eye.

In the evening when he came home and heard that he had a son he was heartily glad, and was going to the bed of his dear wife to see how she was. But the old woman quickly called out, "For your life leave the curtains closed; the Queen ought not to see the light yet, and must have rest." The King went away, and did not find out that a false Queen was lying in the bed.

But at midnight, when all slept, the nurse, who was sitting in the nursery by the cradle, and who was the only person awake, saw the door open and the true Queen walk in. She took the child out of the cradle, laid it on her arm, and suckled it. Then she shook up its pillow, laid the child down again, and covered it with the little quilt. And she did not forget the roebuck, but went into the corner where it lay, and stroked its back. Then she went quite silently out of the door again. The next morning the nurse asked the guards whether any one had come into the palace during the night, but they answered, "No, we have seen no one."

She came thus many nights and never spoke a word: the nurse always saw her, but she did not dare to tell anyone about it.

When some time had passed in this manner, the Queen began to speak in the night, and said—

"How fares my child, how fares my roe?
Twice shall I come, then never more."

The nurse did not answer, but when the Queen had gone again, went to the King and told him all. The King said, "Ah, heavens! what is this? To-morrow night I will watch by the child." In the evening he went into the nursery, and at midnight the Queen again appeared and said—

"How fares my child, how fares my roe?
Once will I come, then never more."

And she nursed the child as she was wont to do before she disappeared. The King dared not speak to her, but on the next night he watched again. Then she said—

"How fares my child, how fares my roe?
This time I come, then never more."

Then the King could not restrain himself; he sprang towards her, and said, "You can be none other than my dear wife." She answered, "Yes, I am your dear wife," and at the same moment she received life again, and by God's grace became fresh, rosy, and full of health.

Then she told the King the evil deed which the wicked witch and her daughter had been guilty of towards her. The King ordered both to be led before the judge, and judgment was delivered against them. The daughter was taken into the forest where she was torn to pieces by wild beasts, but the witch was cast into the fire and miserably burnt. And as soon as she was burnt the roebuck changed his shape, and received his human form again, so the sister and brother lived happily together all their lives.

RAPUNZEL*

THERE WERE once a man and a woman who had long in vain wished for a child. At length the woman hoped that God was about to grant her desire. These people had a little window at the back of their house from which a splendid garden could be seen, which was full of the most beautiful flowers and herbs. It was, however, surrounded by a high wall, and no one dared to go into it because it belonged to an enchantress, who had great power and was dreaded by all the world. One day the woman was standing by this window and looking down into the garden, when she saw a bed which was planted with the most beautiful rampion (rapunzel), and it looked so fresh and green that she longed for it, and had the greatest desire to eat some. This desire increased every day, and as she knew that she could not get any of it, she quite pined away, and looked pale and miserable. Then her husband was alarmed, and asked, "What aileth thee, dear wife?" "Ah," she replied, "if I can't get some of the rampion, which is in the garden behind our house, to eat, I shall die." The man, who loved her, thought, "Sooner than let thy wife die, bring her some of the rampion thyself, let it cost thee what it will." In the twilight of the evening, he clambered down over the wall into the garden of the enchantress, hastily clutched a handful of rampion, and took it to his wife. She at once made herself a salad of it, and ate it with much relish. She, however, liked it so much—so very much, that the next day she longed for it three times as much as before. If he was to have any rest, her husband must once more descend into the garden. In the gloom of evening, therefore, he let himself down again; but when he had clambered down the wall he was terribly afraid, for he saw the enchantress standing before him. "How canst thou dare," said she with angry look, "to

*Rapunzel, *Campanula rapunculus* (rampion), a congener of the common harebell. It has a long white spindle-shaped root which is eaten raw like a radish, and has a pleasant sweet flavour. Its leaves and young shoots are also used in salads—and so are the roots, sliced.—TR.

descend into my garden and steal my rampion like a thief? Thou shalt suffer for it!" "Ah," answered he, "let mercy take the place of justice, I only made up my mind to do it out of necessity. My wife saw your rampion from the window, and felt such a longing for it that she would have died if she had not got some to eat." Then the enchantress allowed her anger to be softened, and said to him, "If the case be as thou sayest, I will allow thee to take away with thee as much rampion as thou wilt, only I make one condition, thou must give me the child which thy wife will bring into the world; it shall be well treated, and I will care for it like a mother." The man in his terror consented to everything, and when the woman was brought to bed, the enchantress appeared at once, gave the child the name of Rapunzel, and took it away with her.

Rapunzel grew into the most beautiful child beneath the sun. When she was twelve years old, the enchantress shut her into a tower, which lay in a forest, and had neither stairs nor door, but quite at the top was a little window. When the enchantress wanted to go in, she placed herself beneath it and cried,

"Rapunzel, Rapunzel,
Let down thy hair to me."

Rapunzel had magnificent long hair, fine as spun gold, and when she heard the voice of the enchantress she unfastened her braided tresses, wound them round one of the hooks of the window above, and then the hair fell twenty ells down, and the enchantress climbed up by it.

After a year or two, it came to pass that the King's son rode through the forest and went by the tower. Then he heard a song, which was so charming that he stood still and listened. This was Rapunzel, who in her solitude passed her time in letting her sweet voice resound. The King's son wanted to climb up to her, and looked for the door of the tower, but none was to be found. He rode home, but the singing had so deeply touched his heart, that every day he went out into the forest and listened to it. Once when he was thus standing behind a tree, he saw that an enchantress came there, and he heard how she cried,

"Rapunzel, Rapunzel,
Let down thy hair."

Then Rapunzel let down the braids of her hair, and the enchantress climbed up to her. "If that is the ladder by which one mounts, I will for once try my fortune," said he, and the next day when it began to grow dark, he went to the tower and cried,

"Rapunzel, Rapunzel,
Let down thy hair."

Immediately the hair fell down and the King's son climbed up.

At first Rapunzel was terribly frightened when a man such as her eyes had never yet beheld, came to her; but the King's son began to talk to her quite like a friend, and told her that his heart had been so stirred that it had let him have no rest, and he had been forced to see her. Then Rapunzel lost her fear, and when he asked her if she would take him for her husband, and she saw that he was young and handsome, she thought, "He will love me more than old Dame Gothel does"; and she said yes, and laid her hand in his. She said, "I will willingly go away with thee, but I do not know how to get down. Bring with thee a skein of silk every time that thou comest, and I will weave a ladder with it, and when that is ready I will descend, and thou wilt take me on thy horse." They agreed that until that time he should come to her every evening, for the old woman came by day. The enchantress remarked nothing of this, until once Rapunzel said to her, "Tell me, Dame Gothel, how it happens that you are so much heavier for me to draw up than the young King's son—he is with me in a moment." "Ah! thou wicked child," cried the enchantress "What do I hear thee say! I thought I had separated thee from all the world, and yet thou hast deceived me. In her anger she clutched Rapunzel's beautiful tresses, wrapped them twice round her left hand, seized a pair of scissors with the right, and snip, snap, they were cut off, and the lovely braids lay on the ground. And she was so pitiless that she took poor Rapunzel into a desert where she had to live in great grief and misery.

On the same day, however, that she cast out Rapunzel, the enchantress in the evening fastened the braids of hair which she had cut off, to the hook of the window, and when the King's son came and cried,

"Rapunzel, Rapunzel,
Let down thy hair,"

she let the hair down. The King's son ascended, but he did not find his dearest Rapunzel above, but the enchantress, who gazed at him with wicked and venomous looks. "Aha!" she cried mockingly, "Thou wouldst fetch thy dearest, but the beautiful bird sits no longer singing in the nest; the cat has got it, and will scratch out thy eyes as well. Rapunzel is lost to thee; thou wilt never see her more." The King's son was beside himself with pain, and in his despair he leapt down from the tower. He escaped with his life, but the thorns into which he fell, pierced his eyes. Then he wandered quite blind about the forest, ate nothing but roots and berries, and did nothing but lament and weep over the loss of his dearest wife. Thus he roamed about in misery for some years, and at length came to the desert where Rapunzel, with the twins to which she had given birth, a boy and a girl, lived in wretchedness. He heard a voice, and it seemed so familiar to him that he went towards it, and when he approached, Rapunzel knew him and fell on his neck and wept. Two of her tears wetted his eyes and they grew clear again, and he could see with them as before. He led her to his kingdom where he was joyfully received, and they lived for a long time afterwards, happy and contented.

THE THREE LITTLE MEN IN THE WOOD

THERE WAS once a man whose wife died, and a woman whose husband died, and the man had a daughter, and the woman also had a daughter. The girls were acquainted with each other, and went out walking together, and afterwards came to the woman in her house. Then said she to the man's daughter, "Listen, tell thy father that I would like to marry him, and then thou shalt wash thyself in milk every morning, and drink wine, but my own daughter shall wash herself in water and drink water." The girl went home, and told her father what the woman had said. The man said, "What shall I do? Marriage is a joy and also a torment." At length as he could come to no decision, he pulled off his boot, and said, "Take this boot, it has a hole in the sole of it. Go with it up to the loft, hang it on the big nail, and then pour water into it. If it hold the water, then I will again take a wife, but if it run through, I will not." The girl did as she was ordered, but the water drew the hole together, and the boot became full to the top. She informed her father how it had turned out. Then he himself went up, and when he saw that she was right, he went to the widow and wooed her, and the wedding was celebrated.

The next morning, when the two girls got up, there stood before the man's daughter, milk for her to wash in and wine for her to drink, but before the woman's daughter stood water to wash herself with and water for drinking. On the second morning, stood water for washing and water for drinking before the man's daughter as well as before the woman's daughter. And on the third morning stood water for washing and water for drinking before the man's daughter, and milk for washing and wine for drinking, before the woman's daughter, and so it continued. The woman became bitterly unkind to her step-daughter, and day by day did her best to treat her still worse. She was envious too because her step-daughter was beautiful and lovable, and her own daughter ugly and repulsive.

Once, in winter, when everything was frozen as hard as a stone, and hill and vale lay covered with snow, the woman made a frock of paper, called her step-daughter, and said, "Here, put on this dress and go out into the wood, and fetch me a little basketful of strawberries,—I have a fancy for some." "Good heavens!" said the girl, "no strawberries grow in winter! The ground is frozen, and besides the snow has covered everything. And why am I to go in this paper frock? It is so cold outside that one's very breath freezes! The wind will blow through the frock, and the thorns will tear it off my body." "Wilt thou contradict me again?" said the stepmother, "See that thou goest, and do not show thy face again until thou hast the basketful of strawberries!" Then she gave her a little piece of hard bread, and said, "This will last thee the day," and thought, "Thou wilt die of cold and hunger outside, and wilt never be seen again by me."

Then the maiden was obedient, and put on the paper frock, and went out with the basket. Far and wide there was nothing but snow, and not a green blade to be seen. When she got into the wood she saw a small house out of which peeped three dwarfs.* She wished them good day, and knocked modestly at the door. They cried, "Come in," and she entered the room and seated herself on the bench by the stove, where she began to warm herself and eat her breakfast. The elves said, "Give us, too, some of it." "Willingly," said she, and divided her bit of bread in two, and gave them the half. They asked, "What dost thou here in the forest in the winter time, in thy thin dress?" "Ah," she answered, "I am to look for a basketful of strawberries, and am not to go home until I can take them with me." When she had eaten her bread, they gave her a broom and said, "Sweep away the snow at the back door with it." But when she was outside, the three little men said to each other, "What shall we give her as she is so good, and has shared her bread with us?" Then said the first, "My gift is, that she shall every day grow more beautiful." The second said, "My gift is, that gold pieces shall fall out of her mouth every time she speaks." The third said, "My gift is, that a king shall come and take her to wife."

The girl, however, did as the little men had bidden her, swept away the snow behind the little house with the broom, and what did she find but real ripe strawberries, which came up quite dark-red out of the snow! In her joy she hastily gathered her basket full, thanked the little men, shook hands with each of them, and ran home to take her step-mother what she had longed for so much. When she went in and

*In the original Haulemännerchen—i.e., Höhlen-Waldmännlein. They are so called because they live in caves in the forests. They are little dwarfs with large heads, and are supposed to steal unbaptized children.—Tr.

said good-evening, a piece of gold at once fell from her mouth. Thereupon she related what had happened to her in the wood, but with every word she spoke, gold pieces fell from her mouth, until very soon the whole room was covered with them. "Now look at her arrogance," cried the step-sister, "to throw about gold in that way!" but she was secretly envious of it, and wanted to go into the forest also to seek strawberries. The mother said, "No, my dear little daughter, it is too cold, thou mightest die of cold." However, as her daughter let her have no peace, the mother at last yielded, made her a magnificent dress of fur, which she was obliged to put on, and gave her bread-and-butter and cake with her.

The girl went into the forest and straight up to the little house. The three little elves peeped out again, but she did not greet them, and without looking round at them and without speaking to them, she went awkwardly into the room, seated herself by the stove, and began to eat her bread-and-butter and cake. "Give us some of it," cried the little men; but she replied, "There is not enough for myself, so how can I give it away to other people?" When she had done eating, they said, "There is a broom for thee, sweep all clean for us outside by the back-door." "Humph! Sweep for yourselves," she answered, "I am not your servant." When she saw that they were not going to give her anything, she went out by the door. Then the little men said to each other, "What shall we give her as she is so naughty, and has a wicked envious heart, that will never let her do a good turn to any one?" The first said, "I grant that she may grow uglier every day." The second said, "I grant that at every word she says, a toad shall spring out of her mouth." The third said, "I grant that she may die a miserable death." The maiden looked for strawberries outside, but as she found none, she went angrily home. And when she opened her mouth, and was about to tell her mother what had happened to her in the wood, with every word she said, a toad sprang out of her mouth, so that every one was seized with horror of her.

Then the step-mother was still more enraged, and thought of nothing but how to do every possible injury to the man's daughter, whose beauty, however, grew daily greater. At length she took a cauldron, set it on the fire, and boiled yarn in it. When it was boiled, she flung it on the poor girl's shoulder, and gave her an axe in order that she might go on the frozen river, cut a hole in the ice, and rinse the yarn. She was obedient, went thither and cut a hole in the ice; and while she was in the midst of her cutting, a splendid carriage came driving up, in which sat the King. The carriage stopped, and the King asked, "My child, who are thou, and what art thou doing here?" "I am a poor girl, and I am rinsing yarn." Then the King felt compassion, and when he saw that she was so very beautiful, he said to her, "Wilt thou go away with me?" "Ah, yes, with all my heart," she answered, for she was glad to get away from the mother and sister.

So she got into the carriage and drove away with the King, and when they arrived at his palace, the wedding was celebrated with great pomp, as the little men had granted to the maiden. When a year was over, the young Queen bore a son, and as the step-mother had heard of her great good-fortune, she came with her daughter to the palace and pretended that she wanted to pay her a visit. Once, however, when the King had gone out, and no one else was present, the wicked woman seized the Queen by the head, and her daughter seized her by the feet, and they lifted her out of the bed, and threw her out of the window into the stream which flowed by. Then the ugly daughter laid herself in the bed, and the old woman covered her up over her head. When the King came home again and wanted to speak to his wife, the old woman cried, "Hush, hush, that can't be now, she is lying in a violent perspiration; you must let her rest to-day." The King suspected no evil, and did not come back again till next morning; and as he talked with his wife and she answered him, with every word a toad leaped out, whereas formerly a piece of gold had fallen out. Then he asked what that could be, but the old woman said that she had got that from the violent perspiration, and would soon lose it again. During the night, however, the scullion saw a duck come swimming up the gutter, and it said,

"King, what art thou doing now?
Sleepest thou, or wakest thou?"

And as he returned no answer it said,

"And my guests, What may they do?"

The scullion said,

"They are sleeping soundly, too."

Then it asked again,

"What does little baby mine?"

He answered,

"Sleepeth in her cradle fine."

Then she went upstairs in the form of the Queen, nursed the baby, shook up its little bed, covered it over, and then swam away again down the gutter in the shape of a duck. She came thus for two nights; on the third, she said to the scullion, "Go and tell the King to take his sword and swing it three times over me on the threshold." Then the scullion ran and told this to the King, who came with his sword and swung it thrice over the spirit, and at the third time, his wife stood before him strong, living, and healthy as she had been before. Thereupon the King was full of great joy, but he kept the Queen hidden in a chamber until the Sunday, when the baby was to be christened. And when it was christened he said, "What does a person deserve who drags another out of bed and throws him in the water?" "The wretch deserves nothing better," answered the old woman, "than to be taken and put in a barrel stuck full of nails, and rolled down hill into the water." "Then," said the King, "Thou hast pronounced thine own sentence;" and he ordered such a barrel to be brought, and the old woman to be put into it with her daughter, and then the top was hammered on, and the barrel rolled down hill until it went into the river.

THE THREE SPINNERS

THERE WAS once a girl who was idle and would not spin, and let her mother say what she would, she could not bring her to it. At last the mother was once so overcome with anger and impatience, that she beat her, on which the girl began to weep loudly. Now at this very moment the Queen drove by, and when she heard the weeping she stopped her carriage, went into the house and asked the mother why she was beating her daughter so that the cries could be heard out on the road? Then the woman was ashamed to reveal the laziness of her daughter and said, "I cannot get her to leave off spinning. She insists on spinning for ever and ever, and I am poor, and cannot procure the flax." Then answered the Queen, "There is nothing that I like better to hear than spinning, and I am never happier than when the wheels are humming. Let me have your daughter with me in the palace, I have flax enough, and there she shall spin as much as she likes." The mother was heartily satisfied with this, and the Queen took the girl with her. When they had arrived at the palace, she led her up into three rooms which were filled from the bottom to the top with the finest flax. "Now spin me this flax," said she, "and when thou hast done it, thou shalt have my eldest son for a husband, even if thou art poor. I care not for that, thy indefatigable industry is dowry enough." The girl was secretly terrified, for she could not have spun the flax, no, not if she had lived till she was three hundred years old, and had sat at it every day from morning till night. When therefore she was alone, she began to weep, and sat thus for three days without moving a finger. On the third day came the Queen, and when she saw that nothing had been spun yet, she was surprised; but the girl excused herself by saying that she had not been able to begin because of her great distress at leaving her mother's house. The queen was satisfied with this, but said when she was going away," To-morrow thou must begin to work."

When the girl was alone again, she did not know what to do, and in her distress went to the window. Then she saw three women coming towards her, the first of whom had a broad flat foot, the second had such a great underlip that it hung down over her chin, and the third had a broad thumb. They remained standing before the window, looked up, and asked the girl what was amiss with her? She complained of her trouble, and then they offered her their help and said, "If thou wilt invite us to the wedding, not be ashamed of us, and wilt call us thine aunts, and likewise wilt place us at thy table, we will spin up the flax for thee, and that in a very short time." "With all my heart," she replied, "do but come in and begin the work at once." Then she let in the three strange women, and cleared a place in the first room, where they seated themselves and began their spinning. The one drew the thread and trod the wheel, the other wetted the thread, the third twisted it, and struck the table with her finger, and as often as she struck it, a skein of thread fell to the ground that was spun in the finest manner possible. The girl concealed the three spinners from the Queen, and showed her whenever she came the great quantity of spun thread, until the latter could not praise her enough. When the first room was empty she went to the second, and at last to the third, and that too was quickly cleared. Then the three women took leave and said to the girl, "Do not forget what thou hast promised us,—it will make thy fortune."

When the maiden showed the Queen the empty rooms, and the great heap of yarn, she gave orders for the wedding, and the bridegroom* rejoiced that he was to have such a clever and industrious wife, and praised her mightily. "I have three aunts," said the girl, "and as they have been very kind to me, I should not like to forget them in my good fortune; allow me to invite them to the wedding, and let them sit with us at table." The Queen and the bridegroom said, "Why should we not allow that?" Therefore when the feast began, the three women entered in strange apparel, and the bride said, "Welcome, dear aunts." "Ah," said the bridegroom, "how comest thou by these odious friends?" Thereupon he went to the one with the broad flat foot, and said, "How do you come by such a broad foot?" "By treading," she answered, "by treading." Then the bridegroom went to the second, and said, "How do you come by your falling lip?" "By licking," she answered, "by licking." Then he asked the third, "How do you come by your broad thumb?" "By twisting the thread," she answered, "by twisting the thread." On this the King's son was alarmed and said, "Neither now nor ever shall my beautiful bride touch a spinning-wheel." And thus she got rid of the hateful flax-spinning.

---

*Braütigam, betrothed. The old English brŷdguma had the same signification, and was only applied to a betrothed man, just as brŷd, bride, was only applied to a betrothed woman.—Tr.

HÄNSEL AND GRETHEL

HARD BY a great forest dwelt a poor wood-cutter with his wife and his two children. The boy was called Hänsel and the girl Grethel. He had little to bite and to break, and once when great scarcity fell on the land, he could no longer procure daily bread. Now when he thought over this by night in his bed, and tossed about in his anxiety, he groaned and said to his wife, "What is to become of us? How are we to feed our poor children, when we no longer have anything even for ourselves?" "I'll tell you what, husband," answered the woman, "Early to-morrow morning we will take the children out into the forest to where it is the thickest, there we will light a fire for them, and give each of them one piece of bread more, and then we will go to our work and leave them alone. They will not find the way home again, and we shall be rid of them." "No, wife," said the man, "I will not do that; how can I bear to leave my children alone in the forest?—the wild animals would soon come and tear them to pieces." "O, thou fool!" said she, "Then we must all four die of hunger, thou mayest as well plane the planks for our coffins," and she left him no peace until he consented. "But I feel very sorry for the poor children, all the same," said the man.

The two children had also not been able to sleep for hunger, and had heard what their step-mother had said to their father. Grethel wept bitter tears, and said to Hänsel, "Now all is over with us." "Be quiet, Grethel," said Hänsel, "do not distress thyself, I will soon find a way to help us." And when the old folks had fallen asleep, he got up, put on his little coat, opened the door below, and crept outside. The moon shone brightly, and the white pebbles which lay in front of the house glittered like real silver pennies. Hänsel stooped and put as many of them in the little pocket of his coat as he could possibly get in. Then he went back and said to Grethel, "Be comforted, dear little sister, and sleep in peace, God will not forsake us," and he lay down again in his bed. When day dawned, but before the sun had risen, the woman came and awoke the two children, saying "Get up, you sluggards! we are going into the forest to fetch wood." She gave each a little piece of bread, and said, "There is something for your dinner, but do not eat it up before then, for you will get nothing else." Grethel took the bread under her apron, as Hänsel had the stones in his pocket. Then they all set out together on the way to the forest. When they had walked a short time, Hänsel stood still and peeped back at the house, and did so again and again. His father said, "Hänsel, what art thou looking at there and staying behind for? Mind what thou art about, and do not forget how to use thy legs." "Ah, father," said Hänsel, "I am looking at my little white cat, which is sitting up on the roof, and wants to say good-bye to me." The wife said, "Fool, that is not thy little cat, that is the morning sun which is shining on the chimneys." Hänsel, however, had not been looking back at the cat, but had been constantly throwing one of the white pebble-stones out of his pocket on the road.

When they had reached the middle of the forest, the father said, "Now, children, pile up some wood, and I will light a fire that you may not be cold." Hänsel and Grethel gathered brushwood together, as high as a little hill. The brushwood was lighted, and when the flames were burning very high, the woman said, "Now, children, lay yourselves down by the fire and rest; we will go into the forest and cut some wood. When we have done, we will come back and fetch you away."

Hänsel and Grethel sat by the fire, and when noon came, each ate a little piece of bread, and as they heard the strokes of the wood-axe they believed that their father was near. It was not, however, the axe, it was a branch which he had fastened to a withered tree which the wind was blowing backwards and forwards. And as they had been sitting such a long time, their eyes shut with fatigue, and they fell fast asleep. When at last they awoke, it was already dark night. Grethel began to cry and said, "How are we to get out of the forest now?" But Hänsel comforted her and said, "Just wait a little, until the moon has risen, and then we will soon find the way." And when the full moon had risen, Hänsel took his little sister by the hand, and followed the pebbles which shone like newly-coined silver pieces, and showed them the way.

They walked the whole night long, and by break of day came once more to their father's house. They knocked at the door, and when the woman opened it and saw that it was Hänsel and Grethel, she said, "You naughty children, why have you slept so long in the forest?—we thought you were never coming back at all!" The father, however, rejoiced, for it had cut him to the heart to leave them behind alone.

Not long afterwards, there was once more great scarcity in all parts, and the children heard their mother saying at night to their father, "Everything is eaten again, we have one half loaf left, and after that there is an end. The children must go, we will take them farther into the wood, so that they will not find their way out again; there is no other means of saving ourselves!" The man's heart was heavy, and he thought "it would be better for thee to share the last mouthful with thy children." The woman, however, would listen to nothing that he had to say, but scolded and reproached him. He who says A must say B, likewise, and as he had yielded the first time, he had to do so a second time also.

The children were, however, still awake and had heard the conversation. When the old folks were asleep, Hänsel again got up, and wanted to go out and pick up pebbles as he had done before, but the woman had locked the door, and Hänsel could not get out. Nevertheless he comforted his little sister, and said, "Do not cry, Grethel, go to sleep quietly, the good God will help us."

Early in the morning came the woman, and took the children out of their beds. Their bit of bread was given to them, but it was still smaller than the time before. On the way into the forest Hänsel crumbled his in his pocket, and often stood still and threw a morsel on the ground. "Hänsel, why dost thou stop and look round?" said the father, "go on." "I am looking back at my little pigeon which is sitting on the roof, and wants to say good-bye to me," answered Hänsel. "Simpleton!" said the woman, "that is not thy little pigeon, that is the morning sun that is shining on the chimney." Hänsel, however, little by little, threw all the crumbs on the path.

The woman led the children still deeper into the forest, where they had never in their lives been before. Then a great fire was again made, and the mother said, "Just sit there, you children, and when you are tired you may sleep a little; we are going into the forest to cut wood, and in the evening when we are done, we will come and fetch you away." When it was noon, Grethel shared her piece of bread with Hänsel, who had scattered his by the way. Then they fell asleep and evening came and went, but no one came to the poor children. They did not awake until it was dark night, and Hänsel comforted his little sister and said, "Just wait, Grethel, until the moon rises, and then we shall see the crumbs of bread which I have strewn about, they will show us our way home again." When the moon came they set out, but they found no crumbs, for the many thousands of birds which fly about in the woods and fields had picked them all up. Hänsel said to Grethel, "We shall soon find the way," but they did not find it. They walked the whole night and all the next day too from morning till evening, but they did not get out of the forest, and were very hungry, for they had nothing to eat but two or three berries, which grew on the ground. And as they were so weary that their legs would carry them no longer, they lay down beneath a tree and fell asleep.

It was now three mornings since they had left their father's house. They began to walk again, but they always got deeper into the forest, and if help did not come soon, they must die of hunger and weariness. When it was mid-day, they saw a beautiful snow-white bird sitting on a bough, which sang so delightfully that they stood still and listened to it. And when it had finished its song, it spread its wings and flew away before them, and they followed it until they reached a little house, on the roof of which it alighted; and when they came quite up to little house they saw that it was built of bread and covered with cakes, but that the windows were of clear sugar. "We will set to work on that," said Hänsel, "and have a good meal. I will eat a bit of the roof, and thou, Grethel, canst eat some of the window, it will taste sweet." Hänsel reached up above, and broke off a little of the roof to try how it tasted, and Grethel leant against the window and nibbled at the panes. Then a soft voice cried from the room,

"Nibble, nibble, gnaw,
Who is nibbling at my little house?"

The children answered,

"The wind, the wind,
The heaven-born wind,"

and went on eating without disturbing themselves. Hänsel, who thought the roof tasted very nice, tore down a great piece of it, and Grethel pushed out the whole of one round window-pane, sat down, and enjoyed herself with it. Suddenly the door opened, and a very, very old woman, who supported herself on crutches, came creeping out. Hänsel and Grethel were so terribly frightened that they let fall what they had in their hands. The old woman, however, nodded her head, and said, "Oh, you dear children, who has brought you here? Do come in, and stay with me. No harm shall happen to you." She took them both by the hand, and led them into her little house. Then good food was set before them, milk and pancakes, with sugar, apples, and nuts. Afterwards two pretty little beds were covered with clean white linen, and Hänsel and Grethel lay down in them, and thought they were in heaven.

The old woman had only pretended to be so kind; she was in reality a wicked witch, who lay in wait for children, and had only built the little bread house in order to entice them there. When a child fell into her power, she killed it, cooked and ate it, and that was a feast day with her. Witches have red eyes, and cannot see far, but they have a keen scent like the beasts, and are aware when human beings draw near. When Hänsel and Grethel came into her neighborhood, she laughed maliciously, and said mockingly, "I have them, they shall not escape me again!" Early in the morning before the children were awake, she was already up, and when she saw both of them sleeping and looking so pretty, with their plump red cheeks, she muttered to herself, "That will be a dainty mouthful!" Then she seized Hänsel with her shrivelled hand, carried him into a little stable, and shut him in with a grated door. He might scream as he liked, that was of no use. Then she went to Grethel, shook her till she awoke, and cried, "Get up, lazy thing, fetch some water, and cook something good for thy brother, he is in the stable outside, and is to be made fat. When he is fat, I will eat him." Grethel began to weep bitterly, but it was all in vain, she was forced to do what the wicked witch ordered her.

And now the best food was cooked for poor Hänsel, but Grethel got nothing but crab-shells. Every morning the woman crept to the little stable, and cried, "Hänsel, stretch out thy finger that I may feel if thou wilt soon be fat." Hänsel, however, stretched out a little bone to her, and the old woman, who had dim eyes, could not see it, and thought it was Hänsel's finger, and was astonished that there was no way of fattening him. When four weeks had gone by, and Hänsel still continued thin, she was seized with impatience and would not wait any longer. "Hola, Grethel," she cried to the girl, "be active, and bring some water. Let Hänsel be fat or lean, to-morrow I will kill him, and cook him." Ah, how the poor little sister did lament when she had to fetch the water, and how her tears did flow down over her cheeks! "Dear God, do help us," she cried. "If the wild beasts in the forest had but devoured us, we should at any rate have died together." "Just keep thy noise to thyself," said the old woman, "all that won't help thee at all."

Early in the morning, Grethel had to go out and hang up the cauldron with the water, and light the fire. "We will bake first," said the old woman, "I have already heated the oven, and kneaded the dough." She pushed poor Grethel out to the oven, from which flames of fire were already darting. "Creep in," said the witch, "and see if it is properly heated, so that we can shut the bread in." And when once Grethel was inside, she intended to shut the oven and let her bake in it, and then she would eat her, too. But Grethel saw what she had in her mind, and said, "I do not know how I am to do it; how do you get in?" "Silly goose," said the old woman, "The door is big enough; just look, I can get in myself!" and she crept up and thrust her head into the oven. Then Grethel gave her a push that drove her far into it, and shut the iron door, and fastened the bolt. Oh! then she began to howl quite horribly, but Grethel ran away, and the godless witch was miserably burnt to death.

Grethel, however, ran like lightning to Hänsel, opened his little stable, and cried, "Hänsel, we are saved! The old witch is dead!" Then Hänsel sprang out like a bird from its cage when the door is opened for it. How they did rejoice and embrace each other, and dance about and kiss each other! And as they had no longer any need to fear her, they went into the witch's house, and in every corner there stood chests full of pearls and jewels. "These are far better than pebbles!" said Hänsel, and thrust into his pockets whatever could be got in, and Grethel said, "I, too, will take something home with me," and filled her pinafore full. "But now we will go away." said Hänsel, "that we may get out of the witch's forest."

When they had walked for two hours, they came to a great piece of water. "We cannot get over," said Hänsel, "I see no foot-plank, and no bridge." "And no boat crosses either," answered Grethel, "but a white duck is swimming there; if I ask her, she will help us over." Then she cried,

"Little duck, little duck, dost thou see,
Hänsel and Grethel are waiting for thee?
There's never a plank, or bridge in sight,
Take us across on thy back so white."

The duck came to them, and Hänsel seated himself on its back, and told his sister to sit by him. "No," replied Grethel, "that will be too heavy for the little duck; she shall take us across, one after the other." The good little duck did so, and when they were once safely across and had walked for a short time, the forest seemed to be more and more familiar to them, and at length they saw from afar their father's house. Then they began to run, rushed into the parlour, and threw themselves into their father's arms. The man had not known one happy hour since he had left the children in the forest; the woman, however, was dead. Grethel emptied her pinafore until pearls and precious stones ran about the room, and Hänsel threw one handful after another out of his pocket to add to them. Then all anxiety was at an end, and they lived together in perfect happiness. My tale is done, there runs a mouse, whosoever catches it, may make himself a big fur cap out of it.

THE THREE SNAKE-LEAVES

THERE WAS once on a time a poor man, who could no longer support his only son. Then said the son, "Dear father, things go so badly with us that I am a burden to you. I would rather go away and see how I can earn my bread." So the father gave him his blessing, and with great sorrow took leave of him. At this time the King of a mighty empire was at war, and the youth took service with him, and with him went out to fight. And when he came before the enemy, there was a battle, and great danger, and it rained shot until his comrades fell on all sides, and when the leader also was killed, those left were about to take flight, but the youth stepped forth, spoke boldly to them, and cried, "We will not let our fatherland be ruined!" Then the others followed him, and he pressed on and conquered the enemy. When the King heard that he owed the victory to him alone, he raised him above all the others, gave him great treasures, and made him the first in the kingdom.

The King had a daughter who was very beautiful, but she was also very strange. She had made a vow to take no one as her lord and husband who did not promise to let himself be buried alive with her if she died first. "If he loves me with all his heart," said she, "of what use will life be to him afterwards?" On her side she would do the same, and if he died first, would go down to the grave with him. This strange oath had up to this time frightened away all wooers, but the youth became so charmed with her beauty that he cared for nothing, but asked her father for her. "But dost thou know what thou must promise?" said the King. "I must be buried with her," he replied, "if I outlive her, but my love is so great that I do not mind the danger." Then the King consented, and the wedding was solemnized with great splendour.

They lived now for a while happy and contented with each other, and then it befell that the young Queen was attacked by a severe illness, and no physician could save her. And as she lay there dead, the young King remembered what he had been obliged to promise, and was horrified at having to lie down alive in the grave, but there was no escape. The King had placed sentries at all the gates, and it was not possible to avoid his fate. When the day came when the corpse was to be buried, he was taken down into the royal vault with it and then the door was shut and bolted.

Near the coffin stood a table on which were four candles, four loaves of bread, and four bottles of wine, and when this provision came to an end, he would have to die of hunger. And now he sat there full of pain and grief, ate every day only a little piece of bread, drank only a mouthful of wine, and nevertheless saw death daily drawing nearer. Whilst he thus gazed before him, he saw a snake creep out of a corner of the vault and approach the dead body. And as he thought it came to gnaw at it, he drew his sword and said, "As long as I live, thou shalt not touch her," and hewed the snake in three pieces. After a time a second snake crept out of the hole, and when it saw the other lying dead and cut in pieces, it went back, but soon came again with three green leaves in its mouth. Then it took the three pieces of the snake, laid them together, as they ought to go, and placed one of the leaves on each wound.* Immediately the severed parts joined themselves together, the snake moved, and became alive again, and both of them hastened away together. The leaves were left lying on the ground, and a desire came into the mind of the unhappy man who had been watching all this, to know if the wondrous power of the leaves which had brought the snake to life again, could not likewise be of service to a human being. So he picked up the leaves and laid one of them on the mouth of his dead wife, and the two others on her eyes. And hardly had he done this than the blood stirred in her veins, rose into her pale face, and coloured it again. Then she drew breath, opened her eyes, and said, "Ah, God, where am I?" "Thou art with me, dear wife," he answered, and told her how everything had happened, and how he had brought her back again to life. Then he gave her some wine and bread, and when she had regained her strength, he raised her up and they went to the door and knocked, and called so loudly that the sentries heard it, and told the King. The King came down himself and opened the door, and there he found both strong and well, and rejoiced with them that now all sorrow was over. The young King, however, took the three snake-leaves with him, gave them to a servant and said, "Keep them for me carefully, and carry

---

*It is strange that it did not occur to the Brothers Grimm that three leaves were not wanted. The snake was cut in three pieces, and there could only have been *two* wounds.—TR.

them constantly about thee; who knows in what trouble they may yet be of service to us!"

A change had, however, taken place in his wife; after she had been restored to life, it seemed as if all love for her husband had gone out of her heart. After some time, when he wanted to make a voyage over the sea, to visit his old father, and they had gone on board a ship, she forgot the great love and fidelity which he had shown her, and which had been the means of rescuing her from death, and conceived a wicked inclination for the skipper. And once when the young King lay there asleep, she called in the skipper and seized the sleeper by the head, and the skipper took him by the feet, and thus they threw him down into the sea. When the shameful deed was done, she said, "Now let us return home, and say that he died on the way. I will extol and praise thee so to my father that he will marry me to thee, and make thee the heir to his crown." But the faithful servant who had seen all that they did, unseen by them, unfastened a little boat from the ship, got into it, sailed after his master, and let the traitors go on their way. He fished up the dead body, and by the help of the three snake-leaves which he carried about with him, and laid on the eyes and mouth, he fortunately brought the young King back to life.

They both rowed with all their strength day and night, and their little boat flew so swiftly that they reached the old King before the others did. He was astonished when he saw them come alone, and asked what had happened to them. When he learnt the wickedness of his daughter he said, "I cannot believe that she has behaved so ill, but the truth will soon come to light," and bade both go into a secret chamber and keep themselves hidden from every one. Soon afterwards the great ship came sailing in, and the godless woman appeared before her father with a troubled countenance. He said, "Why dost thou come back alone? Where is thy husband?" "Ah, dear father," she replied, "I come home again in great grief; during the voyage, my husband became suddenly ill and died, and if the good skipper had not given me his help, it would have gone ill with me. He was present at his death, and can tell you all." The King said, "I will make the dead alive again," and opened the chamber, and bade the two come out. When the woman saw her husband, she was thunderstruck, and fell on her knees and begged for mercy. The King said, "There is no mercy. He was ready to die with thee and restored thee to life again, but thou hast murdered him in his sleep, and shalt receive the reward that thou deservest." Then she was placed with her accomplice in a ship which had been pierced with holes, and sent out to sea, where they soon sank amid the waves.

THE WHITE SNAKE

A LONG time ago there lived a king who was famed for his wisdom through all the land. Nothing was hidden from him, and it seemed as if news of the most secret things was brought to him through the air. But he had a strange custom; every day after dinner, when the table was cleared, and no one else was present, a trusty servant had to bring him one more dish. It was covered, however, and even the servant did not know what was in it, neither did any-one know, for the King never took off the cover to eat of it until he was quite alone.

This had gone on for a long time, when one day the servant, who took away the dish, was overcome with such curiosity that he could not help carrying the dish into his room. When he had carefully locked the door, he lifted up the cover, and saw a white snake lying on the dish. But when he saw it he could not deny himself the pleasure of tasting it, so he cut off a little bit and put it into his mouth. No sooner had it touched his tongue than he heard a strange whispering of little voices outside his window. He went and listened, and then noticed that it was the sparrows who were chattering together, and telling one another of all kinds of things which they had seen in the fields and woods. Eating the snake had given him power of understanding the language of animals.

Now it so happened that on this very day the Queen lost her most beautiful ring, and suspicion of having stolen it fell upon this trusty servant, who was allowed to go everywhere. The King ordered the man to be brought before him, and threatened with angry words that unless he could before the morrow point out the thief, he himself should be looked upon as guilty and executed. In vain he declared his innocence; he was dismissed with no better answer.

In his trouble and fear he went down into the courtyard and took thought how to help himself out of his trouble. Now some ducks were sitting together quietly by a brook and taking their rest; and, whilst they were making their feathers smooth with their bills, they were having a confidential conversation together. The servant stood by and listened. They were telling one another of all the places where they had been waddling about all the morning, and what good food they had found, and one said in a pitiful tone, "Something lies heavy on my stomach; as I was eating in haste I swallowed a ring which lay under the Queen's window." The servant at once seized her by the neck, carried her to the kitchen, and said to the cook, "Here is a fine duck; pray, kill her." "Yes," said the cook, and weighed her in his hand; "she has spared no trouble to fatten herself, and has been waiting to be roasted long enough." So he cut off her head, and as she was being dressed for the spit, the Queen's ring was found inside her.

The servant could now easily prove his innocence; and the King, to make amends for the wrong, allowed him to ask a favor, and promised him the best place in the court that he could wish for. The servant refused everything, and only asked for a horse and some money for travelling, as he had a mind to see the world and go about a little.

When his request was granted he set out on his way, and one day came to a pond, where he saw three fishes caught in the reeds and gasping for water. Now, though it is said that fishes are dumb, he heard them lamenting that they must perish so miserably, and, as he had a kind heart, he got off his horse and put the three prisoners back into the water. They quivered with delight, put out their heads, and cried to him, "We will remember you and repay you for saving us!"

He rode on, and after a while it seemed to him that he heard a voice in the sand at his feet. He listened, and heard an ant-king complain, "Why cannot folks, with their clumsy beasts, keep off our bodies? That stupid horse, with his heavy hoofs, has been treading down my people without mercy!" So he turned on to a side path and the ant-king cried out to him, 'We will remember you—one good turn deserves another!"

The path led him into a wood, and there he saw two old ravens standing by their nest, and throwing out their young ones. "Out with you, you idle, good-for-nothing creatures!" cried they; "we cannot find food for you any longer; you are big enough, and can provide for yourselves." But the poor young ravens lay upon the ground, flapping their wings, and crying, "Oh, what helpless chicks we are! We must shift for ourselves, and yet we cannot fly! What can we do, but lie here and starve?" So the good young fellow alighted and killed his horse with his sword, and gave it to them for food. Then they came hopping up to it, satisfied their hunger, and cried, "We will remember you—one good turn deserves another!"

And now he had to use his own legs, and when he had walked a long way, he came to a large city. There was a great noise and crowd in the streets, and a man rode up on horseback, crying aloud, "The King's daughter wants a husband; but whoever sues for her hand must perform a hard task, and if he does not succeed he will forfeit his life." Many had already made the attempt, but in vain; nevertheless when the youth saw the King's daughter he was so overcome by her great beauty that he forgot all danger, went before the King, and declared himself a suitor.

So he was led out to the sea, and a gold ring was thrown into it, in his sight; then the King ordered him to fetch this ring up from the bottom of the sea, and added, "If you come up again without it you will be thrown in again and again until you perish amid the waves." All the people grieved for the handsome youth; then they went away, leaving him alone by the sea.

He stood on the shore and considered what he should do, when suddenly he saw three fishes come swimming towards him, and they were the very fishes whose lives he had saved. The one in the middle held a mussel in its mouth, which it laid on the shore at the youth's feet, and when he had taken it up and opened it, there lay the gold ring in the shell. Full of joy he took it to the King, and expected that he would grant him the promised reward.

But when the proud princess perceived that he was not her equal in birth, she scorned him, and required him first to perform another task. She went down into the garden and strewed with her own hands ten sacks-full of millet-seed on the grass; then she said, "To-morrow morning before sunrise these must be picked up, and not a single grain be wanting."

The youth sat down in the garden and considered how it might be possible to perform this task, but he could think of nothing, and there he sat sorrowfully awaiting the break of day, when he should be led to death. But as soon as the first rays of the sun shone into the garden he saw all the ten sacks standing side by side, quite full, and not a single grain was missing. The ant-king had come in the night with thousands and thousands of ants, and the grateful creatures had by great industry picked up all the millet-seed and gathered them into the sacks.

Presently the King's daughter herself came down into the garden, and was amazed to see that the young man had done the task she had given him. But she could not yet conquer her proud heart, and said, "Although he has performed both the tasks, he shall not be my husband until he has brought me an apple from the Tree of Life."

The youth did not know where the Tree of Life stood, but he set out, and would have gone on for ever, as long as his legs would carry him, though he had no hope of finding it. After he had wandered through three kingdoms, he came one evening to a wood, and lay down under a tree to sleep. But he heard a rustling in the branches, and a golden apple fell into his hand. At the same time three ravens flew down to him, perched themselves upon his knee, and said, "We are the three young ravens whom you saved from starving; when we had grown big, and heard that you were seeking the Golden Apple, we flew over the sea to the end of the world, where the Tree of Life stands, and have brought you the apple." The youth, full of joy, set out homewards, and took the Golden Apple to the King's beautiful daughter, who had no more excuses left to make. They cut the Apple of Life in two and ate it together; and then her heart became full of love for him, and they lived in undisturbed happiness to a great age.

THE STRAW, THE COAL, AND THE BEAN

IN A village dwelt a poor old woman, who had gathered together a dish of beans and wanted to cook them. So she made a fire on her hearth, and that it might burn the quicker, she lighted it with a handful of straw. When she was emptying the beans into the pan, one dropped without her observing it, and lay on the ground beside a straw, and soon afterwards a burning coal from the fire leapt down to the two. Then the straw began and said, "Dear friends, from whence do you come here?" The coal replied, "I fortunately sprang out of the fire, and if I had not escaped by main force, my death would have been certain,—I should have been burnt to ashes." The bean said, "I too have escaped with a whole skin, but if the old woman had got me into the pan, I should have been made into broth without any mercy, like my comrades." "And would a better fate have fallen to my lot?" said the straw. "The old woman has destroyed all my brethren in fire and smoke; she seized sixty of them at once, and took their lives. I luckily slipped through her fingers."

"But what are we to do now?" said the coal.

"I think," answered the bean, "that as we have so fortunately escaped death, we should keep together like good companions, and lest a new mischance should overtake us here, we should go away together, and repair to a foreign country."

The proposition pleased the two others, and they set out on their way in company. Soon, however, they came to a little brook, and as there was no bridge or foot-plank, they did not know how they were to get over it. The straw hit on a good idea, and said, "I will lay myself straight across, and then you can walk over on me as on a bridge." The straw therefore stretched itself from one bank to the other, and the coal, who was of an impetuous disposition, tripped quite boldly on to the newly-built bridge. But when she had reached the middle, and heard the water rushing beneath her, she was, after all, afraid, and stood still, and ventured no farther. The straw, however, began to burn, broke in two pieces, and fell into the stream. The coal slipped after her, hissed when she got into the water, and breathed her last. The bean, who had prudently stayed behind on the shore, could not but laugh at the event, was unable to stop, and laughed so heartily that she burst. It would have been all over with her, likewise, if, by good fortune, a tailor who was traveling in search of work, had not sat down to rest by the brook. As he had a compassionate heart he pulled out his needle and thread, and sewed her together. The bean thanked him most prettily, but as the tailor used black thread, all beans since then have a black seam.

THE FISHERMAN AND HIS WIFE*

THERE WAS once on a time a Fisherman who lived with his wife in a miserable hovel close by the sea, and every day he went out fishing. And once as he was sitting with his rod, looking at the clear water, his line suddenly went down, far down below, and when he drew it up again he brought out a large Flounder. Then the Flounder said to him, "Hark, you Fisherman, I pray you, let me live, I am no Flounder really, but an enchanted prince. What good will it do you to kill me? I should not be good to eat, put me in the water again, and let me go." "Come," said the Fisherman, "there is no need for so many words about it—a fish that can talk I should certainly let go, anyhow," with that he put him back again into the clear water, and the Flounder went to the bottom, leaving a long streak of blood behind him. Then the Fisherman got up and went home to his wife in the hovel.

"Husband," said the woman, "have you caught nothing to-day?" "No," said the man, "I did catch a Flounder, who said he was an enchanted prince, so I let him go again." "Did you not wish for anything first?" said the woman. "No," said the man; "what should I wish for?" "Ah," said the woman, "it is surely hard to have to live always in this dirty hovel; you might have wished for a small cottage for us. Go back and call him. Tell him we want to have a small cottage, he will certainly give us that." "Ah," said the man, "why should I go there again?" "Why," said the woman, "you did catch him, and you let him go again; he is sure to do it. Go at once." The man still did not quite like to go, but did not like to oppose his wife, and went to the sea.

When he got there the sea was all green and yellow, and no longer so smooth; so he stood and said,

---

*According to the late William Howitt, this story was communicated to the Brothers Grimm by Mr. Henry Crabbe Robinson, who had it from an old woman. See 'Diary of H. C. Robinson.'—TR.

"Flounder, flounder in the sea,
Come, I pray thee, here to me;
For my wife, good Ilsabil,*
Wills not as I'd have her will."

Then the Flounder came swimming to him and said, "Well what does she want, then?" "Ah," said the man, "I did catch you, and my wife says I really ought to have wished for something; she does not like to live in a wretched hovel any longer. She would like to have a cottage." "Go, then," said the Flounder, "she has it already."

When the man went home, his wife was no longer in the hovel, but instead of it there stood a small cottage, and she was sitting on a bench before the door. Then she took him by the hand and said to him, "Just come inside, look, now isn't this a great deal better?" So they went in, and there was a small porch, and a pretty little parlor and bedroom, and a kitchen and pantry, with the best of furniture, and fitted up with the most beautiful things made of tin and brass, whatsoever was wanted. And behind the cottage there was a small yard, with hens and ducks, and a little garden with flowers and fruit. "Look," said the wife, "is not that nice!" "Yes," said the husband, "and so we must always think it,—now we will live quite contented." "We will think about that," said the wife. With that they ate something and went to bed.

Everything went well for a week or a fortnight, and then the woman said, "Hark you, husband, this cottage is far too small for us, and the garden and yard are little; the Flounder might just as well have given us a larger house. I should like to live in a great stone castle; go to the Flounder, and tell him to give us a castle." "Ah, wife," said the man, "the cottage is quite good enough; why should we live in a castle?" "What!" said the woman; "just go there, the Flounder can always do that." "No, wife," said the man, "the Flounder has just given us the cottage, I do not like to go back so soon, it might make him angry." "Go," said the woman, "he can do it quite easily, and will be glad to do it; just you go to him."

The man's heart grew heavy, and he would not go. He said to himself, "It is not right," and yet he went. And when he came to the sea the water was quite purple and dark-blue, and grey and thick, and no longer so green and yellow, but it was still quiet. And he stood there and said—

"Flounder, flounder in the sea,
Come, I pray thee, here to me;
For my wife, good Ilsabil,
Wills not as I'd have her will.

*Isabel.—TR.

"Well, what does she want, then?" said the Flounder. "Alas," said the man, half scared, "she wants to live in a great stone castle." "Go to it, then, she is standing before the door," said the Flounder.

Then the man went away, intending to go home, but when he got there, he found a great stone palace, and his wife was just standing on the steps going in, and she took him by the hand and said, "Come in." So he went in with her, and in the castle was a great hall paved with marble, and many servants, who flung wide the doors; and the walls were all bright with beautiful hangings, and in the rooms were chairs and tables of pure gold, and crystal chandeliers hung from the ceiling, and all the rooms and bed-rooms had carpets, and food and wine of the very best were standing on all the tables so that they nearly broke down beneath it. Behind the house, too, there was a great court-yard, with stables for horses and cows, and the very best of carriages; there was a magnificent large garden, too, with the most beautiful flowers and fruit-trees, and a park quite half a mile long, in which were stags, deer, and hares, and everything that could be desired. "Come," said the woman, "isn't that beautiful?" "Yes, indeed," said the man, "now let it be; and we will live in this beautiful castle and be content." "We will consider about that," said the woman, "and sleep upon it;" thereupon they went to bed.

Next morning the wife awoke first, and it was just daybreak, and from her bed she saw the beautiful country lying before her. Her husband was still stretching himself, so she poked him in the side with her elbow, and said, "Get up, husband, and just peep out of the window. Look you, couldn't we be the King over all that land? Go to the Flounder, we will be the King." "Ah, wife," said the man, "why should we be King? I do not want to be King." "Well," said the wife, "if you won't be King, I will; go to the Flounder, for I will be King." "Ah, wife," said the man, "why do you want to be King? I do not like to say that to him." "Why not?" said the woman; "go to him this instant; I must be King!" So the man went, and was quite unhappy because his wife wished to be King. "It is not right; it is not right," thought he. He did not wish to go, but yet he went.

And when he came to the sea, it was quite dark-grey, and the water heaved up from below, and smelt putrid. Then he went and stood by it, and said,

"Flounder, flounder in the sea,
Come, I pray thee, here to me;
For my wife, good Ilsabil,
Wills not as I'd have her will."

"Well, what does she want, then?" said the Flounder. "Alas," said the man, "she wants to be King." "Go to her; she is King already."

So the man went, and when he came to the palace, the castle had become much larger, and had a great tower and magnificent ornaments, and the sentinel was standing before the door, and there were numbers of soldiers with kettle-drums and trumpets. And when he went inside the house, everything was of real marble and gold, with velvet covers and great golden tassels. Then the doors of the hall were opened, and there was the court in all its splendour, and his wife was sitting on a high throne of gold and diamonds, with a great crown of gold on her head, and a sceptre of pure gold and jewels in her hand, and on both sides of her stood her maids-in-waiting in a row, each of them always one head shorter than the last.

Then he went and stood before her, and said, "Ah, wife, and now you are King." "Yes," said the woman, "now I am King." So he stood and looked at her, and when he had looked at her thus for some time, he said, "And now that you are King, let all else be, now we will wish for nothing more." "Nay, husband," said the woman, quite anxiously, "I find time pass very heavily, I can bear it no longer; go to the Flounder—I am King, but I must be Emperor, too." "Alas, wife, why do you wish to be Emperor?" "Husband," said she, "go to the Flounder. I will be Emperor." "Alas, wife," said the man, "he cannot make you Emperor; I may not say that to the fish. There is only one Emperor in the land. An Emperor the Flounder cannot make you! I assure you he cannot."

"What!" said the woman, "I am the King, and you are nothing but my husband; will you go this moment? go at once! If he can make a king he can make an emperor. I will be Emperor; go instantly." So he was forced to go. As the man went, however, he was troubled in mind, and thought to himself, "It will not end well; it will not end well! Emperor is too shameless! The Flounder will at last be tired out."

With that he reached the sea, and the sea was quite black and thick, and began to boil up from below, so that it threw up bubbles, and such a sharp wind blew over it that it curdled, and the man was afraid. Then he went and stood by it, and said,

"Flounder, flounder in the sea,
Come, I pray thee, here to me;
For my wife, good Ilsabil,
Wills not as I'd have her will."

"Well, what does she want, then?" said the Flounder. "Alas, Flounder," said he, "my wife wants to be Emperor." "Go to her," said the Flounder; "she is Emperor already."

So the man went, and when he got there the whole palace was made of polished marble with alabaster figures and golden ornaments, and soldiers were marching before the door blowing trumpets, and beating cymbals and drums; and in the house, barons, and counts, and dukes were going about as servants. Then they opened the doors to him, which were of pure gold. And when he entered, there sat his wife on a throne, which was made of one piece of gold, and was quite two miles high; and she wore a great golden crown that was three yards high, and set with diamonds and carbuncles, and in one hand she had the sceptre, and in the other the imperial orb; and on both sides of her stood the yeomen of the guard in two rows, each being smaller than the one before him, from the biggest giant, who was two miles high, to the very smallest dwarf, just as big as my little finger. And before it stood a number of princes and dukes.

Then the man went and stood among them, and said, "Wife, are you Emperor now?" "Yes," said she, "now I am Emperor." Then he stood and looked at her well, and when he had looked at her thus for some time, he said, "Ah, wife, be content, now that you are Emperor." "Husband," said she, "why are you standing there? Now, I am Emperor, but I will be Pope too; go to the Flounder." "Alas, wife," said the man, "what will you not wish for? You cannot be Pope; there is but one in Christendom; he cannot make you Pope." "Husband," said she, "I will be Pope; go immediately, I must be Pope this very day." "No, wife," said the man, "I do not like to say that to him; that would not do, it is too much; the Flounder can't make you Pope." "Husband," said she, "what nonsense! If he can make an emperor he can make a pope. Go to him directly. I am Emperor, and you are nothing but my husband; will you go at once?"

Then he was afraid and went; but he was quite faint, and shivered and shook, and his knees and legs trembled. And a high wind blew over the land, and the clouds flew, and towards evening all grew dark, and the leaves fell from the trees, and the water rose and roared as if it were boiling, and splashed upon the shore. And in the distance he saw ships which were firing guns in their sore need, pitching and tossing on the waves. And yet in the midst of the sky there was still a small bit of blue, though on every side it was as red as in a heavy storm. So, full of despair, he went and stood in much fear and said,

"Flounder, flounder in the sea,
Come, I pray thee, here to me;
For my wife, good Ilsabil,
Wills not as I'd have her will.

"Well, what does she want, then?" said the Flounder. "Alas," said the man, "she wants to be Pope." "Go to her then," said the Flounder; "she is Pope already."

So he went, and when he got there, he saw what seemed to be a large church surrounded by palaces. He pushed his way through the crowd. Inside, however, everything was lighted up with thousands and thousands of candles, and his wife was clad in gold, and she was sitting on a much higher throne, and had three great golden crowns on, and round about her there was much ecclesiastical splendour; and on both sides of her was a row of candles the largest of which was as tall as the very tallest tower, down to the very smallest kitchen candle, and all the emperors and kings were on their knees before her, kissing her shoe. "Wife," said the man, and looked attentively at her, "are you now Pope?" "Yes," said she, "I am Pope." So he stood and looked at her, and it was just as if he was looking at the bright sun. When he had stood looking at her thus for a short time, he said, "Ah, wife, if you are Pope, do let well alone!" But she looked as stiff as a post, and did not move or show any signs of life. Then said he, "Wife, now that you are Pope, be satisfied, you cannot become anything greater now." "I will consider about that," said the woman. Thereupon they both went to bed, but she was not satisfied, and greediness let her have no sleep, for she was continually thinking what there was left for her to be.

The man slept well and soundly, for he had run about a great deal during the day; but the woman could not fall asleep at all, and flung herself from one side to the other the whole night through, thinking always what more was left for her to be, but unable to call to mind anything else. At length the sun began to rise, and when the woman saw the red of dawn, she sat up in bed and looked at it. And when, through the window, she saw the sun thus rising, she said, "Cannot I, too, order the sun and moon to rise?" "Husband," said she, poking him in the ribs with her elbows, "wake up! go to the Flounder, for I wish to be even as God is." The man was still half asleep, but he was so horrified that he fell out of bed. He thought he must have heard amiss, and rubbed his eyes, and said, "Alas, wife, what are you saying?" "Husband," said she, "if I can't order the sun and moon to rise, and have to look on and see the sun and moon rising, I can't bear it. I shall not know what it is to have another happy hour, unless I can make them rise myself." Then she looked at him so terribly that a shudder ran over him, and said, "Go at once; I wish to be like unto God." "Alas, wife," said the man, falling on his knees before her, "the Flounder cannot do that; he can make an emperor and a pope; I beseech you, go on as you are, and be Pope." Then she fell into a rage, and her hair flew wildly about her head, and she cried, "I will not endure this, I'll not bear it any longer; wilt thou go?" Then he put on his trousers and ran away like a madman. But outside a great storm was raging, and blowing so hard that he could scarcely keep his feet; houses and trees toppled over, the mountains trembled, rocks rolled into the sea, the sky was pitch black, and it thundered and lightened, and the sea came in with black waves as high as church-towers and mountains, and all with crests of white foam at the top. Then he cried, but could not hear his own words,

"Flounder, flounder in the sea,
Come, I pray thee, here to me;
For my wife, good Ilsabil,
Wills not as I'd have her will."

"Well, what does she want, then?" said the Flounder. "Alas," said he, "she wants to be like unto God." "Go to her, and you will find her back again in the dirty hovel." And there they are living still at this very time.

THE VALIANT LITTLE TAILOR

One summer's morning a little tailor was sitting on his table by the window; he was in good spirits, and sewed with all his might. Then came a peasant woman down the street crying, "Good jams, cheap! Good jams, cheap!" This rang pleasantly in the tailor's ears; he stretched his delicate head out of the window, and called, "Come up here, dear woman; here you will get rid of your goods." The woman came up the three steps to the tailor with her heavy basket, and he made her unpack the whole of the pots for him. He inspected all of them, lifted them up, put his nose to them, and at length said, "The jam seems to me to be good, so weigh me out four ounces, dear woman, and if it is a quarter of a pound that is of no consequence." The woman who had hoped to find a good sale, gave him what he desired, but went away quite angry and grumbling. "Now, God bless the jam to my use," cried the little tailor, "and give me health and strength"; so he brought the bread out of the cupboard, cut himself a piece right across the loaf and spread the jam over it. "This won't taste bitter," said he, "but I will just finish the jacket before I take a bite." He laid the bread near him, sewed on, and in his joy, made bigger and bigger stitches. In the meantime the smell of the sweet jam ascended so to the wall, where the flies were sitting in great numbers, that they were attracted and descended on it in hosts. "Hola! who invited you?" said the little tailor, and drove the unbidden guests away. The flies, however, who understood no German, would not be turned away, but came back again in ever-increasing companies. Then the little tailor at last lost all patience, and got a bit of cloth from the hole under his work-table, and saying, "Wait, and I will give it to you," struck it mercilessly on them. When he drew it away and counted, there lay before him no fewer than seven, dead and with legs stretched out. "Art thou a fellow of that sort?" said he, and could not help admiring his own bravery. "The whole town shall know of this!" And the little tailor hastened to cut himself a girdle, stitched it, and embroidered on it in large letters, "Seven at one stroke!" "What, the town!" he continued, "The whole world shall hear of it!" and his heart wagged with joy like a lamb's tail. The tailor put on the girdle, and resolved to go forth into the world, because he thought his workshop was too small for his valour. Before he went away, he sought about in the house to see if there was anything which he could take with him; however, he found nothing but an old cheese, and that he put in his pocket. In front of the door he observed a bird which had caught itself in the thicket. It had to go into his pocket with the cheese. Now he took to the road boldly, and as he was light and nimble, he felt no fatigue. The road led him up a mountain, and when he had reached the highest point of it, there sat a powerful giant looking about him quite comfortably. The little tailor went bravely up, spoke to him, and said, "Good day, comrade, so thou art sitting there overlooking the wide-spread world! I am just on my way thither, and want to try my luck. Hast thou any inclination to go with me?" The giant looked contemptuously at the tailor, and said, "Thou ragamuffin! Thou miserable creature!"

"Oh, indeed?" answered the little tailor, and unbuttoned his coat, and showed the giant the girdle, "There mayst thou read what kind of a man I am!" The giant read, "Seven at one stroke," and thought that they had been men whom the tailor had killed, and began to feel a little respect for the tiny fellow. Nevertheless, he wished to try him first, and took a stone in his hand and squeezed it together so that water dropped out of it. "Do that likewise," said the giant, "if thou hast strength?" "Is that all?" said the tailor, "that is child's play with us!" and put his hand into his pocket, brought out the soft cheese, and pressed it until the liquid ran out of it. "Faith," said he, "that was a little better, wasn't it?" The giant did not know what to say, and could not believe it of the little man. Then the giant picked up a stone and threw it so high that the eye could scarcely follow it. "Now, little mite of a man, do that likewise." "Well thrown," said the tailor, "but after all the stone came down to earth again; I will throw you one which shall never come back at all," and he put his hand into his pocket, took out the bird, and threw it into the air. The bird, delighted with its liberty, rose, flew away and did not come back. "How does that shot please you, comrade?" asked the tailor. "Thou canst certainly throw," said the giant, "but now we will see if thou art able to carry anything properly." He took the little tailor to a mighty oak tree which lay there felled on the ground, and said, "If thou art strong enough, help me to carry the tree out of the forest." "Readily," answered the little man; "take thou the trunk on thy shoulders, and I will raise up the branches and twigs; after all, they are the heaviest." The giant took the trunk on his shoulder, but the tailor seated himself on a branch, and the giant who could not look round, had to carry away the whole tree, and the little tailor into the bargain: he behind, was quite merry and happy, and whistled the song, "Three tailors rode forth from the gate," as if carrying the tree were child's play. The giant, after he had dragged the heavy burden part of the way, could go no further, and cried, "Hark you, I shall have to let the tree fall!" The tailor sprang nimbly down, seized the tree with both arms as if he had been carrying it, and said to the giant, "Thou art such a great fellow, and yet canst not even carry the tree!"

They went on together, and as they passed a cherry-tree, the giant laid hold of the top of the tree where the ripest fruit was hanging, bent it down, gave it into the tailor's hand, and bade him eat. But the little tailor was much too weak to hold the tree, and when the giant let it go, it sprang back again, and the tailor was hurried into the air with it. When he had fallen down again without injury, the giant said, "What is this? Hast thou not strength enough to hold the weak twig?" "There is no lack of strength," answered the little tailor. "Dost thou think that could be anything to a man who has struck down seven at one blow? I leapt over the tree because the huntsmen are shooting down there in the thicket. Jump as I did, if thou canst do it." The giant made the attempt, but could not get over the tree, and remained hanging in the branches, so that in this also the tailor kept the upper hand.

The giant said, "If thou art such a valiant fellow, come with me into our cavern and spend the night with us." The little tailor was willing, and followed him. When they went into the cave, other giants were sitting there by the fire, and each of them had a roasted sheep in his hand and was eating it. The little tailor looked round and thought, "It is much more spacious here than in my workshop." The giant showed him a bed, and said he was to lie down in it and sleep. The bed was, however, too big for the little tailor; he did not lie down in it, but crept into a corner. When it was midnight, and the giant thought that the little tailor was lying in a sound sleep, he got up, took a great iron bar, cut through the bed with one blow, and thought he had given the grasshopper his finishing stroke. With the earliest dawn the giants went into the forest, and had quite forgotten the little tailor, when all at once he walked up to them quite merrily and boldly. The giants were terrified, they were afraid that he would strike them all dead, and ran away in a great hurry.

The little tailor went onwards, always following his own pointed nose. After he had walked for a long time, he came to the court-yard of a royal palace, and as he felt weary, he lay down on the grass and fell asleep. Whilst he lay there, the people came and inspected him on all sides, and read on his girdle, "Seven at one stroke." "Ah," said they, "What does the great warrior here in the midst of peace? He must be a mighty lord." They went and announced him to the King, and gave it as their opinion that if war should break out, this would be a weighty and useful man who ought on no account to be allowed to depart. The counsel pleased the King, and he sent one of his courtiers to the little tailor to offer him military service when he awoke. The ambassador remained standing by the sleeper, waited until he stretched his limbs and opened his eyes, and then conveyed to him this proposal. "For this very reason have I come here," the tailor replied, "I am ready to enter the King's service." He was therefore honorably received and a special dwelling was assigned him.

The soldiers, however, were set against the little tailor, and wished him a thousand miles away. "What is to be the end of this?" they said amongst themselves. "If we quarrel with him, and he strikes about him, seven of us will fall at every blow; not one of us can stand against him." They came therefore to a decision, betook themselves in a body to the King, and begged for their dismissal. "We are not prepared," said they, "to stay with a man who kills seven at one stroke." The King was sorry that for the sake of one he should lose all his faithful servants, wished that he had never set eyes on the tailor, and would willingly have been rid of him again. But he did not venture to give him his dismissal, for he dreaded lest he should strike him and all his people dead, and place himself on the royal throne. He thought about it for a long time, and at last found good counsel. He sent to the little tailor and caused him to be informed that as he was such a great warrior, he had one request to make to him. In a forest of his country lived two giants who caused great mischief with their robbing, murdering, ravaging, and burning, and no one could approach them without putting himself in danger of death. If the tailor conquered and killed these two giants, he would give him his only daughter to wife, and half of his kingdom as a dowry, likewise one hundred horsemen should go with him to assist him. "That would indeed be a fine thing for a man like me!" thought the little tailor. "One is not offered a beautiful princess and half a kingdom every day of one's life!" "Oh, yes," he replied, "I will soon subdue the giants, and do not require the help of the hundred horsemen to do it; he who can hit seven with one blow has no need to be afraid of two."

The little tailor went forth, and the hundred horsemen followed him. When he came to the outskirts of the forest, he said to his followers, "Just stay waiting here, I alone will soon finish off the giants." Then he bounded into the forest and looked about right and left. After a while he perceived both giants. They lay sleeping under a tree, and snored so that the branches waved up and down. The little tailor, not idle, gathered two pocketsful of stones, and with these climbed up the tree. When he was half-way up, he slipped down by a branch, until he sat just above the sleepers, and then let one stone after another fall on the breast of one of the giants. For a long time the giant felt nothing, but at last he awoke, pushed his comrade, and said, "Why art thou knocking me?" "Thou must be dreaming," said the other, "I am not knocking thee." They laid themselves down to sleep again, and then the tailor threw a stone down on the second. "What is the meaning of this?" cried the other. "Why art thou pelting me?" "I am not pelting thee," answered the first, growling. They disputed about it for a time, but as they were weary they let the matter rest, and their eyes closed once more. The little tailor began his game again, picked out the biggest stone, and threw it with all his might on the breast of the first giant. "That is too bad!" cried he, and sprang up like a madman, and pushed his companion against the tree until it shook. The other paid him back in the same coin, and they got into such a rage that they tore up trees and belabored each other so long, that at last they both fell down dead on the ground at the same time. Then the little tailor leapt down. "It is a lucky thing," said he, "that they did not tear up the tree on which I was sitting, or I should have had to spring on to another like a squirrel; but we tailors are nimble." He drew out his sword and gave each of them a couple of thrusts in the breast, and then went out to the horsemen and said, "The work is done; I have given both of them their finishing stroke, but it was hard work! They tore up trees in their sore need, and defended themselves with them, but all that is to no purpose when a man like myself comes, who can kill seven at one blow." "But are you not wounded?" asked the horsemen. "You need not concern yourself about that," answered the tailor, "They have not bent one hair of mine." The horsemen would not believe him, and rode into the forest; there they found the giants swimming in their blood, and all round about lay the torn-up trees.

The little tailor demanded of the King the promised reward; he, however, repented of his promise, and again bethought himself how he could get rid of the hero. "Before thou receivest my daughter, and the half of my kingdom," said he to him, "thou must perform one more heroic deed. In the forest roams a unicorn which does great harm, and thou must catch it first." "I fear one unicorn still less than two giants. Seven at one blow, is my kind of affair." He took a rope and an axe with him, went forth into the forest, and again bade those who were sent with him to wait outside. He had not to seek long. The unicorn soon came towards him, and rushed directly on the tailor, as if it would spit him on his horn without more ceremony.

"Softly, softly; it can't be done as quickly as that," said he, and stood still and waited until the animal was quite close, and then sprang nimbly behind the tree. The unicorn ran against the tree with all its strength, and struck its horn so fast in the trunk that it had not strength enough to draw it out again, and thus it was caught. "Now, I have got the bird," said the tailor, and came out from behind the tree and put the rope round its neck, and then with his axe he hewed the horn out of the tree, and when all was ready he led the beast away and took it to the King.

The King still would not give him the promised reward, and made a third demand. Before the wedding the tailor was to catch him a wild boar that made great havoc in the forest, and the huntsmen should give him their help. "Willingly," said the tailor, "that is child's play!" He did not take the huntsmen with him into the forest, and they were well pleased that he did not, for the wild boar had several times received them in such a manner that they had no inclination to lie in wait for him. When the boar perceived the tailor, it ran on him with foaming mouth and whetted tusks, and was about to throw him to the ground, but the active hero sprang into a chapel which was near, and up to the window at once, and in one bound out again. The boar ran in after him, but the tailor ran round outside and shut the door behind it, and then the raging beast, which was much too heavy and awkward to leap out of the window, was caught. The little tailor called the huntsmen thither that they might see the prisoner with their own eyes. The hero, however went to the King, who was now, whether he liked it or not, obliged to keep his promise, and gave him his daughter and the half of his kingdom. Had he known that it was no warlike hero, but a little tailor who was standing before him, it would have gone to his heart still more than it did. The wedding was held with great magnificence and small joy, and out of a tailor a king was made.

After some time the young Queen heard her husband say in his dreams at night, "Boy, make me the doublet, and patch the pantaloons, or else I will rap the yard-measure over thine ears." Then she discovered in what state of life the young lord had been born, and next morning complained of her wrongs to her father, and begged him to help her to get rid of her husband, who was nothing else but a tailor. The King comforted her and said, "Leave thy bed-room door open this night, and my servants shall stand outside, and when he has fallen asleep shall go in, bind him, and take him on board a ship which shall carry him into the wide world." The woman was satisfied with this; but the King's armour-bearer, who had heard all, was friendly with the young lord, and informed him of the whole plot. "I'll put a screw into that business," said the little tailor. At night he went to bed with his wife at the usual time, and when she thought that he had fallen asleep, she got up, opened the door, and then lay down again. The little tailor, who was only pretending to be asleep, began to cry out in a clear voice, "Boy, make me the doublet and patch me the pantaloons, or I will rap the yard-measure over thine ears. I smote seven at one blow. I killed two giants, I brought away one unicorn, and caught a wild boar, and am I to fear those who are standing outside the room." When these men heard the tailor speaking thus, they were overcome by a great dread, and ran as if the wild huntsman were behind them, and none of them would venture anything further against him. So the little tailor was a king and remained one, to the end of his life.

CINDERELLA

THE WIFE of a rich man fell sick, and as she felt that her end was drawing near, she called her only daughter to her bedside and said, "Dear child, be good and pious, and then the good God will always protect thee, and I will look down on thee from heaven and be near thee." Thereupon she closed her eyes and departed. Every day the maiden went out to her mother's grave and wept, and she remained pious and good. When winter came the snow spread a white sheet over the grave, and when the spring sun had drawn it off again, the man had taken another wife.

The woman had brought two daughters into the house with her, who were beautiful and fair of face, but vile and black of heart. Now began a bad time for the poor step-child. "Is the stupid goose to sit in the parlour with us?" said they. "He who wants to eat bread must earn it; out with the kitchen-wench." They took her pretty clothes away from her, put an old grey bedgown on her, and gave her wooden shoes. "Just look at the proud princess, how decked out she is!" they cried, and laughed, and led her into the kitchen. There she had to do hard work from morning till night, get up before daybreak, carry water, light fires, cook and wash. Besides this, the sisters did her every imaginable injury—they mocked her and emptied her peas and lentils into the ashes, so that she was forced to sit and pick them out again. In the evening when she had worked till she was weary she had no bed to go to, but had to sleep by the fireside in the ashes. And as on that account she always looked dusty and dirty, they called her Cinderella. It happened that the father was once going to the fair, and he asked his two step-daughters what he should bring back for them. "Beautiful dresses," said one, "Pearls and jewels," said the second. "And thou, Cinderella," said he, "what wilt thou have?" "Father, break off for me the first branch which knocks against your hat on your way home." So he bought beautiful dresses, pearls and jewels for his two step-daughters, and on his way home, as he was riding through a green thicket, a hazel twig brushed against him and knocked off his hat. Then he broke off the branch and took it with him. When he reached home he gave his step-daughters the things which they had wished for, and to Cinderella he gave the branch from the hazel-bush. Cinderella thanked him, went to her mother's grave and planted the branch on it, and wept so much that the tears fell down on it and watered it. It grew, however, and became a handsome tree. Thrice a day Cinderella went and sat beneath it, and wept and prayed, and a little white bird always came on the tree, and if Cinderella expressed a wish, the bird threw down to her what she had wished for.

It happened, however, that the King appointed a festival which was to last three days, and to which all the beautiful young girls in the country were invited, in order that his son might choose himself a bride. When the two step-sisters heard that they too were to appear among the number, they were delighted, called Cinderella and said, "Comb our hair for us, brush our shoes and fasten our buckles, for we are going to the festival at the King's palace." Cinderella obeyed, but wept, because she too would have liked to go with them to the dance, and begged her step-mother to allow her to do so. "Thou go, Cinderella!" said she; "Thou art dusty and dirty and wouldst go to the festival? Thou hast no clothes and shoes, and yet wouldst dance!" As, however, Cinderella went on asking, the step-mother at last said, "I have emptied a dish of lentils into the ashes for thee, if thou hast picked them out again in two hours, thou shalt go with us." The maiden went through the back-door into the garden, and called, "You tame pigeons, you turtle-doves, and all you birds beneath the sky, come and help me to pick

"The good into the pot,
The bad into the crop."

Then two white pigeons came in by the kitchen-window, and afterwards the turtle-doves, and at last all the birds beneath the sky, came whirring and crowding in, and alighted amongst the ashes. And the pigeons nodded with their heads and began pick, pick, pick, pick, and the rest began also pick, pick, pick, pick, and gathered all the good grains into the dish. Hardly had one hour passed before they had finished, and all flew out again. Then the girl took the dish to her step-mother, and was glad, and believed that now she would be allowed to go with them to the festival. But the step-mother said, "No, Cinderella, thou hast no clothes and thou canst not dance; thou wouldst only be laughed at." And as Cinderella wept at this, the step-mother said, "If thou canst pick two dishes of lentils out of the ashes for me in one hour, thou shalt go with us." And she thought to herself, "That she most certainly cannot do." When the step-mother had emptied the two dishes of lentils amongst the ashes, the maiden went through the back-door into the garden and cried, You tame pigeons, you turtle-doves, and all you birds under heaven, come and help me to pick

"The good into the pot,
The bad into the crop."

Then two white pigeons came in by the kitchen-window, and afterwards the turtle-doves, and at length all the birds beneath the sky, came whirring and crowding in, and alighted amongst the ashes. And the doves nodded with their heads and began pick, pick, pick, pick, and the others began also pick, pick, pick, pick, and gathered all the good seeds into the dishes, and before half an hour was over they had already finished, and all flew out again. Then the maiden carried the dishes to the step-mother and was delighted, and believed that she might now go with them to the festival. But the step-mother said, "All this will not help thee; thou goest not with us, for thou hast no clothes and canst not dance; we should be ashamed of thee!" On this she turned her back on Cinderella, and hurried away with her two proud daughters.

As no one was now at home, Cinderella went to her mother's grave beneath the hazel-tree, and cried,

"Shiver and quiver, little tree,
Silver and gold throw down over me."

Then the bird threw a gold and silver dress down to her, and slippers embroidered with silk and silver. She put on the dress with all speed, and went to the festival. Her step-sisters and the step-mother however did not know her, and thought she must be a foreign princess, for she looked so beautiful in the golden dress. They never once thought of Cinderella, and believed that she was sitting at home in the dirt, picking lentils out of the ashes. The prince went to meet her, took her by the hand and danced with her. He would dance with no other maiden, and never left loose of her hand, and if any one else came to invite her, he said, "This is my partner."

She danced till it was evening, and then she wanted to go home. But the King's son said, "I will go with thee and bear thee company," for he wished to see to whom the beautiful maiden belonged. She escaped from him, however, and sprang into the pigeon-house. The King's son waited until her father came, and then he told him that the stranger maiden had leapt into the pigeon-house. The old man thought, "Can it be Cinderella?" and they had to bring him an axe and a pickaxe that he might hew the pigeon-house to pieces, but no one was inside it. And when they got home Cinderella lay in her dirty clothes among the ashes, and a dim little oil-lamp was burning on the mantle-piece, for Cinderella had jumped quickly down from the back of the pigeon-house and had run to the little hazel-tree, and there she had taken off her beautiful clothes and laid them on the grave, and the bird had taken them away again, and then she had placed herself in the kitchen amongst the ashes in her grey gown.

Next day when the festival began afresh, and her parents and the step-sisters had gone once more, Cinderella went to the hazel-tree and said—

"Shiver and quiver, my little tree,
Silver and gold throw down over me."

Then the bird threw down a much more beautiful dress than on the preceding day. And when Cinderella appeared at the festival in this dress, every one was astonished at her beauty. The King's son had waited until she came, and instantly took her by the hand and danced with no one but her. When others came and invited her, he said, "She is my partner." When evening came she wished to leave, and the King's son followed her and wanted to see into which house she went. But she sprang away from him, and into the garden behind the house. Therein stood a beautiful tall tree on which hung the most magnificent pears. She clambered so nimbly between the branches like a squirrel that the King's son did not know where she was gone. He waited until her father came, and said to him, "The stranger-maiden has escaped from me, and I believe she has climbed up the pear-tree." The father thought, "Can it be Cinderella?" and had an axe brought and cut the tree down, but no one was on it. And when they got into the kitchen, Cinderella lay there amongst the ashes, as usual, for she had jumped down on the other side of the tree, had taken the beautiful dress to the bird on the little hazel-tree, and put on her grey gown.

On the third day, when the parents and sisters had gone away, Cinderella once more went to her mother's grave and said to the little tree—

"Shiver and quiver, my little tree,
Silver and gold throw down over me."

And now the bird threw down to her a dress which was more splendid and magnificent than any she had yet had, and the slippers were golden. And when she went to the festival in the dress, no one knew how to speak for astonishment. The King's son danced with her only, and if any one invited her to dance, he said, "She is my partner."

When evening came, Cinderella wished to leave, and the King's son was anxious to go with her, but she escaped from him so quickly that he could not follow her. The King's son had, however, used a strategem, and had caused the whole staircase to be smeared with pitch, and there, when she ran down, had the maiden's left slipper remained sticking. The King's son picked it up, and it was small and dainty, and all golden. Next morning, he went with it to the father, and said to him, "No one shall be my wife but she whose foot this golden slipper fits." Then were the two sisters glad, for they had pretty feet. The eldest went with the shoe into her room and wanted to try it on, and her mother stood by. But she could not get her big toe into it, and the shoe was too small for her. Then her mother gave her a knife and said, "Cut the toe off; when thou art Queen thou wilt have no more need to go on foot." The maiden cut the toe off, forced the foot into the shoe, swallowed the pain, and went out to the King's son. Then he took her on his his horse as his bride and rode away with her. They were, however, obliged to pass the grave, and there, on the hazel-tree, sat the two pigeons and cried,

"Turn and peep, turn and peep,
There's blood within the shoe,
The shoe it is too small for her,
The true bride waits for you."

Then he looked at her foot and saw how the blood was streaming from it. He turned his horse round and took the false bride home again, and said she was not the true one, and that the other sister was to put the shoe on. Then this one went into her chamber and got her toes safely into the shoe, but her heel was too large. So her mother gave her a knife and said, "Cut a bit off thy heel; when thou art Queen thou wilt have no more need to go on foot." The maiden cut a bit off her heel, forced her foot into the shoe, swallowed the pain, and went out to the King's son. He took her on his horse as his bride, and rode away with her, but when they passed by the hazel-tree, two little pigeons sat on it and cried,

"Turn and peep, turn and peep,
There's blood within the shoe
The shoe it is too small for her,
The true bride waits for you."

He looked down at her foot and saw how the blood was running out of her shoe, and how it had stained her white stocking. Then he turned his horse and took the false bride home again. "This also is not the right one," said he, "have you no other daughter?" "No," said the man, "There is still a little stunted kitchen-wench which my late wife left behind her, but she cannot possibly be the bride." The King's son said he was to send her up to him; but the mother answered, "Oh no, she is much too dirty, she cannot show herself!" He absolutely insisted on it, and Cinderella had to be called. She first washed her hands and face clean, and then went and bowed down before the King's son, who gave her the golden shoe. Then she seated herself on a stool, drew her foot out of the heavy wooden shoe, and put it into the slipper, which fitted like a glove. And when she rose up and the King's son looked at her face he recognized the beautiful maiden who had danced with him and cried, "That is the true bride!" The step-mother and the two sisters were terrified and became pale with rage; he, however, took Cinderella on his horse and rode away with her. As they passed by the hazel-tree, the two white doves cried—

> "Turn and peep, turn and peep,
> No blood is in the shoe,
> The shoe is not too small for her,
> The true bride rides with you,"

and when they had cried that, the two came flying down and placed themselves on Cinderella's shoulders, one on the right, the other on the left, and remained sitting there.

When the wedding with the King's son had to be celebrated, the two false sisters came and wanted to get into favour with Cinderella and share her good fortune. When the betrothed couple went to church, the elder was at the right side and the younger at the left, and the pigeons pecked out one eye of each of them. Afterwards as they came back, the elder was at the left, and the younger at the right, and then the pigeons pecked out the other eye of each. And thus, for their wickedness and falsehood, they were punished with blindness as long as they lived.

MOTHER HOLLE

THERE WAS once a widow who had two daughters—one of whom was pretty and industrious, whilst the other was ugly and idle. But she was much fonder of the ugly and idle one, because she was her own daughter; and the other, who was a step-daughter, was obliged to do all the work, and be the Cinderella of the house. Every day the poor girl had to sit by a well, in the highway, and spin and spin till her fingers bled.

Now it happened that one day the shuttle was marked with her blood, so she dipped it in the well, to wash the mark off; but it dropped out of her hand and fell to the bottom. She began to weep, and ran to her step-mother and told her of the mishap. But she scolded her sharply, and was so merciless as to say, "Since you have let the shuttle fall in, you must fetch it out again."

So the girl went back to the well, and did not know what to do; and in the sorrow of her heart she jumped into the well to get the shuttle. She lost her senses; and when she awoke and came to herself again, she was in a lovely meadow where the sun was shining and many thousands of flowers were growing. Along this meadow she went, and at last came to a baker's oven full of bread, and the bread cried out, "Oh, take me out! take me out! or I shall burn; I have been baked a long time!" So she went up to it, and took out all the loaves one after another with the bread-shovel. After that she went on till she came to a tree covered with apples, which called out to her, "Oh, shake me! shake me! we apples are all ripe!" So she shook the tree till the apples fell like rain, and went on shaking till they were all down, and when she had gathered them into a heap, she went on her way.

At last she came to a little house, out of which an old woman peeped; but she had such large teeth that the girl was frightened, and was about to run away.

But the old woman called out to her, "What are you afraid of, dear child? Stay with me; if you will do all the work in the house properly, you shall be the better for it. Only you must take care to make my bed well, and shake it thoroughly till the feathers fly—for then there is snow on the earth. I am Mother Holle.*

As the old woman spoke so kindly to her, the girl took courage and agreed to enter her service. She attended to everything to the satisfaction of her mistress, and always shook her bed so vigorously that the feathers flew about like snow-flakes. So she had a pleasant life with her; never an angry word; and boiled or roast meat every day.

She stayed some time with Mother Holle, and then she became sad. At first she did not know what was the matter with her, but found at length that it was home-sickness: although she was many thousand times better off here than at home, still she had a longing to be there. At last she said to the old woman, "I have a longing for home; and however well off I am down here, I cannot stay any longer; I must go up again to my own people." Mother Holle said, "I am pleased that you long for your home again, and as you have served me so truly, I myself will take you up again." Thereupon she took her by the hand, and led her to a large door. The door was opened, and just as the maiden was standing beneath the doorway, a heavy shower of golden rain fell, and all the gold remained sticking to her, so that she was completely covered over with it.

"You shall have that because you have been so industrious," said Mother Holle; and at the same time she gave her back the shuttle which she had let fall into the well. Thereupon the door closed, and the maiden found herself up above upon the earth, not far from her mother's house.

And as she went into the yard the cock was standing by the well-side, and cried—

"Cock-a-doodle-doo!
Your golden girl's come back to you!"

So she went in to her mother, and as she arrived thus covered with gold, she was well received, both by her and her sister.

The girl told all that had happened to her; and as soon as the mother heard how she had come by so much wealth, she was very anxious to obtain the same good luck for the ugly and lazy daughter. She had to seat herself by the well and spin; and in order that her shuttle might be stained with blood, she stuck her hand into a thorn bush and pricked her finger. Then she threw her shuttle into the well, and jumped in after it.

She came, like the other, to the beautiful meadow and walked along

---

*Thus in Hesse, when it snows, they say, "Mother Holle is making her bed."

the very same path. When she got to the oven the bread again cried, "Oh, take me out! take me out! or I shall burn; I have been baked a long time!" But the lazy thing answered, "As if I had any wish to make myself dirty?" and on she went. Soon she came to the apple-tree, which cried, "Oh, shake me! shake me! we apples are all ripe!" But she answered, "I like that! one of you might fall on my head," and so went on.

When she came to Mother Holle's house she was not afraid, for she had already heard of her big teeth, and she hired herself to her immediately.

The first day she forced herself to work diligently, and obeyed Mother Holle when she told her to do anything, for she was thinking of all the gold that she would give her. But on the second day she began to be lazy, and on the third day still more so, and then she would not get up in the morning at all. Neither did she make Mother Holle's bed as she ought, and did not shake it so as to make the feathers fly up. Mother Holle was soon tired of this, and gave her notice to leave. The lazy girl was willing enough to go, and thought that now the golden rain would come. Mother Holle led her too to the great door; but while she was standing beneath it, instead of the gold a big kettleful of pitch was emptied over her. "That is the reward for your service," said Mother Holle, and shut the door.

So the lazy girl went home; but she was quite covered with pitch, and the cock by the well-side, as soon as he saw her, cried out—

"Cock-a-doodle-doo!
Your pitchy girl's come back to you!"

But the pitch stuck fast to her, and could not be got off as long as she lived.

THE SEVEN RAVENS

THERE WAS once a man who had seven sons, and still he had no daughter, however much he wished for one. At length his wife again gave him hope of a child, and when it came into the world it was a girl. The joy was great, but the child was sickly and small, and had to be privately baptized on account of its weakness. The father sent one of the boys in haste to the spring to fetch water for the baptism. The other six went with him, and as each of them wanted to be first to fill it, the jug fell into the well. There they stood and did not know what to do, and none of them dared to go home. As they still did not return, the father grew impatient, and said, "They have certainly forgotten it for some game, the wicked boys!" He became afraid that the girl would have to die without being baptized, and in his anger cried, "I wish the boys were all turned into ravens." Hardly was the word spoken before he heard a whirring of wings over his head in the air, looked up and saw seven coal-black ravens flying away. The parents could not recall the curse, and however sad they were at the loss of their seven sons, they still to some extent comforted themselves with their dear little daughter, who soon grew strong and every day became more beautiful. For a long time she did not know that she had had brothers, for her parents were careful not to mention them before her, but one day she accidentally heard some people saying of herself, "that the girl was certainly beautiful, but that in reality she was to blame for the misfortune which had befallen her seven brothers." Then she was much troubled, and went to her father and mother and asked if it was true that she had had brothers, and what had become of them? The parents now dared keep the secret no longer, but said that what had befallen her brothers was the will of Heaven, and that her birth had only been the innocent cause. But the maiden laid it to heart daily, and thought she must deliver her brothers. She had no rest or peace until she set out secretly, and went forth into the wide world to trace out her brothers and set them free, let it cost what it might. She took nothing with her but a little ring belonging to her parents as a keepsake, a loaf of bread against hunger, a little pitcher of water against thirst, and a little chair as a provision against weariness.

And now she went continually onwards, far, far, to the very end of the world. Then she came to the sun, but it was too hot and terrible, and devoured little children. Hastily she ran away, and ran to the moon, but it was far too cold, and also awful and malicious, and when it saw the child, it said, "I smell, I smell the flesh of men." On this she ran swiftly away, and came to the stars, which were kind and good to her, and each of them sat on its own particular little chair. But the morning star arose, and gave her the drumstick of a chicken, and said, "If thou hast not that drumstick thou canst not open the Glass mountain, and in the Glass mountain are thy brothers."

The maiden took the drumstick, wrapped it carefully in a cloth, and went onwards again until she came to the Glass mountain. The door was shut, and she thought she would take out the drumstick; but when she undid the cloth, it was empty, and she had lost the good star's present. What was she now to do? She wished to rescue her brothers, and had no key to the Glass mountain. The good sister took a knife, cut off one of her little fingers, put it in the door, and succeeded in opening it. When she had gone inside, a little dwarf came to meet her, who said, "My child, what are you looking for?" "I am looking for my brothers, the seven ravens," she replied. The dwarf said, "The lord ravens are not at home, but if you will wait here until they come, step in." Thereupon the little dwarf carried the ravens' dinner in, on seven little plates, and in seven little glasses, and the little sister ate a morsel from each plate, and from each little glass she took a sip, but in the last little glass she dropped the ring which she had brought away with her.

Suddenly she heard a whirring of wings and a rushing through the air, and then the little dwarf said, "Now the lord ravens are flying home." Then they came, and wanted to eat and drink, and looked for their little plates and glasses. Then said one after the other, "Who has eaten something from my plate? Who has drunk out of my little glass? It was a human mouth." And when the seventh came to the bottom of the glass, the ring rolled against his mouth. Then he looked at it, and saw that it was a ring belonging to his father and mother, and said, "God grant that our sister may be here, and then we shall be free." When the maiden, who was standing behind the door watching, heard that wish, she came forth, and on this all the ravens were restored to their human form again. And they embraced and kissed each other, and went joyfully home.

LITTLE RED-CAP*

ONCE UPON a time there was a dear little girl who was loved by every one who looked at her, but most of all by her grandmother, and there was nothing that she would not have given to the child. Once she gave her a little cap of red velvet, which suited her so well that she would never wear anything else; so she was always called "Little Red-Cap."

One day her mother said to her, "Come, Little Red-Cap, here is a piece of cake and a bottle of wine; take them to your grandmother, she is ill and weak, and they will do her good. Set out before it gets hot, and when you are going, walk nicely and quietly and do not run off the path, or you may fall and break the bottle, and then your grandmother will get nothing; and when you go into her room, don't forget to say, 'Good-morning,' and don't peep into every corner before you do it."

"I will take great care," said Little Red-Cap to her mother, and gave her hand on it.

The grandmother lived out in the wood, half a league from the village, and just as Little Red-Cap entered the wood, a wolf met her. Red-Cap did not know what a wicked creature he was, and was not at all afraid of him.

"Good-day, Little Red-Cap," said he.

"Thank you kindly, wolf."

"Whither away so early, Little Red-Cap?"

"To my grandmother's."

"What have you got in your apron?"

"Cake and wine; yesterday was baking-day, so poor sick grandmother is to have something good, to make her stronger."

"Where does your grandmother live, Little Red-Cap?"

*The English version of this story, the well-known Little Red-Riding-Hood, is probably derived more immediately from the French, "Le Petit Chaperon Rouge," as given by Perrault, where it ends with the death of the girl.

"A good quarter of a league farther on in the wood; her house stands under the three large oak-trees, the nut-trees are just below; you surely must know it," replied Little Red-Cap.

The wolf thought to himself, "What a tender young creature! what a nice plump mouthful—she will be better to eat than the old woman. I must act craftily, so as to catch both." So he walked for a short time by the side of Little Red-Cap, and then he said, "See, Little Red-Cap, how pretty the flowers are about here—why do you not look round? I believe, too, that you do not hear how sweetly the little birds are singing; you walk gravely along as if you were going to school, while everything else out here in the wood is merry."

Little Red-Cap raised her eyes, and when she saw the sunbeams dancing here and there through the trees, and pretty flowers growing everywhere, she thought, "Suppose I take grandmother a fresh nosegay; that would please her too. It is so early in the day that I shall still get there in good time"; and so she ran from the path into the wood to look for flowers. And whenever she had picked one, she fancied that she saw a still prettier one farther on, and ran after it, and so got deeper and deeper into the wood.

Meanwhile the wolf ran straight to the grandmother's house and knocked at the door.

"Who is there?"

"Little Red-Cap," replied the wolf. "She is bringing cake and wine; open the door."

"Lift the latch," called out the grandmother, "I am too weak, and cannot get up."

The wolf lifted the latch, the door flew open, and without saying a word he went straight to the grandmother's bed, and devoured her. Then he put on her clothes, dressed himself in her cap, laid himself in bed and drew the curtains.

Little Red-Cap, however, had been running about picking flowers, and when she had gathered so many that she could carry no more, she remembered her grandmother, and set out on the way to her.

She was surprised to find the cottage-door standing open, and when she went into the room, she had such a strange feeling that she said to herself, "Oh dear! how uneasy I feel to-day, and at other times I like being with grandmother so much." She called out, "Good morning," but received no answer; so she went to the bed and drew back the curtains. There lay her grandmother with her cap pulled far over her face, and looking very strange.

"Oh! grandmother," she said, "what big ears you have!"

"The better to hear you with, my child," was the reply.

"But, grandmother, what big eyes you have!" she said.

"The better to see you with, my dear."

"But, grandmother, what large hands you have!"

"The better to hug you with."

"Oh! but, grandmother, what a terrible big mouth you have!"

"The better to eat you with!"

And scarcely had the wolf said this, than with one bound he was out of bed and swallowed up Red-Cap.

When the wolf had appeased his appetite, he lay down again in the bed, fell asleep and began to snore very loud. The huntsman was just passing the house, and thought to himself, "How the old woman is snoring! I must just see if she wants anything." So he went into the room, and when he came to the bed, he saw that the wolf was lying in it. "Do I find thee here, thou old sinner!" said he. "I have long sought thee!" Then just as he was going to fire at him, it occurred to him that the wolf might have devoured the grandmother, and that she might still be saved, so he did not fire, but took a pair of scissors, and began to cut open the stomach of the sleeping wolf. When he had made two snips, he saw the little Red-Cap shining, and then he made two snips more, and the little girl sprang out, crying, "Ah, how frightened I have been! How dark it was inside the wolf"; and after that the aged grandmother came out alive also, but scarcely able to breathe. Red-Cap, however, quickly fetched great stones with which they filled the wolf's body, and when he awoke, he wanted to run away, but the stones were so heavy that he fell down at once, and fell dead.

Then all three were delighted. The huntsman drew off the wolf's skin and went home with it; the grandmother ate the cake and drank the wine which Red-Cap had brought, and revived, but Red-Cap thought to herself, "As long as I live, I will never by myself leave the path, to run into the wood, when my mother has forbidden me to do so."

⋆

It is also related that once when Red-Cap was again taking cakes to the old grandmother, another wolf spoke to her, and tried to entice her from the path. Red-Cap was, however, on her guard, and went straight forward on her way, and told her grandmother that she had met the wolf, and that he had said "good-morning" to her, but with such a wicked look in his eyes, that if they had not been on the public road she was certain he would have eaten her up. "Well," said the grandmother, "we will shut the door, that he may not come in." Soon afterwards the wolf knocked, and cried, "Open the door, grandmother, I am little Red-Cap, and am fetching you some cakes." But they did not speak, or open the door, so the grey-beard stole twice or thrice round the house, and at last jumped on the roof, intending to wait until Red-Cap went home in the evening, and then to steal after her and devour her in the darkness. But the grandmother saw what was in his thoughts. In front of the house was a great stone trough, so she said to the child, "Take the pail, Red-Cap; I made some sausages yesterday, so carry the water in which I boiled them to the trough." Red-Cap carried until the great trough was quite full. Then the smell of the sausages reached the wolf, and he sniffed and peeped down, and at last stretched out his neck so far that he could no longer keep his footing and began to slip, and slipped down from the roof straight into the great trough, and was drowned. But Red-Cap went joyously home, and never did anything to harm any one.

THE BREMEN TOWN-MUSICIANS

A CERTAIN man had a donkey, which had carried the corn-sacks to the mill indefatigably for many a long year; but his strength was going, and he was growing more and more unfit for work. Then his master began to consider how he might best save his keep; but the donkey, seeing that no good wind was blowing, ran away and set out on the road to Bremen. "There," he thought, "I can surely be town-musician." When he had walked some distance, he found a hound lying on the road, gasping like one who had run till he was tired. "What are you gasping so for, you big fellow?" asked the donkey.

"Ah," replied the hound, "as I am old, and daily grow weaker, and no longer can hunt, my master wanted to kill me, so I took to flight; but now how am I to earn my bread?"

"I tell you what," said the donkey, "I am going to Bremen, and shall be town-musician there; go with me and engage yourself also as a musician. I will play the lute, and you shall beat the kettledrum."

The hound agreed, and on they went.

Before long they came to a cat, sitting on the path, with a face like three rainy days! "Now then, old shaver, what has gone askew with you?" asked the donkey.

"Who can be merry when his neck is in danger?" answered the cat. "Because I am now getting old, and my teeth are worn to stumps, and I prefer to sit by the fire and spin, rather than hunt about after mice, my mistress wanted to drown me, so I ran away. But now good advice is scarce. Where am I to go?"

"Go with us to Bremen. You understand night-music, you can be a town-musician."

The cat thought well of it, and went with them. After this the three fugitives came to a farm-yard, where the cock was sitting upon the gate, crowing with all his might. "Your crow goes through and through one," said the donkey. "What is the matter?"

"I have been foretelling fine weather, because it is the day on which Our Lady washes the Christ-child's little shirts, and wants to dry them," said the cock; "but guests are coming for Sunday, so the housewife has no pity, and has told the cook that she intends to eat me in the soup to-morrow, and this evening I am to have my head cut off. Now I am crowing at full pitch while I can."

"Ah, but red-comb," said the donkey, "you had better come away with us. We are going to Bremen; you can find something better than death everywhere: you have a good voice, and if we make music together it must have some quality!"

The cock agreed to this plan, and all four went on together. They could not, however, reach the city of Bremen in one day, and in the evening they came to a forest where they meant to pass the night. The donkey and the hound laid themselves down under a large tree, the cat and the cock settled themselves in the branches; but the cock flew right to the top, where he was most safe. Before he went to sleep he looked round on all the four sides, and thought he saw in the distance a little spark burning; so he called out to his companions that there must be a house not far off, for he saw a light. The donkey said, "If so, we had better get up and go on, for the shelter here is bad." The hound thought that a few bones with some meat on would do him good too!

So they made their way to the place where the light was, and soon saw it shine brighter and grow larger, until they came to a well-lighted robber's house. The donkey, as the biggest, went to the window and looked in.

"What do you see, my grey-horse?" asked the cock. "What do I see?" answered the donkey; "a table covered with good things to eat and drink, and robbers sitting at it enjoying themselves." "That would be the sort of thing for us," said the cock. "Yes, yes; ah, how I wish we were there!" said the donkey.

Then the animals took counsel together how they should manage to drive away the robbers, and at last they thought of a plan. The donkey was to place himself with his fore-feet upon the window-ledge, the hound was to jump on the donkey's back, the cat was to climb upon the dog, and lastly the cock was to fly up and perch upon the head of the cat.

When this was done, at a given signal, they began to perform their music together: the donkey brayed, the hound barked, the cat mewed, and the cock crowed; then they burst through the window into the room, so that the glass clattered! At this horrible din, the robbers sprang up, thinking no otherwise than that a ghost had come in, and fled in a great fright out into the forest. The four companions now sat down at the table, well content with what was left, and ate as if they were going to fast for a month.

As soon as the four minstrels had done, they put out the light, and each sought for himself a sleeping-place according to his nature and to what suited him. The donkey laid himself down upon some straw in the yard, the hound behind the door, the cat upon the hearth near the warm ashes, and the cock perched himself upon a beam of the roof; and being tired from their long walk, they soon went to sleep.

When it was past midnight, and the robbers saw from afar that the light was no longer burning in their house, and all appeared quiet, the captain said, "We ought not to have let ourselves be frightened out of our wits"; and ordered one of them to go and examine the house.

The messenger finding all still, went into the kitchen to light a candle, and, taking the glistening fiery eyes of the cat for live coals, he held a lucifer-match to them to light it. But the cat did not understand the joke, and flew in his face, spitting and scratching. He was dreadfully frightened, and ran to the back-door, but the dog, who lay there sprang up, and bit his leg; and as he ran across the yard by the straw-heap, the donkey gave him a smart kick with its hind foot. The cock, too, who had been awakened by the noise, and had become lively, cried down from the beam, "Cock-a-doodle-doo!"

Then the robber ran back as fast as he could to his captain, and said, "Ah, there is a horrible witch sitting in the house, who spat on me and scratched my face with her long claws; and by the door stands a man with a knife, who stabbed me in the leg; and in the yard there lies a black monster, who beat me with a wooden club; and above, upon the roof, sits the judge, who called out, 'Bring the rogue here to me!' so I got away as well as I could."

After this the robbers did not trust themselves in the house again; but it suited the four musicians of Bremen so well that they did not care to leave it any more. And the mouth of him who last told this story is still warm.

CLEVER HANS

THE MOTHER of Hans said, "Whither away, Hans?" Hans answered, "To Grethel." "Behave well, Hans." "Oh, I'll behave well. Good-bye, mother." "Good-bye, Hans." Hans comes to Grethel, "Good day, Grethel." "Good day, Hans. What dost thou bring that is good?" "I bring nothing, I want to have something given me." Grethel presents Hans with a needle. Hans says, "Good-bye, Grethel." "Good-bye, Hans."

Hans takes the needle, sticks it into a hay-cart, and follows the cart home. "Good evening, mother." "Good evening, Hans. Where hast thou been?" "With Grethel." "What didst thou take her?" "Took nothing; had something given me." "What did Grethel give thee?" "Gave me a needle." "Where is the needle, Hans?" "Stuck in the hay-cart." "That was ill done, Hans. Thou shouldst have stuck the needle in thy sleeve." "Never mind, I'll do better next time."

"Whither away, Hans?" "To Grethel, mother." "Behave well, Hans." "Oh, I'll behave well. Good-bye, mother." "Good-bye, Hans."

Hans comes to Grethel. "Good day, Grethel." "Good day, Hans. What dost thou bring that is good?" "I bring nothing; I want to have something given to me." Grethel presents Hans with a knife. "Good-bye, Grethel." "Good-bye Hans." Hans takes the knife, sticks it in his sleeve, and goes home. "Good evening, mother." "Good evening, Hans. Where hast thou been?" "With Grethel." "What didst thou take her?" "Took her nothing, she gave me something." "What did Grethel give thee?" "Gave me a knife." "Where is the knife, Hans?" "Stuck in my sleeve." "That's ill done, Hans, thou shouldst have put the knife in thy pocket." "Never mind, will do better next time." "Whither away, Hans?" "To Grethel, mother. " "Behave well, Hans." "Oh, I'll behave well. Good-bye, mother." "Good-bye, Hans."

Hans comes to Grethel. "Good day, Grethel." "Good day, Hans. What good thing dost thou bring?" "I bring nothing, I want something given me." Grethel presents Hans with a young goat. "Good-bye, Grethel." "Good-bye, Hans." Hans takes the goat, ties its legs, and puts it in his pocket. When he gets home it is suffocated. "Good evening, mother." "Good evening, Hans. Where hast thou been?" "With Grethel." "What didst thou take her?" "Took nothing, she gave me something." "What did Grethel give thee?" "She gave me a goat." "Where is the goat, Hans?" "Put it in my pocket." "That was ill done, Hans, thou shouldst have put a rope round the goat's neck." "Never mind, will do better next time."

"Whither away, Hans?" "To Grethel, mother." "Behave well, Hans." "Oh, I'll behave well. Good-bye, mother." "Good-bye, Hans." Hans comes to Grethel. "Good day, Grethel." "Good day, Hans. What good thing dost thou bring?" "I bring nothing, I want something given me." Grethel presents Hans with a piece of bacon. "Good-bye, Grethel." "Good-bye, Hans."

Hans takes the bacon, ties it to a rope, and drags it away behind him. The dogs come and devour the bacon. When he gets home, he has the rope in his hand, and there is no longer anything hanging to it. "Good evening, mother." "Good evening, Hans." "Where hast thou been?" "With Grethel." What didst thou take her?" "I took her nothing, she gave me something." "What did Grethel give thee?" "Gave me a bit of bacon." "Where is the bacon, Hans?" "I tied it to a rope, brought it home, dogs took it." "That was ill done, Hans, thou shouldst have carried the bacon on thy head." "Never mind, will do better next time." "Whither away, Hans?" "To Grethel, mother." "Behave well, Hans." "I'll behave well. Good-bye, mother." "Good-bye, Hans."

Hans comes to Grethel. "Good day, Grethel." "Good day, Hans." "What good thing dost thou bring?" "I bring nothing, but would have something given." Grethel presents Hans with a calf. "Good-bye, Grethel." "Good-bye, Hans."

Hans takes the calf, puts it on his head, and the calf kicks his face. Good evening, mother." "Good evening, Hans. Where hast thou been?" "With Grethel." "What didst thou take her?" "I took nothing, but had something given me." "What did Grethel give thee?" "A calf." "Where hast thou the calf, Hans?" "I set it on my head and it kicked my face." "That was ill done, Hans, thou shouldst have led the calf, and put it in the stall." "Never mind, will do better next time."

"Whither away, Hans?" "To Grethel, mother." "Behave well, Hans." "I'll behave well. Good-bye, mother." "Good-bye, Hans."

Hans comes to Grethel. "Good day, Grethel." "Good day, Hans. What good thing dost thou bring?" "I bring nothing, but would have something given." Grethel says to Hans, "I will go with thee."

Hans takes Grethel, ties her to a rope, leads her to the rack and binds her fast. Then Hans goes to his mother. "Good evening, mother." "Good evening, Hans. Where hast thou been?" "With Grethel." "What didst thou take her?" "I took her nothing." "What did Grethel give thee?" "She gave me nothing, she came with me." "Where hast thou left Grethel?" "I led her by the rope, tied her to the rack, and scattered some grass for her." "That was ill done, Hans, thou shouldst have cast friendly eyes on her." "Never mind, will do better."

Hans went into the stable, cut out all the calves', and sheep's eyes, and threw them in Grethel's face. Then Grethel became angry, tore herself loose and ran away, and became the bride of Hans.

THE WISHING-TABLE, THE GOLD-ASS, AND THE CUDGEL IN THE SACK

THERE WAS once upon a time a tailor who had three sons, and only one goat. But as the goat supported the whole of them with her milk, she was obliged to have good food, and to be taken every day to pasture. The sons, therefore, did this, in turn. Once the eldest took her to the churchyard, where the finest herbs were to be found, and let her eat and run about there. At night when it was time to go home he asked, "Goat, hast thou had enough?" The goat answered,

"I have eaten so much,
Not a leaf more I'll touch, meh! meh!"

"Come home, then," said the youth, and took hold of the cord round her neck, led her into the stable and tied her up securely. "Well," said the old tailor, "has the goat had as much food as she ought?" "Oh," answered the son, "she has eaten so much, not a leaf more she'll touch." But the father wished to satisfy himself, and went down to the stable, stroked the dear animal and asked, "Goat, art thou satisfied?" The goat answered,

"Wherewithal should I be satisfied?
Among the graves I leapt about,
And found no food, so went without, meh! meh!"

"What do I hear?" cried the tailor, and ran upstairs and said to the youth, "Hollo, thou liar: thou saidest the goat had had enough, and hast let her hunger!" and in his anger he took the yard-measure from the wall, and drove him out with blows.

Next day it was the turn of the second son, who looked out for a place in the fence of the garden, where nothing but good herbs grew, and the goat cleared them all off. At night when he wanted to go home, he asked, "Goat, art thou satisfied?" The goat answered,

"I have eaten so much,
Not a leaf more I'll touch, meh! meh!"

"Come home, then," said the youth, and led her home, and tied her up in the stable. "Well," said the old tailor, "has the goat had as much food as she ought?" "Oh," answered the son, "she has eaten so much, not a leaf more she'll touch." The tailor would not rely on this, but went down to the stable and said, "Goat, hast thou had enough?" The goat answered,

"Wherewithal should I be satisfied?
Among the graves I leapt about,
And found no food, so went without, meh! meh!"

"The godless wretch!" cried the tailor, "to let such a good animal hunger," and he ran up and drove the youth out of doors with the yard-measure.

Now came the turn of the third son, who wanted to do the thing well, and sought out some bushes with the finest leaves, and let the goat devour them. In the evening when he wanted to go home, he asked, "Goat, hast thou had enough?" The goat answered,

"I have eaten so much,
Not a leaf more I'll touch, meh! meh!"

"Come home, then," said the youth, and led her into the stable, and tied her up. "Well," said the old tailor, "has the goat had a proper amount of food?" "She has eaten so much, not a leaf more she'll touch." The tailor did not trust to that, but went down and asked, "Goat, hast thou had enough?" The wicked beast answered,

"Wherewithal should I be satisfied?
Among the graves I leapt about,
And found no leaves, so went without, meh! meh!"

"Oh, the brood of liars!" cried the tailor, "each as wicked and forgetful of his duty as the other! Ye shall no longer make a fool of me," and quite beside himself with anger, he ran upstairs and belabored the poor young fellow so vigorously with the yard-measure that he sprang out of the house.

The old tailor was now alone with his goat. Next morning he went down into the stable, caressed the goat and said, "Come, my dear little animal, I will take thee to feed myself." He took her by the rope and conducted her to green hedges, and amongst milfoil, and whatever else goats like to eat. "There thou mayest for once eat to thy heart's content," said he to her, and let her browse till evening. Then he asked, "Goat, art thou satisfied?" She replied,

"I have eaten so much,
Not a leaf more I'll touch, meh! meh!"

"Come home, then," said the tailor, and led her into the stable, and tied her fast. When he was going away, he turned round again and said, "Well, art thou satisfied for once?" But the goat did not behave the better to him, and cried,

> "Wherewithal should I be satisfied?
> Among the graves I leapt about,
> And found no leaves, so went without, meh! meh!"

When the tailor heard that, he was shocked, and saw clearly that he had driven away his three sons without cause. "Wait, thou ungrateful creature," cried he, "it is not enough to drive thee forth, I will mark thee so that thou wilt no more dare to show thyself amongst honest tailors." In great haste he ran upstairs, fetched his razor, lathered the goat's head, and shaved her as clean as the palm of his hand. And as the yard-measure would have been too good for her, he brought the horsewhip, and gave her such cuts with it that she ran away in violent haste.

When the tailor was thus left quite alone in his house he fell into great grief, and would gladly have had his sons back again, but no one knew whither they were gone. The eldest had apprenticed himself to a joiner, and learnt industriously and indefatigably, and when the time came for him to go travelling,* his master presented him with a little table which had no particular appearance, and was made of common wood, but it had one good property; if any one set it out, and said, "Little table, spread thyself," the good little table was at once covered with a clean little cloth, and a plate was there, and a knife and fork beside it, and dishes with boiled meats and roasted meats, as many as there was room for, and a great glass of red wine shone so that it made the heart glad. The young journeyman thought, "With this thou hast enough for thy whole life," and went joyously about the world and never troubled himself at all whether an inn was good or bad, or if anything was to be found in it or not. When it suited him he did not enter an inn at all, but either on the plain, in a wood, a meadow, or wherever he fancied, he took his little table off his back, set it down before him, and said, "Cover thyself," and then everything appeared that his heart desired. At length he took it into his head to go back to his father, whose anger would now be appeased, and who would now willingly receive him with his wishing-table. It came to pass that on his way home, he came one evening to an inn which was filled with

*On the completion of his apprenticeship (*Lehrjahre*) a German artisan's travels (*Wanderjahre*) begin. This is a certain period during which he is obliged by law, or custom, to travel about from place to place, to perfect his knowledge of his craft. He cannot become a master until he has gone through this.—TR.

guests. They bade him welcome, and invited him to sit and eat with them, for otherwise he would have difficulty in getting anything. "No," answered the joiner, "I will not take the few bites out of your mouths; rather than that, you shall be my guests." They laughed, and thought he was jesting with them; he, however, placed his wooden table in the middle of the room, and said, "Little table, cover thyself." Instantly it was covered with food, so good that the host could never have procured it, and the smell of it ascended pleasantly to the nostrils of the guests. "Fall to, dear friends," said the joiner; and the guests when they saw that he meant it, did not need to be asked twice, but drew near, pulled out their knives and attacked it valiantly. And what surprised them the most was that when a dish became empty, a full one instantly took its place of its own accord. The innkeeper stood in one corner and watched the affair; he did not at all know what to say, but thought, "Thou couldst easily find a use for such a cook as that in thy kitchen." The joiner and his comrades made merry until late into the night; at length they lay down to sleep, and the young apprentice also went to bed, and set his magic table against the wall. The host's thoughts, however, let him have no rest; it occurred to him that there was a little old table in his lumber-room, which looked just like the apprentice's and he brought it out quite softly, and exchanged it for the wishing-table. Next morning, the joiner paid for his bed, took up his table, never thinking that he had got a false one, and went his way. At mid-day he reached his father, who received him with great joy. "Well, my dear son, what hast thou learnt?" said he to him. "Father, I have become a joiner."

"A good trade," replied the old man; "but what hast thou brought back with thee from thy apprenticeship?" "Father, the best thing which I have brought back with me is this little table." The tailor inspected it on all sides and said, "Thou didst not make a masterpiece* when thou mad'st that; it is a bad old table." "But it is a table which furnishes itself," replied the son. "When I set it out, and tell it to cover itself, the most beautiful dishes stand on it, and a wine also, which gladdens the heart. Just invite all our relations and friends, they shall refresh and enjoy themselves for once, for the table will give them all they require." When the company was assembled, he put his table in the middle of the room and said, "Little table, cover thyself," but the little table did not bestir itself, and remained just as bare as any other table which did not understand language. Then the poor apprentice became aware that his table had been changed, and was ashamed at

*Masterpiece—the piece of work which a journeyman has to make at the end of his *Wanderjahre* to prove his right to become a master craftsman.

having to stand there like a liar. The relations, however, mocked him, and were forced to go home without having eaten or drunk. The father brought out his patches again, and went on tailoring, but the son went to a master in the craft.

The second son had gone to a miller and had apprenticed himself to him. When his years were over, the master said, "As thou hast conducted thyself so well, I give thee an ass of a peculiar kind, which neither draws a cart nor carries a sack." "To what use is he put, then?" asked the young apprentice. "He lets gold drop from his mouth," answered the miller. "If thou settest him on a cloth and sayest 'Bricklebrit,' the good animal will drop gold pieces for thee." "That is a fine thing," said the apprentice, and thanked the master, and went out into the world. When he had need of gold, he had only to say "Bricklebrit" to his ass, and it rained gold pieces, and he had nothing to do but pick them off the ground. Wheresoever he went, the best of everything was good enough for him, and the dearer the better, for he had always a full purse. When he had looked about the world for some time, he thought, "Thou must seek out thy father; if thou goest to him with the gold-ass he will forget his anger, and receive thee well." It came to pass that he came to the same public-house in which his brother's table had been exchanged. He led his ass by the bridle, and the host was about to take the animal from him and tie him up, but the young apprentice said, "Don't trouble yourself, I will take my grey horse into the stable, and tie him up myself too, for I must know where he stands." This struck the host as odd, and he thought that a man who was forced to look after his ass himself, could not have much to spend; but when the stranger put his hand in his pocket and brought out two gold pieces, and said he was to provide something good for him, the host opened his eyes wide, and ran and sought out the best he could muster. After dinner the guest asked what he owed. The host did not see why he should not double the reckoning, and said the apprentice must give two more gold pieces. He felt in his pocket, but his gold was just at an end. "Wait an instant, sir host," said he, "I will go and fetch some money"; but he took the table-cloth with him. The host could not imagine what this could mean, and being curious, stole after him, and as the guest bolted the stable-door, he peeped through a hole left by a knot in the wood. The stranger spread out the cloth under the animal and cried, "Bricklebrit," and immediately the beast began to let gold pieces fall, so that it fairly rained down money on the ground. "Eh, my word," said the host, "ducats are quickly coined there! A purse like that is not amiss." The guest paid his score, and went to bed, but in the night the host stole down into the stable, led away the master of the mint, and tied up another ass in his place. Early next morning the apprentice travelled away with his ass, and thought that he had his gold-ass. At mid-day he reached his father, who rejoiced to see him again, and gladly took him in. "What hast thou made of thyself, my son?" asked the old man. "A miller, dear father," he answered. "What hast thou brought back with thee from thy travels?" "Nothing else but an ass." "There are asses enough here," said the father, "I would rather have had a good goat." "Yes," replied the son, "but it is no common ass, but a gold-ass, when I say 'Bricklebrit,' the good beast opens its mouth and drops a whole sheetful of gold pieces. Just summon all our relations hither, and I will make them rich folks." "That suits me well," said the tailor, "for then I shall have no need to torment myself any longer with the needle," and ran out himself and called the relations together. As soon as they were assembled, the miller bade them make way, spread out his cloth, and brought the ass into the room. "Now watch," said he, and cried, "Bricklebrit," but no gold pieces fell, and it was clear that the animal knew nothing of the art, for every ass does not attain such perfection. Then the poor miller pulled a long face, saw that he was betrayed, and begged pardon of the relatives, who went home as poor as they came. There was no help for it, the old man had to betake him to his needle once more, and the youth hired himself to a miller.

The third brother had apprenticed himself to a turner, and as that is skilled labour, he was the longest in learning. His brothers, however, told him in a letter how badly things had gone with them, and how the inn-keeper had cheated them of their beautiful wishing-gifts on the last evening before they reached home. When the turner had served his time, and had to set out on his travels, as he had conducted himself so well, his master presented him with a sack and said, "There is a cudgel in it." "I can put on the sack," said he, "and it may be of good service to me, but why should the cudgel be in it? It only makes it heavy." "I will tell thee why," replied the master; "if any one has done anything to injure thee, do but say, 'Out of the sack, Cudgel!' and the cudgel will leap forth among the people, and play such a dance on their backs that they will not be able to stir or move for a week, and it will not leave off until thou sayest, "Into the sack, Cudgel!" The apprentice thanked him, and put the sack on his back, and when any one came too near him, and wished to attack him, he said, "Out of the sack, Cudgel!" and instantly the cudgel sprang out, and dusted the coat or jacket of one after the other on their backs, and never stopped until it had stripped it off them, and it was done so quickly, that before anyone was aware, it was already his own turn. In the evening the young turner reached the inn where his brothers had been cheated. He laid his sack on the table before him, and began to talk of all the wonderful things which he had seen in the world. "Yes," said he, "people may easily find a table which will cover itself, a gold-ass, and things of that kind—extremely good things which I by no means despise—but these are nothing in comparison with the treasure which I have won for myself, and am carrying about with me in my sack there." The inn-keeper pricked up his ears, "What in the world can that be?" thought he; "the sack must be filled with nothing but jewels; I ought to get them cheap too, for all good things go in threes." When it was time for sleep, the guest stretched himself on the bench, and laid his sack beneath him for a pillow. When the inn-keeper thought his guest was lying in a sound sleep, he went to him and pushed and pulled quite gently and carefully at the sack to see if he could possibly draw it away and lay another in its place. The turner had, however, been waiting for this for a long time, and now just as the inn-keeper was about to give a hearty tug, he cried, "Out of the sack, Cudgel!" Instantly the little cudgel came forth, and fell on the inn-keeper and gave him a sound thrashing.

The host cried for mercy; but the louder he cried, so much the more heavily the cudgel beat the time on his back, until at length he fell to the ground exhausted. Then the turner said, "If thou dost not give back the table which covers itself, and the gold-ass, the dance shall begin afresh." "Oh, no," cried the host, quite humbly, "I will gladly produce everything, only make the accursed kobold creep back into the sack." Then said the apprentice, "I will let mercy take the place of justice, but beware of getting into mischief again!" So he cried, "Into the sack, Cudgel!" and let him have rest.

Next morning the turner went home to his father with the wishing-table, and the gold-ass. The tailor rejoiced when he saw him once more, and asked him likewise what he had learned in foreign parts. "Dear father," said he, "I have become a turner." "A skilled trade," said the father. "What hast thou brought back with thee from thy travels?"

"A precious thing, dear father," replied the son, "a cudgel in the sack."

"What!" cried the father, "a cudgel! That's worth thy trouble, indeed! From every tree thou can cut thyself one." "But not one like this, dear father. If I say, 'Out of the sack, Cudgel!' the cudgel springs out and leads any one who means ill with me a weary dance, and never stops until he lies on the ground and prays for fair weather. Look you, with this cudgel have I got back the wishing-table and the gold-ass which the thievish inn-keeper took away from my brothers. Now let them both be sent for, and invite all our kinsmen. I will give them to eat and to drink, and will fill their pockets with gold into the bargain." The old tailor would not quite believe, but nevertheless got the relatives together. Then the turner spread a cloth in the room and led in the gold-ass, and said to his brother, "Now, dear brother, speak to him." The miller said, "Bricklebrit," and instantly the gold pieces fell down on the cloth like a thunder-shower, and the ass did not stop until every one of them had so much that he could carry no more. (I can see in thy face that thou also wouldst have liked to be there.)

Then the turner brought the little table, and said, "Now dear brother, speak to it." And scarcely had the carpenter said, "Table, cover thyself," than it was spread and amply covered with the most exquisite dishes. Then such a meal took place as the good tailor had never yet known in his house, and the whole party of kinsmen stayed together till far in the night, and were all merry and glad. The tailor locked away needle and thread, yard-measure and goose, in a press, and lived with his three sons in joy and splendour.

(What, however, has become of the goat who was to blame for the tailor driving out his three sons? That I will tell thee. She was ashamed that she had a bald head, and ran to a fox's hole and crept into it. When the fox came home, he was met by two great eyes shining out of the darkness, and was terrified and ran away. A bear met him, and as the fox looked quite disturbed, he said, "What is the matter with thee, brother Fox, why dost thou look like that?" "Ah," answered Redskin, "a fierce beast is in my cave and stared at me with its fiery eyes." "We will soon drive him out," said the bear, and went with him to the cave and looked in, but when he saw the fiery eyes, fear seized on him likewise; he would have nothing to do with the furious beast, and took to his heels. The bee met him, and as she saw that he was ill at ease, she said, "Bear, thou art really pulling a very pitiful face; what has become of all thy gaiety?" "It is all very well for thee to talk," replied the bear, "a furious beast with staring eyes is in Redskin's house, and we can't drive him out." The bee said, "Bear, I pity thee, I am a poor weak creature whom thou wouldst not turn aside to look at, but still, I believe, I can help thee." She flew into the fox's cave, lighted on the goat's smoothly-shorn head, and stung her so violently, that she sprang up, crying "Meh, meh," and ran forth into the world as if mad, and to this hour no one knows where she has gone.)

THUMBLING

THERE WAS once a poor peasant who sat in the evening by the hearth and poked the fire, and his wife sat and span. Then said he, "How sad it is that we have no children! With us all is so quiet, and in other houses it is noisy and lively."

"Yes," replied the wife, and sighed, "even if we had only one, and it were quite small, and only as big as a thumb, I should be quite satisfied, and we would still love it with all our hearts." Now it so happened that the woman fell ill, and after seven months gave birth to a child, that was perfect in all its limbs, but no longer than a thumb. Then said they, "It is as we wished it to be, and it shall be our dear child"; and because of its size, they called it Thumbling. They did not let it want for food, but the child did not grow taller, but remained as it had been at the first, nevertheless it looked sensibly out of its eyes, and soon showed itself to be a wise and nimble creature, for everything it did turned out well.

One day the peasant was getting ready to go into the forest to cut wood, when he said as if to himself, "How I wish that there was any one who would bring the cart to me!" "Oh, father," cried Thumbling, "I will soon bring the cart, rely on that; it shall be in the forest at the appointed time." The man smiled and said, "How can that be done, thou art far too small to lead the horse by the reins?" "That's of no consequence, father, if my mother will only harness it, I will sit in the horse's ear and call out to him how he is to go." "Well," answered the man, "for once we will try it."

When the time came, the mother harnessed the horse, and placed Thumbling in its ear, and then the little creature cried, "Gee up, gee up!"

Then it went quite properly as if with its master, and the cart went the right way into the forest. It so happened that just as he was turning a corner, and the little one was crying "Gee up," two strange men came towards him. "My word!" said one of them. "What is this?

There is a cart coming, and a driver is calling to the horse and still he is not to be seen!" "That can't be right," said the other, "we will follow the cart and see where it stops." The cart, however, drove right into the forest, and exactly to the place where the wood had been cut. When Thumbling saw his father, he cried to him, "Seest thou, father, here I am with the cart; now take me down." The father got hold of the horse with his left hand and with the right took his little son out of the ear. Thumbling sat down quite merrily on a straw, but when the two strange men saw him, they did not know what to say for astonishment. Then one of them took the other aside and said, "Hark, the little fellow would make our fortune if we exhibited him in a large town, for money. We will buy him." They went to the peasant and said, "Sell us the little man. He shall be well treated with us." "No," replied the father, "he is the apple of my eye, and all the money in the world cannot buy him from me." Thumbling, however, when he heard of the bargain, had crept up the folds of his father's coat, placed himself on his shoulder, and whispered in his ear, "Father do give me away, I will soon come back again." Then the father parted with him to the two men for a handsome bit of money. "Where wilt thou sit?" they said to him. "Oh, just set me on the rim of your hat, and then I can walk backwards and forwards and look at the country, and still not fall down." They did as he wished, and when Thumbling had taken leave of his father, they went away with him. They walked until it was dusk, and then the little fellow said, "Do take me down, I want to come down." The man took his hat off, and put the little fellow on the ground by the wayside, and he leapt and crept about a little between the sods, and then he suddenly slipped into a mouse-hole which he had sought out. "Good evening, gentlemen, just go home without me," he cried to them, and mocked them. They ran thither and stuck their sticks into the mouse-hole, but it was all lost labour. Thumbling crept still farther in, and as it soon became quite dark, they were forced to go home with their vexation and their empty purses.

When Thumbling saw that they were gone, he crept back out of the subterranean passage. "It is so dangerous to walk on the ground in the dark," said he; "how easily a neck or a leg is broken!" Fortunately he knocked against an empty snail-shell. "Thank God!" said he. "In that I can pass the night in safety," and got into it. Not long afterwards, when he was just going to sleep, he heard two men go by, and one of them was saying, "How shall we contrive to get hold of the rich pastor's silver and gold?" "I could tell thee that," cried Thumbling, interrupting them. "What was that?" said one of the thieves in fright, "I heard some one speaking." They stood still listening, and

Thumbling spoke again, and said, "Take me with you, and I'll help you."

"But where art thou?" "Just look on the ground, and observe from whence my voice comes," he replied. There the thieves at length found him, and lifted him up. "Thou little imp, how wilt thou help us?" they said. "A great deal," said he, "I will creep into the pastor's room through the iron bars, and will reach out to you whatever you want to have." "Come then," they said, "and we will see what thou canst do." When they got to the pastor's house, Thumbling crept into the room, but instantly cried out with all his might, "Do you want to have everything that is here?" The thieves were alarmed, and said, "But do speak softly, so as not to waken any one!" Thumbling however, behaved as if he had not understood this, and cried again, "What do you want? Do you want to have everything that is here?" The cook, who slept in the next room, heard this and sat up in bed, and listened. The thieves, however, had in their fright run some distance away, but at last they took courage, and thought, "The little rascal wants to mock us." They came back and whispered to him, "Come, be serious, and reach something out to us." Then Thumbling again cried as loudly as he could, "I really will give you everything, only put your hands in." The maid who was listening, heard this quite distinctly, and jumped out of bed and rushed to the door. The thieves took flight, and ran as if the Wild Huntsman were behind them, but as the maid could not see anything, she went to strike a light. When she came to the place with it, Thumbling, unperceived, betook himself to the granary, and the maid, after she had examined every corner and found nothing, lay down in her bed again, and believed that, after all, she had only been dreaming with open eyes and ears.

Thumbling had climbed up among the hay and found a beautiful place to sleep in; there he intended to rest until day, and then go home again to his parents. But he had other things to go through. Truly there is much affliction and misery in this world! When day dawned, the maid arose from her bed to feed the cows. Her first walk was into the barn, where she laid hold of an armful of hay, and precisely that very one in which poor Thumbling was lying asleep. He, however, was sleeping so soundly that he was aware of nothing, and did not awake until he was in the mouth of the cow, who had picked him up with the hay. "Ah, heavens!" cried he, "how have I got into the fulling mill?" but he soon discovered where he was. Then it was necessary to be careful not to let himself go between the teeth and be dismembered, but he was nevertheless forced to slip down into the stomach with the hay. "In this little room the windows are forgotten," said he, "and no sun shines in, neither will a candle be brought." His quarters were especially unpleasing to him, and the worst was, more and more hay was always coming in by the door, and the space grew less and less. Then, at length in his anguish, he cried as loud as he could, "Bring me no more fodder, bring me no more fodder." The maid was just milking the cow, and when she heard some one speaking, and saw no one, and perceived that it was the same voice that she had heard in the night, she was so terrified that she slipped off her stool, and spilt the milk. She ran in the greatest haste to her master, and said, "Oh, heavens, pastor, the cow has been speaking!" "Thou art mad," replied the pastor; but he went himself to the byre to see what was there. Hardly, however, had he set his foot inside when Thumbling again cried, "Bring me no more fodder, bring me no more fodder." Then the pastor himself was alarmed, and thought that an evil spirit had gone into the cow, and ordered her to be killed. She was killed, but the stomach, in which Thumbling was, was thrown on the midden. Thumbling had great difficulty in working his way; however, he succeeded so far as to get some room, but just as he was going to thrust his head out, a new misfortune occurred. A hungry wolf ran thither, and swallowed the whole stomach at one gulp. Thumbling did not lose courage. "Perhaps," thought he, "the wolf will listen to what I have got to say," and he called to him from out of his stomach, "Dear wolf, I know of a magnificent feast for thee."

"Where is it to be had?" said the wolf.

"In such and such a house; thou must creep into it through the kitchen-sink, and wilt find cakes, and bacon, and sausages, and as much of them as thou canst eat," and he described to him exactly his father's house. The wolf did not require to be told this twice, squeezed himself in at night through the sink, and ate to his heart's content in the larder. When he had eaten his fill, he wanted to go out again, but he had become so big that he could not go out by the same way. Thumbling had reckoned on this, and now began to make a violent noise in the wolf's body, and raged and screamed as loudly as he could. "Wilt thou be quiet," said the wolf, "thou wilt waken up the people!" "Eh, what," replied the little fellow, "thou hast eaten thy fill, and I will make merry likewise," and began once more to scream with all his strength. At last his father and mother were aroused by it, and ran to the room and looked in through the opening in the door. When they saw that a wolf was inside, they ran away, and the husband fetched his axe, and the wife the scythe. "Stay behind," said the man, when they entered the room. "When I have given him a blow, if he is not killed by it, thou must cut him down and hew his body to pieces." Then Thumbling heard his parents' voices and cried, "Dear father, I am here; I am in the wolf's body." Said the father, full of joy, "Thank God, our dear child has found us again," and bade the woman take away her scythe, that Thumbling might not be hurt with it. After that he raised his arm, and struck the wolf such a blow on his head that he fell down dead, and then they got knives and scissors and cut his body open and drew the little fellow forth. "Ah," said the father, "what sorrow we have gone through for thy sake." "Yes father, I have gone about the world a great deal. Thank heaven, I breathe fresh air again!" "Where hast thou been, then?" "Ah, father, I have been in a mouse's hole, in a cow's stomach, and then in a wolf's; now I will stay with you." "And we will not sell thee again, no, not for all the riches in the world," said his parents, and they embraced and kissed their dear Thumbling. They gave him to eat and to drink, and had some new clothes made for him, for his own had been spoiled on his journey.

THE ELVES

FIRST STORY

A SHOEMAKER, by no fault of his own, had become so poor that at last he had nothing left but leather for one pair of shoes. So in the evening, he cut out the shoes which he wished to begin to make the next morning, and as he had a good conscience, he lay down quietly in his bed, commended himself to God, and fell asleep. In the morning, after he had said his prayers, and was just going to sit down to work, the two shoes stood quite finished on his table. He was astounded, and did not know what to say to it. He took the shoes in his hands to observe them closer, and they were so neatly made that there was not one bad stitch in them, just as if they were intended as a masterpiece. Soon after, too, a buyer came in, and as the shoes pleased him so well, he paid more for them than was customary, and, with the money, the shoemaker was able to purchase leather for two pairs of shoes. He cut them out at night, and next morning was about to set to work with fresh courage; but he had no need to do so, for, when he got up, they were already made, and buyers also were not wanting, who gave him money enough to buy leather for four pairs of shoes. The following morning, too, he found the four pairs made; and so it went on constantly, what he cut out in the evening was finished by the morning, so that he soon had his honest independence again, and at last became a wealthy man. Now it befell that one evening not long before Christmas, when the man had been cutting out, he said to his wife, before going to bed, "What think you if we were to stay up tonight to see who it is that lends us this helping hand?" The woman liked the idea, and lighted a candle, and then they hid themselves in a corner of the room, behind some clothes which were hanging up there, and watched. When it was midnight, two pretty little naked men came, sat down by the shoemaker's table, took all the work which was cut out before them and began to stitch, and sew, and hammer so skilfully and so quickly with their little fingers that the shoemaker could not turn away his eyes for astonishment. They did not stop until all was done, and stood finished on the table, and then they ran quickly away.

Next morning the woman said, "The little men have made us rich, and we really must show that we are grateful for it. They run about so, and have nothing on, and must be cold. I'll tell thee what I'll do: I will make them little shirts, and coats, and vests, and trousers, and knit both of them a pair of stockings, and do thou, too, make them two little pairs of shoes." The man said, "I shall be very glad to do it"; and one night, when everything was ready, they laid their presents all together on the table instead of the cut-out work, and then concealed themselves to see how the little men would behave. At midnight they came bounding in, and wanted to get to work at once, but as they did not find any leather cut out, but only the pretty little articles of clothing, they were at first astonished, and then they showed intense delight. They dressed themselves with the greatest rapidity, putting the pretty clothes on, and singing,

"Now we are boys so fine to see,
Why should we longer cobblers be?"

Then they danced and skipped and leapt over chairs and benches. At last they danced out of doors. From that time forth they came no more, but as long as the shoemaker lived all went well with him, and all his undertakings prospered.

SECOND STORY

THERE WAS once a poor servant-girl, who was industrious and cleanly, and swept the house every day, and emptied her sweepings on the great heap in front of the door. One morning when she was just going back to her work, she found a letter on this heap, and as she could not read, she put her broom in the corner, and took the letter to her master and mistress, and behold it was an invitation from the elves, who asked the girl to hold a child for them at its christening. The girl did not know what to do, but at length, after much persuasion, and as they told her that it was not right to refuse an invitation of this kind, she consented. Then three elves came and conducted her to a hollow mountain, where the little folks lived. Everything there was small, but more elegant and beautiful than can be described. The baby's mother lay in a bed of black ebony ornamented with pearls, the coverlids were embroidered with gold, the cradle was of ivory, the bath of gold. The girl stood as godmother, and then wanted to go home again, but the little elves urgently entreated her to stay three days with them. So she stayed, and passed the time in pleasure and gaiety, and the little folks did all they could to make her happy. At last she set out on her way home. Then first they filled her pockets quite full of money, and after that they led her out of the mountain again. When she got home, she wanted to begin her work, and took the broom, which was still standing in the corner, in her hand and began to sweep. Then some strangers came out of the house, who asked her who she was, and what business she had there? And she had not, as she thought, been three days with the little men in the mountains, but seven years, and in the meantime her former masters had died.

THIRD STORY

A CERTAIN mother's child had been taken away out of its cradle by the elves, and a changeling with a large head and staring eyes, which would do nothing but eat and drink, laid in its place. In her trouble she went to her neighbour, and asked her advice. The neighbour said that she was to carry the changeling into the kitchen, set it down on the hearth, light a fire, and boil some water in two egg-shells, which would make the changeling laugh, and if he laughed, all would be over with him. The woman did everything that her neighbour bade her. When she put the egg-shells with water on the fire, the imp said, "I am as old now as the Wester forest, but never yet have I seen any one boil anything in an egg-shell!" And he began to laugh at it. Whilst he was laughing, suddenly came a host of little elves, who brought the right child, set it down on the hearth, and took the changeling away with them.

THE ROBBER BRIDEGROOM

THERE WAS once on a time a miller, who had a beautiful daughter, and as she was grown up, he wished that she was provided for, and well married. He thought, "If any good suitor comes and asks for her, I will give her to him." Not long afterwards, a suitor came, who appeared to be very rich, and as the miller had no fault to find with him, he promised his daughter to him. The maiden, however, did not like him quite so much as a girl should like the man to whom she is engaged, and had no confidence in him. Whenever she saw, or thought of him, she felt a secret horror. Once he said to her, "Thou art my betrothed, and yet thou hast never once paid me a visit." The maiden replied, "I know not where thy house is." Then said the bridegroom, "My house is out there in the dark forest." She tried to excuse herself and said she could not find the way there. The bridegroom said, "Next Sunday thou must come out there to me; I have already invited the guests, and I will strew ashes in order that thou mayst find thy way through the forest." When Sunday came, and the maiden had to set out on her way, she became very uneasy, she herself knew not exactly why, and to mark her way she filled both her pockets full of peas and lentils. Ashes were strewn at the entrance of the forest, and these she followed, but at every step she threw a couple of peas on the ground. She walked almost the whole day until she reached the middle of the forest, where it was the darkest, and there stood a solitary house, which she did not like, for it looked so dark and dismal. She went inside it, but no one was within, and the most absolute stillness reigned. Suddenly a voice cried,

"Turn back, turn back, young maiden dear,
'Tis a murderer's house you enter here."

The maiden looked up, and saw that the voice came from a bird, which was hanging in a cage on the wall. Again it cried,

"Turn back, turn back, young maiden dear,
'Tis a murderer's house you enter here."

Then the young maiden went on farther from one room to another, and walked through the whole house, but it was entirely empty and not one human being was to be found. At last she came to the cellar, and there sat an extremely aged woman, whose head shook constantly. "Can you not tell me," said the maiden, "if my betrothed lives here?"

"Alas, poor child," replied the old woman, "whither hast thou come? Thou art in a murderer's den. Thou thinkest thou art a bride soon to be married, but thou wilt keep thy wedding with death. Look, I have been forced to put a great kettle on there, with water in it, and when they have thee in their power, they will cut thee to pieces without mercy, will cook thee, and eat thee, for they are eaters of human flesh. If I do not have compassion on thee, and save thee, thou art lost.

Thereupon the old woman led her behind a great hogshead where she could not be seen. "Be as still as a mouse," said she, "do not make a sound, or move, or all will be over with thee. At night, when the robbers are asleep, we will escape; I have long waited for an opportunity." Hardly was this done, than the godless crew came home. They dragged with them another young girl. They were drunk, and paid no heed to her screams and lamentations. They gave her wine to drink, three glasses full, one glass of white wine, one glass of red, and a glass of yellow, and with this her heart burst in twain. Thereupon they tore off her delicate raiment, laid her on a table, cut her beautiful body in pieces and strewed salt thereon. The poor bride behind the cask trembled and shook, for she saw right well what fate the robbers had destined for her. One of them noticed a gold ring on the little finger of the murdered girl, and as it would not come off at once, he took an axe and cut the finger off, but it sprang up in the air, away over the cask and fell straight into the bride's bosom. The robber took a candle and wanted to look for it, but could not find it. Then another of them said, "Hast thou looked behind the great hogshead?" But the old woman cried, "Come and get something to eat, and leave off looking till the morning, the finger won't run away from you."

Then the robbers said, "The old woman is right," and gave up their search, and sat down to eat, and the old woman poured a sleeping-draught in their wine, so that they soon lay down in the cellar, and slept and snored. When the bride heard that, she came out from behind the hogshead, and had to step over the sleepers, for they lay in rows on the ground, and great was her terror lest she should waken one of them. But God helped her, and she got safely over. The old woman went up with her, opened the doors, and they hurried out of the murderers' den with all the speed in their power. The wind had blown away the strewn ashes, but the peas and lentils had sprouted and grown up, and showed them the way in the moonlight. They walked the whole night, until in the morning they arrived at the mill, and then the maiden told her father everything exactly as it had happened.

When the day came when the wedding was to be celebrated, the bridegroom appeared, and the Miller had invited all his relations and friends. As they sat at table, each was bidden to relate something. The bride sat still, and said nothing. Then said the bridegroom to the bride, "Come, my darling, dost thou know nothing? Relate something to us like the rest." She replied, "Then I will relate a dream. I was walking alone through a wood, and at last I came to a house, in which no living soul was, but on the wall there was a bird in a cage which cried,

"Turn back, turn back, young maiden dear,
'Tis a murderer's house you enter here."

And this it cried once more. My darling, I only dreamt this. Then I went through all the rooms, and they were all empty, and there was something so horrible about them! At last I went down into the cellar, and there sat a very very old woman, whose head shook; I asked her, 'Does my bridegroom live in this house? She answered, 'Alas, poor child, thou hast got into a murderer's den, thy bridegroom does live here, but he will hew thee in pieces, and kill thee, and then he will cook thee, and eat thee.' My darling, I only dreamt this. But the old woman hid me behind a great hogshead, and, scarcely was I hidden, when the robbers came home, dragging a maiden with them, to whom they gave three kinds of wine to drink, white, red, and yellow, with which her heart broke in twain. My darling, I only dreamt this. Thereupon they pulled off her pretty clothes, and hewed her fair body in pieces on a table, and sprinkled them with salt. My darling, I only dreamt this. And one of the robbers saw that there was still a ring on her little finger, and as it was hard to draw off, he took an axe and cut it off, but the finger sprang up in the air, and sprang behind the great hogshead, and fell in my bosom. And there is the finger with the ring!" And with these words she drew it forth, and showed it to those present.

The robber, who had during this story become as pale as ashes, leapt up and wanted to escape, but the guests held him fast, and delivered him over to justice. Then he and his whole troop were executed for their infamous deeds.

THE SIX SWANS

ONCE UPON a time, a certain King was hunting in a great forest, and he chased a wild beast so eagerly that none of his attendants could follow him. When evening drew near he stopped and looked around him, and then he saw that he had lost his way. He sought a way out, but could find none. Then he perceived an aged woman with a head which nodded perpetually, who came towards him, but she was a witch. "Good woman," said he to her, "Can you not show me the way through the forest?" "Oh, yes, Lord King," she answered, "that I certainly can, but on one condition, and if you do not fulfil that, you will never get out of the forest, and will die of hunger in it."

"What kind of condition is it?" asked the King.

"I have a daughter," said the old woman, "who is as beautiful as any one in the world, and well deserves to be your consort, and if you will make her your Queen, I will show you the way out of the forest." In the anguish of his heart the King consented, and the old woman led him to her little hut, where her daughter was sitting by the fire. She received the King as if she had been expecting him, and he saw that she was very beautiful, but still she did not please him, and he could not look at her without secret horror. After he had taken the maiden up on his horse, the old woman showed him the way, and the King reached his royal palace again, where the wedding was celebrated.

The King had already been married once, and had by his first wife, seven children, six boys and a girl, whom he loved better than anything else in the world. As he now feared that the step-mother might not treat them well, and even do them some injury, he took them to a lonely castle which stood in the midst of a forest. It lay so concealed, and the way was so difficult to find that he himself would not have found it, if a wise woman had not given him a ball of yarn with wonderful properties. When he threw it down before him, it unrolled itself and showed him his path. The King, however, went so frequently away to his dear children that the Queen observed his absence; she was curious and wanted to know what he did when he was quite alone in the forest. She gave a great deal of money to his servants, and they betrayed the secret to her, and told her likewise of the ball which alone could point out the way. And now she knew no rest until she had learnt where the King kept the ball of yarn, and then she made little shirts of white silk, and as she had learnt the art of witchcraft from her mother, she sewed a charm inside them. And once when the King had ridden forth to hunt, she took the little shirts and went into the forest, and the ball showed her the way. The children, who saw from a distance that some one was approaching, thought that their dear father was coming to them, and full of joy, ran to meet him. Then she threw one of the little shirts over each of them, and no sooner had the shirts touched their bodies than they were changed into swans, and flew away over the forest. The Queen went home quite delighted, and thought she had got rid of her step-children, but the girl had not run out with her brothers, and the Queen knew nothing about her. Next day the King went to visit his children, but he found no one but the little girl. "Where are thy brothers?' asked the King. "Alas, dear father," she answered, "they have gone away and left me alone!" and she told him that she had seen from her little window how her brothers had flown away over the forest in the shape of swans, and she showed him the feathers, which they had let fall in the courtyard, and which she had picked up. The King mourned, but he did not think that the Queen had done this wicked deed, and as he feared that the girl would also be stolen away from him, he wanted to take her away with him. But she was afraid of her step-mother, and entreated the King to let her stay just this one night more in the forest castle.

The poor girl thought, "I can no longer stay here. I will go and seek my brothers." And when night came, she ran away, and went straight into the forest. She walked the whole night long, and next day also without stopping, until she could go no farther for weariness. Then she saw a forest-hut, and went into it, and found a room with six little beds, but she did not venture to get into one of them, but crept under one, and lay down on the hard ground, intending to pass the night there. Just before sunset, however, she heard a rustling, and saw six swans come flying in at the window. They alighted on the ground and blew at each other, and blew all the feathers off, and their swan's skins stripped off like a shirt. Then the maiden looked at them and recognized her brothers, was glad and crept forth from beneath the bed. The brothers were not less delighted to see their little sister, but their joy was of short duration. "Here canst thou not abide," they said to her. "This is a shelter for robbers, if they come home and find thee, they will kill thee." "But can you not protect me?" asked the little sister. "No," they replied, "only for one quarter of an hour each evening can we lay aside our swan's skins and have during that time our human form; after that, we are once more turned into swans." The little sister wept and said, "Can you not be set free?" "Alas, no," they answered, "the conditions are too hard! For six years thou mayst neither speak nor laugh, and in that time thou must sew together six little shirts of starwort for us. And if one single word falls from thy lips, all thy work will be lost." And when the brothers had said this, the quarter of an hour was over, and they flew out of the window again as swans.

The maiden, however, firmly resolved to deliver her brothers, even if it should cost her her life. She left the hut, went into the midst of the forest, seated herself on a tree, and there passed the night. Next morning she went out and gathered starwort and began to sew. She could not speak to any one, and she had no inclination to laugh; she sat there and looked at nothing but her work. When she had already spent a long time there it came to pass that the King of the country was hunting in the forest, and his huntsmen came to the tree on which the maiden was sitting. They called to her and said, "Who art thou?" But she made no answer. "Come down to us," said they. "We will not do thee any harm." She only shook her head. As they pressed her further with questions she threw her golden necklace down to them, and thought to content them thus. They, however, did not cease, and then she threw her girdle down to them, and as this also was to no purpose, her garters, and by degrees everything that she had on that she could do without until she had nothing left but her shift. The huntsmen, however, did not let themselves be turned aside by that, but climbed the tree and fetched the maiden down and led her before the King. The King asked, "Who art thou? What art thou doing on the tree?" But she did not answer. He put the question in every language that he knew, but she remained as mute as a fish. As she was so beautiful, the King's heart was touched, and he was smitten with a great love for her. He put his mantle on her, took her before him on his horse, and carried her to his castle. Then he caused her to be dressed in rich garments, and she shone in her beauty like bright daylight, but no word could be drawn from her. He placed her by his side at table, and her modest bearing and courtesy pleased him so much that he said, "She is the one whom I wish to marry, and no other woman in the world." And after some days he united himself to her.

The King, however, had a wicked mother who was dissatisfied with this marriage and spoke ill of the young Queen. "Who knows," said she, "from whence the creature who can't speak, comes? She is not worthy of a king!" After a year had passed, when the Queen brought her first child into the world, the old woman took it away from her, and smeared her mouth with blood as she slept. Then she went to the King and accused the Queen of being a man-eater. The King would not believe it, and would not suffer any one to do her any injury. She, however, sat continually sewing at the shirts, and cared for nothing else. The next time, when she again bore a beautiful boy, the false step-mother used the same treachery, but the King could not bring himself to give credit to her words. He said, "She is too pious and good to do anything of that kind; if she were not dumb, and could defend herself, her innocence would come to light." But when the old woman stole away the newly-born child for the third time, and accused the Queen, who did not utter one word of defence, the King could do no otherwise than deliver her over to justice, and she was sentenced to suffer death by fire.

When the day came for the sentence to be executed, it was the last day of the six years during which she was not to speak or laugh, and she had delivered her dear brothers from the power of the enchantment. The six shirts were ready, only the left sleeve of the sixth was wanting. When, therefore, she was led to the stake, she laid the shirts on her arm, and when she stood on high and the fire was just going to be lighted, she looked around and six swans came flying through the air towards her. Then she saw that her deliverance was near, and her heart leapt with joy. The swans swept towards her and sank down so that she could throw the shirts over them, and as they were touched by them, their swan's skins fell off, and her brothers stood in their own bodily form before her, and were vigorous and handsome. The youngest only lacked his left arm, and had in the place of it a swan's wing on his shoulder. They embraced and kissed each other, and the Queen went to the King, who was greatly moved, and she began to speak and said, "Dearest husband, now I may speak and declare to thee that I am innocent, and falsely accused." And she told him of the treachery of the old woman who had taken away her three children and hidden them. Then to the great joy of the King they were brought thither, and as a punishment, the wicked step-mother was bound to the stake, and burnt to ashes. But the King and the Queen with their six brothers lived many years in happiness and peace.

LITTLE BRIAR-ROSE (SLEEPING BEAUTY)

A LONG time ago there were a King and Queen who said every day, "Ah, if only we had a child!" but they never had one. But it happened that once when the Queen was bathing, a frog crept out of the water on to the land, and said to her, "Your wish shall be fulfilled; before a year has gone by you shall have a daughter."

What the frog had said came true, and the Queen had a little girl who was so pretty that the King could not contain himself for joy, and ordered a great feast. He invited not only his kindred, friends and acquaintance, but also the Wise Women, in order that they might be kind and well-disposed towards the child. There were thirteen of them in his kingdom, but, as he had only twelve golden plates for them to eat out of, one of them had to be left at home.

The feast was held with all manner of splendour, and when it came to an end the Wise Women bestowed their magic gifts upon the baby: one gave virtue, another beauty, a third riches, and so on with everything in the world that one can wish for.

When eleven of them had made their promises, suddenly the thirteenth came in. She wished to avenge herself for not having been invited, and without greeting, or even looking at any one, she cried with a loud voice, "The King's daughter shall in her fifteenth year prick herself with a spindle, and fall down dead." And, without saying a word more, she turned round and left the room.

They were all shocked; but the twelfth, whose good wish still remained unspoken, came forward, and as she could not undo the evil sentence, but only soften it, she said, "It shall not be death, but a deep sleep of a hundred years, into which the princess shall fall."

The King, who would fain keep his dear child from the misfortune, gave orders that every spindle in the whole kingdom should be burnt. Meanwhile the gifts of the Wise Women were plenteously fulfilled on the young girl, for she was so beautiful, modest, good-natured, and wise, that every one who saw her was bound to love her.

It happened that on the very day when she was fifteen years old, the King and Queen were not at home, and the maiden was left in the palace quite alone. So she went round into all sorts of places, looked into rooms and bed-chambers just as she liked, and at last came to an old tower. She climbed up the narrow winding-staircase, and reached a little door. A rusty key was in the lock, and when she turned it the door sprang open, and there in a little room sat an old woman with a spindle, busily spinning her flax.

"Good day, old dame," said the King's daughter; "what are you doing there?" "I am spinning," said the old woman, and nodded her head. "What sort of thing is that, that rattles round so merrily?" said the girl, and she took the spindle and wanted to spin too. But scarcely had she touched the spindle when the magic decree was fulfilled, and she pricked her finger with it.

And, in the very moment when she felt the prick, she fell down upon the bed that stood there, and lay in a deep sleep. And this sleep extended over the whole palace; the King and Queen who had just come home, and had entered the great hall, began to go to sleep, and the whole of the court with them. The horses, too, went to sleep in the stable, the dogs in the yard, the pigeons upon the roof, the flies on the wall; even the fire that was flaming on the hearth became quiet and slept, the roast meat left off frizzling, and the cook, who was just going to pull the hair of the scullery boy, because he had forgotten something, let him go, and went to sleep. And the wind fell, and on the trees before the castle not a leaf moved again.

But round about the castle there began to grow a hedge of thorns, which every year became higher, and at last grew close up round the castle and all over it, so that there was nothing of it to be seen, not even the flag upon the roof. But the story of the beautiful sleeping "Briar-rose," for so the princess was named, went about the country, so that from time to time kings' sons came and tried to get through the thorny hedge into the castle.

But they found it impossible, for the thorns held fast together, as if they had hands, and the youths were caught in them, could not get loose again, and died a miserable death.

After long, long years a King's son came again to that country, and heard an old man talking about the thorn-hedge, and that a castle was said to stand behind it in which a wonderfully beautiful princess, named Briar-rose, had been asleep for a hundred years; and that the King and Queen and the whole court were asleep likewise. He had heard, too, from his grandfather, that many kings' sons had already come, and had tried to get through the thorny hedge, but they had remained sticking fast in it, and had died a pitiful death. Then the youth said, "I am not afraid, I will go and see the beautiful Briar-rose." The good old man might dissuade him as he would, he did not listen to his words.

But by this time the hundred years had just passed, and the day had come when Briar-rose was to awake again. When the King's son came near to the thorn-hedge, it was nothing but large and beautiful flowers, which parted from each other of their own accord, and let him pass unhurt, then they closed again behind him like a hedge. In the castle-yard he saw the horses and the spotted hounds lying asleep; on the roof sat the pigeons with their heads under their wings. And when he entered the house, the flies were asleep upon the wall, the cook in the kitchen was still holding out his hand to seize the boy, and the maid was sitting by the black hen which she was going to pluck.

He went on farther, and in the great hall he saw the whole of the court lying asleep, and up by the throne lay the King and Queen.

Then he went on still farther, and all was so quiet that a breath could be heard, and at last he came to the tower, and opened the door into the little room where Briar-rose was sleeping. There she lay, so beautiful that he could not turn his eyes away; and he stooped down and gave her a kiss. But as soon as he kissed her, Briar-rose opened her eyes and awoke, and looked at him quite sweetly.

Then they went down together, and the King awoke, and the Queen, and the whole court, and looked at each other in great astonishment. And the horses in the court-yard stood up and shook themselves; the hounds jumped up and wagged their tails; the pigeons upon the roof pulled out their heads from under their wings, looked round, and flew into the open country; the flies on the wall crept again; the fire in the kitchen burned up and flickered and cooked the meat; the joint began to turn and frizzle again, and the cook gave the boy such a box on the ear that he screamed, and the maid plucked the fowl ready for the spit.

And then the marriage of the King's son with Briar-rose was celebrated with all splendour, and they lived contented to the end of their days.

KING THRUSHBEARD

A KING had a daughter who was beautiful beyond all measure, but so proud and haughty withal that no suitor was good enough for her. She sent away one after the other, and ridiculed them as well.

Once the King made a great feast and invited thereto, from far and near, all the young men likely to marry. They were all marshalled in a row according to their rank and standing; first came the kings, then the grand-dukes, then the princes, the earls, the barons, and the gentry. Then the King's daughter was led through the ranks, but to every one she had some objection to make; one was too fat, "The wine-cask," she said. Another was too tall, "Long and thin has little in." The third was too short, "Short and thick is never quick." The fourth was too pale, "As pale as death." The fifth too red, "A fighting-cock." The sixth was not straight enough, "A green log dried behind the stove."

So she had something to say against every one, but she made herself especially merry over a good king who stood quite high up in the row, and whose chin had grown a little crooked. "Well," she cried and laughed, "he has a chin like a thrush's beak!" and from that time he got the name of King Thrushbeard.

But the old King, when he saw that his daugher did nothing but mock the people, and despised all the suitors who were gathered there, was very angry, and swore that she should have for her husband the very first beggar that came to his doors.

A few days afterwards a fiddler came and sang beneath the windows, trying to earn a small alms. When the King heard him he said, "Let him come up." So the fiddler came in, in his dirty, ragged clothes, and sang before the King and his daughter, and when he had ended he asked for a trifling gift. The King said, "Your song has pleased me so well that I will give you my daughter there, to wife."

The King's daughter shuddered, but the King said, "I have taken an oath to give you to the very first beggar-man, and I will keep it." All she could say was in vain; the priest was brought, and she had to let herself be wedded to the fiddler on the spot. When that was done the King said, "Now it is not proper for you, a beggar-woman, to stay any longer in my palace, you may just go away with your husband."

The beggar-man led her out by the hand, and she was obliged to walk away on foot with him. When they came to a large forest she asked, "To whom does that beautiful forest belong?" "It belongs to King Thrushbeard; if you had taken him, it would have been yours." "Ah, unhappy girl that I am, if I had but taken King Thrushbeard!"

Afterwards they came to a meadow, and she asked again, "To whom does this beautiful green meadow belong?" "It belongs to King Thrushbeard; if you had taken him, it would have been yours." "Ah, unhappy girl that I am, if I had but taken King Thrushbeard!"

Then they came to a large town, and she asked again, "To whom does this fine large town belong?" "It belongs to King Thrushbeard; if you had taken him, it would have been yours." "Ah, unhappy girl that I am, if I had but taken King Thrushbeard!"

"It does not please me," said the fiddler, "to hear you always wishing for another husband; am I not good enough for you?" At last they came to a very little hut, and she said, "Oh, goodness! what a small house; to whom does this miserable, mean hovel belong?" The fiddler answered, "That is my house and yours, where we shall live together."

She had to stoop in order to go in at the low door. "Where are the servants?" said the King's daughter. "What servants?" answered the beggar-man; "you must yourself do what you wish to have done. Just make a fire at once, and set on water to cook my supper, I am quite tired." But the King's daughter knew nothing about lighting fires or cooking, and the beggar-man had to lend a hand himself to get anything fairly done. When they had finished their scanty meal they went to bed; but he forced her to get up quite early in the morning in order to look after the house.

For a few days they lived in this way as well as might be, and finished all their provisions. Then the man said, "Wife, we cannot go on any longer eating and drinking here and earning nothing. You weave baskets." He went out, cut some willows, and brought them home. Then she began to weave, but the tough willows wounded her delicate hands.

"I see that this will not do," said the man; "you had better spin, perhaps you can do that better." She sat down and tried to spin, but the hard thread soon cut her soft fingers so that the blood ran down. "See," said the man, "you are fit for no sort of work; I have made a bad bargain with you. Now I will try to make a business with pots and earthenware; you must sit in the market-place and sell the ware." "Alas," thought she, "if any of the people from my father's kingdom come to the market and see me sitting there, selling, how they will mock me?" But it was of no use, she had to yield unless she chose to die of hunger.

For the first time she succeeded well, for the people were glad to buy the woman's wares because she was good-looking, and they paid her what she asked; many even gave her the money and left the pots with her as well. So they lived on what she had earned as long as it lasted, then the husband bought a lot of new crockery. With this she sat down at the corner of the market-place, and set it out round about her ready for sale. But suddenly there came a drunken hussar galloping along, and he rode right amongst the pots so that they were all broken into a thousand bits. She began to weep, and did now know what to do for fear. "Alas! what will happen to me?" cried she; "what will my husband say to this?"

She ran home and told him of the misfortune. "Who would seat herself at a corner of the market-place with crockery?" said the man; "leave off crying, I see very well that you cannot do any ordinary work, so I have been to our King's palace and have asked whether they cannot find a place for a kitchen-maid, and they have promised me to take you; in that way you will get your food for nothing."

The King's daughter was now a kitchen-maid, and had to be at the cook's beck and call, and do the dirtiest work. In both her pockets she fastened a little jar, in which she took home her share of the leavings, and upon this they lived.

It happened that the wedding of the King's eldest son was to be celebrated, so the poor woman went up and placed herself by the door of the hall to look on. When all the candles were lit, and people, each more beautiful than the other, entered, and all was full of pomp and splendour, she thought of her lot with a sad heart, and cursed the pride and haughtiness which had humbled her and brought her to so great poverty.

The smell of the delicious dishes which were being taken in and out reached her, and now and then the servants threw her a few morsels of them: these she put in her jars to take home.

All at once the King's son entered, clothed in velvet and silk, with gold chains about his neck. And when he saw the beautiful woman standing by the door he seized her by the hand, and would have danced with her; but she refused and shrank with fear, for she saw that it was King Thrushbeard, her suitor whom she had driven away with scorn. Her struggles were of no avail, he drew her into the hall; but the string by which her pockets were hung broke, the pots fell down, the soup ran out, and the scraps were scattered all about. And when the people saw it, there arose general laughter and derision, and she was so ashamed that she would rather have been a thousand fathoms below the ground. She sprang to the door and would have run away, but on the stairs a man caught her and brought her back; and when she looked at him it was King Thrushbeard again. He said to her kindly, "Do not be afraid, I and the fiddler who has been living with you in that wretched hovel are one. For love of you I disguised myself so; and I also was the hussar who rode through your crockery. This was all done to humble your proud spirit, and to punish you for the insolence with which you mocked me."

Then she wept bitterly and said, "I have done great wrong, and am not worthy to be your wife." But he said, "Be comforted, the evil days are past; now we will celebrate our wedding." Then the maids-in-waiting came and put on her the most splendid clothing, and her father and his whole court came and wished her happiness in her marriage with King Thrushbeard, and the joy now began in earnest. I wish you and I had been there too.

LITTLE SNOW-WHITE

ONCE UPON a time in the middle of winter, when the flakes of snow were falling like feathers from the sky, a queen sat at a window sewing, and the frame of the window was made of black ebony. And whilst she was sewing and looking out of the window at the snow, she pricked her finger with the needle, and three drops of blood fell upon the snow. And the red looked pretty upon the white snow, and she thought to herself, "Would that I had a child as white as snow, as red as blood, and as black as the wood of the window-frame."

Soon after that she had a little daughter, who was as white as snow, and as red as blood, and her hair was as black as ebony; and she was therefore called Little Snow-white. And when the child was born, the Queen died.

After a year had passed the King took to himself another wife. She was a beautiful woman, but proud and haughty, and she could not bear that anyone else should surpass her in beauty. She had a wonderful looking-glass, and when she stood in front of it and looked at herself in it, and said—

"Looking-glass, Looking-glass, on the wall,
Who in this land is the fairest of all?"

the looking-glass answered—

"Thou, O Queen, art the fairest of all!"

Then she was satisfied, for she knew that the looking-glass spoke the truth.

But Snow-white was growing up, and grew more and more beautiful; and when she was seven years old she was as beautiful as the day, and more beautiful than the Queen herself. And once when the Queen asked her looking-glass—

"Looking-glass, Looking-glass, on the wall,
Who in this land is the fairest of all?"

it answered—

> "Thou art fairer than all who are here, Lady Queen."
> But more beautiful still is Snow-white, as I ween."

Then the Queen was shocked, and turned yellow and green with envy. From that hour, whenever she looked at Snow-white, her heart heaved in her breast, she hated the girl so much.

And envy and pride grew higher and higher in her heart like a weed, so that she had no peace day or night. She called a huntsman, and said, "Take the child away into the forest; I will no longer have her in my sight. Kill her, and bring me back her heart as a token." The huntsman obeyed, and took her away; but when he had drawn his knife, and was about to pierce Snow-white's innocent heart, she began to weep, and said, "Ah, dear huntsman, leave me my life! I will run away into the wild forest, and never come home again."

And as she was so beautiful the huntsman had pity on her and said, "Run away, then, you poor child." "The wild beasts will soon have devoured you," thought he, and yet it seemed as if a stone had been rolled from his heart since it was no longer needful for him to kill her. And as a young boar just then came running by he stabbed it, and cut out its heart and took it to the Queen as proof that the child was dead. The cook had to salt this, and the wicked Queen ate it, and thought she had eaten the heart of Snow-white.

But now the poor child was all alone in the great forest, and so terrified that she looked at every leaf of every tree, and did not know what to do. Then she began to run, and ran over sharp stones and through thorns, and the wild beasts ran past her, but did her no harm.

She ran as long as her feet would go until it was almost evening; then she saw a little cottage and went into it to rest herself. Everything in the cottage was small, but neater and cleaner than can be told. There was a table on which was a white cover, and seven little plates, and on each plate a little spoon; moreover, there were seven little knives and forks, and seven little mugs. Against the wall stood seven little beds side by side, and covered with snow-white counterpanes.

Little Snow-white was so hungry and thirsty that she ate some vegetables and bread from each plate and drank a drop of wine out of each mug, for she did not wish to take all from one only. Then, as she was so tired, she laid herself down on one of the little beds, but none of them suited her; one was too long, another too short, but at last she found that the seventh one was right, and so she remained in it, said a prayer and went to sleep.

When it was quite dark the owners of the cottage came back; they were seven dwarfs who dug and delved in the mountains for ore.

They lit their seven candles, and as it was now light within the cottage they saw that someone had been there, for everything was not in the same order in which they had left it.

The first said, "Who has been sitting on my chair?"

The second, "Who has been eating off my plate?"

The third, "Who has been taking some of my bread?"

The fourth, "Who has been eating my vegetables?"

The fifth, "Who has been using my fork?"

The sixth, "Who has been cutting with my knife?"

The seventh, "Who has been drinking out of my mug?"

Then the first looked round and saw that there was a little hole on his bed, and he said, "Who has been getting into my bed?" The others came up and each called out, "Somebody has been lying in my bed too." But the seventh when he looked at his bed saw little Snow-white, who was lying asleep therein. And he called the others, who came running up, and they cried out with astonishment, and brought their seven little candles and let the light fall on little Snow-white. "Oh, heavens! oh, heavens!" cried they, "what a lovely child!" and they were so glad that they did not wake her up, but let her sleep on in the bed. And the seventh dwarf slept with his companions, one hour with each, and so got through the night.

When it was morning little Snow-white awoke, and was frightened when she saw the seven dwarfs. But they were friendly and asked her what her name was. "My name is Snow-white," she answered. "How have you come to our house?" said the dwarfs. Then she told them that her step-mother had wished to have her killed, but that the huntsman had spared her life, and that she had run for the whole day, until at last she had found their dwelling. The dwarfs said, "If you will take care of our house, cook, make the beds, wash, sew, and knit, and if you will keep everything neat and clean, you can stay with us and you shall want for nothing." "Yes," said Snow-white, "with all my heart," and she stayed with them. She kept the house in order for them; in the mornings they went to the mountains and looked for copper and gold, in the evenings they came back, and then their supper had to be ready. The girl was alone the whole day, so the good dwarfs warned her and said, "Beware of your step-mother, she will soon know that you are here; be sure to let no one come in."

But the Queen, believing that she had eaten Snow-white's heart, could not but think that she was again the first and most beautiful of all; and she went to her looking-glass and said—

"Looking-glass, Looking-glass, on the wall,
Who in this land is the fairest of all?"

and the glass answered—

"Oh, Queen, thou art fairest of all I see,
But over the hills, where the seven dwarfs dwell,
Snow-white is still alive and well,
And none is so fair as she."

Then she was astounded, for she knew that the looking-glass never spoke falsely, and she knew that the huntsman had betrayed her, and that little Snow-white was still alive.

And so she thought and thought again how she might kill her, for so long as she was not the fairest in the whole land, envy let her have no rest. And when she had at last thought of something to do, she painted her face, and dressed herself like an old pedler-woman, and no one could have known her. In this disguise she went over the seven mountains to the seven dwarfs, and knocked at the door and cried, "Pretty things to sell, very cheap, very cheap." Little Snow-white looked out of the window and called out, "Good-day, my good woman, what have you to sell?" "Good things, pretty things," she answered; "stay-laces of all colours," and she pulled out one which was woven of bright-coloured silk. "I may let the worthy old woman in," thought Snow-white, and she unbolted the door and bought the pretty laces. "Child," said the old woman, "what a fright you look; come, I will lace you properly for once." Snow-white had no suspicion, but stood before her, and let herself be laced with the new laces. But the old woman laced so quickly and so tightly that Snow-white lost her breath and fell down as if dead. "Now I am the most beautiful," said the Queen to herself, and ran away.

Not long afterwards, in the evening, the seven dwarfs came home, but how shocked they were when they saw their dear little Snow-white lying on the ground, and that she neither stirred nor moved, and seemed to be dead. They lifted her up, and, as they saw that she was laced too tightly, they cut the laces; then she began to breathe a little, and after a while came to life again. When the dwarfs heard what had happened they said, "The old pedler-woman was no one else than the wicked Queen; take care and let no one come in when we are not with you."

But the wicked woman when she had reached home went in front of the glass and asked—

"Looking-glass, Looking-glass, on the wall,
Who in this land is the fairest of all?"

and it answered as before—

"Oh, Queen, thou art fairest of all I see,

But over the hills, where the seven dwarfs dwell,
Snow-white is still alive and well,
And none is so fair as she."

When she heard that, all her blood rushed to her heart with fear, for she saw plainly that little Snow-white was again alive. "But now," she said, "I will think of something that shall put an end to you," and by the help of witchcraft, which she understood, she made a poisonous comb. Then she disguised herself and took the shape of another old woman. So she went over the seven mountains to the seven dwarfs, knocked at the door, and cried, "Good things to sell, cheap, cheap!" Little Snow-white looked out and said, "Go away; I cannot let any one come in." "I suppose you can look," said the old woman, and pulled the poisonous comb out and held it up. It pleased the girl so well that she let herself be beguiled, and opened the door. When they had made a bargain the old woman said, "Now I will comb you properly for once." Poor little Snow-white had no suspicion, and let the old woman do as she pleased, but hardly had she put the comb in her hair than the poison in it took effect, and the girl fell down senseless. "You paragon of beauty," said the wicked woman, "you are done for now," and she went away.

But fortunately it was almost evening, when the seven dwarfs came home. When they saw Snow-white lying as if dead upon the ground they at once suspected the step-mother, and they looked and found the poisoned comb. Scarcely had they taken it out when Snow-white came to herself, and told them what had happened. Then they warned her once more to be upon her guard and to open the door to no one.

The Queen, at home, went in front of the glass and said—

"Looking-glass, Looking-glass, on the wall,
Who in this land is the fairest of all?"

then it answered as before—

"Oh, Queen, thou art fairest of all I see,
But over the hills, where the seven dwarfs dwell,
Snow-white is still alive and well,
And none is so fair as she."

When she heard the glass speak thus she trembled and shook with rage. "Snow-white shall die," she cried, "even if it costs me my life!"

Thereupon she went into a quite secret, lonely room, where no one ever came, and there she made a very poisonous apple. Outside it looked pretty, white with a red cheek, so that everyone who saw it longed for it; but whoever ate a piece of it must surely die.

When the apple was ready she painted her face, and dressed herself up as a country-woman, and so she went over the seven mountains to the seven dwarfs. She knocked at the door. Snow-white put her head out of the window and said, "I cannot let any one in; the seven dwarfs have forbidden me." "It is all the same to me," answered the woman, "I shall soon get rid of my apples. There, I will give you one."

"No," said Snow-white, "I dare not take anything." "Are you afraid of poison?" said the old woman; "look, I will cut the apple in two pieces; you eat the red cheek, and I will eat the white." The apple was so cunningly made that only the red cheek was poisoned. Snow-white longed for the fine apple, and when she saw that the woman ate part of it she could resist no longer, and stretched out her hand and took the poisonous half. But hardly had she a bit of it in her mouth than she fell down dead. Then the Queen looked at her with a dreadful look, and laughed aloud and said, "White as snow, red as blood, black as ebony-wood! this time the dwarfs cannot wake you up again."

And when she asked of the Looking-glass at home—

"Looking-glass, Looking-glass, on the wall,
Who in this land is the fairest of all?"

it answered at last—

"Oh, Queen, in this land thou art fairest of all."

Then her envious heart had rest, so far as an envious heart can have rest.

The dwarfs, when they came home in the evening, found Snow-white lying upon the ground; she breathed no longer and was dead. They lifted her up, looked to see whether they could find anything poisonous, unlaced her, combed her hair, washed her with water and wine, but it was all of no use; the poor child was dead, and remained dead. They laid her upon a bier, and all seven of them sat round it and wept for her, and wept three days long.

Then they were going to bury her, but she still looked as if she were living, and still had her pretty red cheeks. They said, "We could not bury her in the dark ground," and they had a transparent coffin of glass made, so that she could be seen from all sides, and they laid her in it, and wrote her name upon it in golden letters, and that she was a king's daughter. Then they put the coffin out upon the mountain, and one of them always stayed by it and watched it. And birds came too, and wept for Snow-white; first an owl, then a raven, and last a dove.

And now Snow-white lay a long, long time in the coffin, and she did not change, but looked as if she were asleep; for she was as white as snow, as red as blood, and her hair was as black as ebony.

It happened, however, that a king's son came into the forest, and went to the dwarfs' house to spend the night. He saw the coffin on the mountain, and the beautiful Snow-white within it, and read what was written upon it in golden letters. Then he said to the dwarfs, "Let me have the coffin, I will give you whatever you want for it." But the dwarfs answered, "We will not part with it for all the gold in the world." Then he said, "Let me have it as a gift, for I cannot live without seeing Snow-white. I will honour and prize her as my dearest possession." As he spoke in this way the good dwarfs took pity upon him, and gave him the coffin.

And now the King's son had it carried away by his servants on their shoulders. And it happened that they stumbled over a tree-stump, and with the shock the poisonous piece of apple which Snow-white had bitten off came out of her throat. And before long she opened her eyes, lifted up the lid of the coffin, sat up, and was once more alive. "Oh, heavens, where am I?" she cried. The King's son, full of joy, said, "You are with me," and told her what had happened, and said, "I love you more than everything in the world; come with me to my father's palace, you shall be my wife."

And Snow-white was willing, and went with him, and their wedding was held with great show and splendour. But Snow-white's wicked step-mother was also bidden to the feast. When she had arrayed herself in beautiful clothes she went before the Looking-glass, and said—

"Looking-glass, Looking-glass, on the wall,
Who in this land is the fairest of all?"

the glass answered—

"Oh, Queen, of all here the fairest art thou,
But the young Queen is fairer by far as I trow."

Then the wicked woman uttered a curse, and was so wretched, so utterly wretched, that she knew not what to do. At first she would not go to the wedding at all, but she had no peace, and must go to see the young Queen. And when she went in she knew Snow-white; and she stood still with rage and fear, and could not stir. But iron slippers had already been put upon the fire, and they were brought in with tongs, and set before her. Then she was forced to put on the red-hot shoes, and dance until she dropped down dead.

THE KNAPSACK, THE HAT, AND THE HORN

THERE WERE once three brothers who had fallen deeper and deeper into poverty, and at last their need was so great that they had to endure hunger, and had nothing to eat or drink. Then said they, "We cannot go on thus, we had better go into the world and seek our fortune." They therefore set out, and had already walked over many a long road and many a blade of grass, but had not yet met with good luck. One day they arrived in a great forest, and in the midst of it was a hill, and when they came nearer they saw that the hill was all silver. Then spake the eldest, "Now I have found the good luck I wished for, and I desire nothing more." He took as much of the silver as he could possibly carry, and then turned back and went home again. But the two others said, "We want something more from good luck than mere silver," and did not touch it, but went onwards. After they had walked for two days longer without stopping, they came to a hill which was all gold. The second brother stopped, took thought with himself, and was undecided. "What shall I do?" said he; "shall I take for myself so much of this gold, that I have sufficient for all the rest of my life, or shall I go farther?" At length he made a decision, and putting as much into his pockets as would go in, said farewell to his brother, and went home. But the third said, "Silver and gold do not move me, I will not renounce my chance of fortune, perhaps something better still will be given me." He journeyed onwards, and when he had walked for three days, he got into a forest which was still larger than the one before, and never would come to an end, and as he found nothing to eat or to drink, he was all but exhausted. Then he climbed up a high tree to find out if up there he could see the end of the forest, but so far as his eye could pierce he saw nothing but the tops of trees. Then he began to descend the tree again, but hunger tormented him, and he thought to himself, "If I could but eat my fill once more!" When he got down he saw with astonishment a table beneath the tree richly spread with food, the steam of which rose up to meet him. "This time," said he, "my wish has been fulfilled at the right moment." And without inquiring who had brought the food, or who had cooked it, he approached the table, and ate with enjoyment until he had appeased his hunger. When he was done, he thought, "It would after all be a pity if the pretty little table-cloth were to be spoilt in the forest here," and folded it up tidily and put it in his pocket. Then he went onwards, and in the evening, when hunger once more made itself felt, he wanted to make a trial of his little cloth, and spread it out and said, "I wish thee to be covered with good cheer again," and scarcely had the wish crossed his lips than as many dishes with the most exquisite food on them stood on the table as there was room for. "Now I perceive," said he, "in what kitchen my cooking is done. Thou shalt be dearer to me than the mountains of silver and gold." For he saw plainly that it was a wishing-cloth. The cloth, however, was still not enough to enable him to sit down quietly at home; he preferred to wander about the world and pursue his fortune farther.

One night he met, in a lonely wood, a dusty, black charcoal-burner, who was burning charcoal there, and had some potatoes by the fire, on which he was going to make a meal. "Good evening, blackbird!" said the youth. "How dost thou get on in thy solitude?"

"One day is like another," replied the charcoal-burner, "and every night potatoes! Hast thou a mind to have some, and wilt thou be my guest?" "Many thanks," replied the traveller, "I won't rob thee of thy supper; thou didst not reckon on a visitor, but if thou wilt put up with what I have, thou shalt have an invitation."

"Who is to prepare it for thee?" said the charcoal-burner. "I see that thou hast nothing with thee, and there is no one within a two hours' walk who could give thee anything." "And yet there shall be a meal," answered the youth, "and better than any thou hast ever tasted." Thereupon he brought his cloth out of his knapsack, spread it on the ground, and said, "Little cloth, cover thyself," and instantly boiled meat and baked meat stood there, and as hot as if it had just come out of the kitchen. The charcoal-burner stared, but did not require much pressing; he fell to, and thrust larger and larger mouthfuls into his black mouth. When they had eaten everything, the charcoal-burner smiled contentedly, and said, "Hark thee, thy table-cloth has my approval; it would be a fine thing for me in this forest, where no one ever cooks me anything good. I will propose an exchange to thee; there in the corner hangs a soldier's knapsack, which is certainly old and shabby, but in it lie concealed wonderful powers; but, as I no longer use it, I will give it to thee for the table-cloth."

"I must first know what these wonderful powers are," answered the youth.

"That will I tell thee," replied the charcoal-burner; "every time thou tappest it with thy hand, a corporal comes with six men armed from head to foot, and they do whatsoever thou commandest them." "So far as I am concerned," said the youth, "if nothing else can be done, we will exchange," and he gave the charcoal-burner the cloth, took the knapsack from the hook, put it on, and bade farewell. When he had walked a while, he wished to make a trial of the magical powers of his knapsack and tapped it. Immediately the seven warriors stepped up to him, and the corporal said, "What does my lord and ruler wish for?"

"March with all speed to the charcoal-burner, and demand my wishing-cloth back." They faced to the left, and it was not long before they brought what he required, and had taken it from the charcoal-burner without asking many questions. The young man bade them retire, went onwards, and hoped fortune would shine yet more brightly on him. By sunset he came to another charcoal-burner, who was making his supper ready by the fire. "If thou wilt eat some potatoes with salt, but with no dripping, come and sit down with me," said the sooty fellow.

"No," he replied, "this time thou shalt be my guest," and he spread out his cloth, which was instantly covered with the most beautiful dishes. They ate and drank together, and enjoyed themselves heartily. After the meal was over, the charcoal-burner said, "Up there on that shelf lies a little old worn-out hat which has strange properties: when any one puts it on, and turns it round on his head, the cannons go off as if twelve were fired all together, and they shoot down everything so that no one can withstand them. The hat is of no use to me, and I will willingly give it for thy table-cloth."

"That suits me very well," he answered, took the hat, put it on, and left his table-cloth behind him. Hardly, however, had he walked away than he tapped on his knapsack, and his soldiers had to fetch the cloth back again. "One thing comes on the top of another," thought he, "and I feel as if my luck had not yet come to an end." Neither had his thoughts deceived him. After he had walked on for the whole of one day, he came to a third charcoal-burner, who like the previous ones, invited him to potatoes without dripping. But he let him also dine with him from his wishing-cloth, and the charcoal-burner liked it so well, that at last he offered him a horn for it, which had very different properties from those of the hat. When any one blew it all the walls and fortifications fell down, and all towns and villages became ruins. He certainly gave the charcoal-burner the cloth for it, but he afterwards sent his soldiers to demand it back again, so that at length he had the knapsack, hat and horn, all three. "Now," said he, "I am a made man, and it is time for me to go home and see how my brothers are getting on."

When he reached home, his brothers had built themselves a handsome house with their silver and gold, and were living in clover. He went to see them, but as he came in a ragged coat, with his shabby hat on his head, and his old knapsack on his back, they would not acknowledge him as their brother. They mocked and said, "Thou givest out that thou art our brother who despised silver and gold, and craved for something still better for himself. He will come in his carriage in full splendour like a mighty king, not like a beggar," and they drove him out of doors. Then he fell into a rage, and tapped his knapsack until a hundred and fifty men stood before him armed from head to foot. He commanded them to surround his brothers' house, and two of them were to take hazel-sticks with them, and beat the two insolent men until they knew who he was. A violent disturbance arose, people ran together, and wanted to lend the two some help in their need, but against the soldiers they could do nothing. News of this at length came to the King, who was very angry, and ordered a captain to march out with his troop, and drive this disturber of the peace out of the town; but the man with the knapsack soon got a greater body of men together, who repulsed the captain and his men, so that they were forced to retire with bloody noses. The King said, "This vagabond is not brought to order yet," and next day sent a still larger troop against him, but they could do even less. The youth set still more men against them, and in order to be done the sooner, he turned his hat twice round on his head, and heavy guns began to play, and the king's men were beaten and put to flight. "And now," said he, "I will not make peace until the King gives me his daughter to wife, and I govern the whole kingdom in his name." He caused this to be announced to the King, and the latter said to his daughter, "Necessity is a hard nut to crack,—what remains to me but to do what he desires? If I want peace and to keep the crown on my head, I must give thee away."

So the wedding was celebrated, but the King's daughter was vexed that her husband should be a common man, who wore a shabby hat, and put on an old knapsack. She wished much to get rid of him, and night and day studied how she could accomplish this. Then she thought to herself, "Is it possible that his wonderful powers lie in the knapsack?" and she dissembled and caressed him, and when his heart was softened, she said, "If thou wouldst but lay aside that ugly knapsack, it disfigures thee so, that I can't help being ashamed of thee."

"Dear child," said he, "this knapsack is my greatest treasure; as long as I have it, there is no power on earth that I am afraid of." And he revealed to her the wonderful virtue with which it was endowed. Then she threw herself in his arms as if she were going to kiss him, but dexterously took the knapsack off his shoulders, and ran away with it. As soon as she was alone she tapped it, and commanded the warriors to seize their former master, and take him out of the royal palace. They obeyed, and the false wife sent still more men after him, who were to drive him quite out of the country. Then he would have been ruined if he had not had the little hat. But his hands were scarcely at liberty before he turned it twice. Immediately the cannon began to thunder, and struck down everything, and the King's daughter herself was forced to come and beg for mercy. As she entreated in such moving terms, and promised amendment, he allowed himself to be persuaded and granted her peace. She behaved in a friendly manner to him, and acted as if she loved him very much, and after some time managed so to befool him, that he confided to her that even if someone got the knapsack into his power, he could do nothing against him so long as the old hat was still his. When she knew the secret, she waited until he was asleep, and then she took the hat away from him, and had it thrown out into the street. But the horn still remained to him, and in great anger he blew it with all his strength. Instantly all walls, fortifications, towns, and villages, toppled down, and crushed the King and his daughter to death. And had he not put down the horn and had blown just a little longer, everything would have been in ruins, and not one stone would have been left standing on another. Then no one opposed him any longer, and he made himself King of the whole country.

RUMPELSTILTSKIN

ONCE THERE was a miller who was poor, but who had a beautiful daughter. Now it happened that he had to go and speak to the King, and in order to make himself appear important he said to him, "I have a daughter who can spin straw into gold." The King said to the miller, "That is an art which pleases me well; if your daughter is as clever as you say, bring her to-morrow to my palace, and I will try what she can do."

And when the girl was brought to him he took her into a room which was quite full of straw, gave her a spinning-wheel and a reel, and said, "Now set to work, and if by to-morrow morning early you have not spun this straw into gold during the night, you must die." Thereupon he himself locked up the room, and left her in it alone. So there sat the poor miller's daughter, and for the life of her could not tell what to do; she had no idea how straw could be spun into gold, and she grew more and more miserable, until at last she began to weep.

But all at once the door opened, and in came a little man, and said, "Good evening, Mistress Miller; why are you crying so?" "Alas!" answered the girl, "I have to spin straw into gold, and I do not know how to do it." "What will you give me," said the manikin, "if I do it for you?" "My necklace," said the girl. The little man took the necklace, seated himself in front of the wheel, and "whirr, whirr, whirr," three turns, and the reel was full; then he put another on, and whirr, whirr, whirr, three times round, and the second was full too. And so it went on until the morning, when all the straw was spun, and all the reels were full of gold. By daybreak the King was already there, and when he saw the gold he was astonished and delighted, but his heart became only more greedy. He had the miller's daughter taken into another room full of straw, which was much larger, and commanded her to spin that also in one night if she valued her life. The girl knew not how to help herself, and was crying, when the door again opened, and the little man appeared, and said, "What will you give me if I spin the straw into gold for you?" "The ring on my finger," answered the girl. The little man took the ring, again began to turn the wheel, and by morning had spun all the straw into glittering gold.

The King rejoiced beyond measure at the sight, but still he had not gold enough; and he had the miller's daughter taken into a still larger room full of straw, and said, "You must spin this, too, in the course of this night; but if you succeed, you shall be my wife." "Even if she be a miller's daughter," thought he, "I could not find a richer wife in the whole world."

When the girl was alone the manikin came again for the third time, and said, "What will you give me if I spin the straw for you this time also?" "I have nothing left that I could give," answered the girl. "Then promise me, if you should become Queen, your first child." "Who knows whether that will ever happen?" thought the miller's daughter; and, not knowing how else to help herself in this strait, she promised the manikin what he wanted, and for that he once more span the straw into gold.

And when the King came in the morning, and found all as he had wished, he took her in marriage, and the pretty miller's daughter became a Queen.

A year after, she had a beautiful child, and she never gave a thought to the manikin. But suddenly he came into her room, and said, "Now give me what you promised." The Queen was horror-struck, and offered the manikin all the riches of the kingdom if he would leave her the child. But the manikin said, "No, something that is living is dearer to me than all the treasures in the world." Then the Queen began to weep and cry, so that the manikin pitied her. "I will give you three days' time," said he; "if by that time you find out my name, then shall you keep your child."

So the Queen thought the whole night of all the names that she had ever heard, and she sent a messenger over the country to inquire, far and wide, for any other names that there might be. When the manikin came the next day, she began with Caspar, Melchior, Balthazar, and said all the names she knew, one after another; but to every one the little man said, "That is not my name." On the second day she had inquiries made in the neighborhood as to the names of the people there, and she repeated to the manikin the most uncommon and curious. "Perhaps your name is Shortribs, or Sheepshanks, or Laceleg?" but he always answered, "That is not my name."

On the third day the messenger came back again, and said, "I have not been able to find a single new name, but as I came to a high mountain at the end of the forest, where the fox and the hare bid each other good night, there I saw a little house, and before the house a fire was burning, and round about the fire quite a ridiculous little man was jumping: he hopped upon one leg, and shouted—

> "'To-day I bake, to-morrow brew,
> The next I'll have the young Queen's child.
> Ha! glad am I that no one knew
> That Rumpelstiltskin I am styled.'"

You may think how glad the Queen was when she heard the name! And when soon afterwards the little man came in, and asked, "Now, Mistress Queen, what is my name?" at first she said, "Is your name Conrad?" " No." "Is your name Harry?" "No."

"Perhaps your name is Rumpelstiltskin?"

"The devil has told you that! the devil has told you that!" cried the little man, and in his anger he plunged his right foot so deep into the earth that his whole leg went in; and then in rage he pulled at his left leg so hard with both hands that he tore himself in two.

THE GOLDEN BIRD

IN THE olden time there was a king, who had behind his palace a beautiful pleasure-garden in which there was a tree that bore golden apples. When the apples were getting ripe they were counted, but on the very next morning one was missing. This was told to the King, and he ordered that a watch should be kept every night beneath the tree.

The King had three sons, the eldest of whom he sent, as soon as night came on, into the garden; but when midnight came he could not keep himself from sleeping, and next morning again an apple was gone.

The following night the second son had to keep watch, it fared no better with him; as soon as twelve o'clock had struck he fell asleep, and in the morning an apple was gone.

Now it came to the turn of the third son to watch; and he was quite ready, but the King had not much trust in him, and thought that he would be of less use even than his brothers; but at last he let him go. The youth lay down beneath the tree, but kept awake, and did not let sleep master him. When it struck twelve, something rustled through the air, and in the moonlight he saw a bird coming whose feathers were all shining with gold. The bird alighted on the tree, and had just plucked off an apple, when the youth shot an arrow at him. The bird flew off, but the arrow had struck his plumage, and one of his golden feathers fell down. The youth picked it up, and the next morning took it to the King and told him what he had seen in the night. The King called his council together, and every one declared that a feather like this was worth more than the whole kingdom. "If the feather is so precious," declared the King, "one alone will not do for me; I must and will have the whole bird!"

The eldest son set out; he trusted to his cleverness, and thought that he would easily find the Golden Bird. When he had gone some distance he saw a Fox sitting at the edge of a wood, so he cocked his gun and took aim at him. The Fox cried, "Do not shoot me! and in return I will give you some good counsel. You are on the way to the Golden Bird; and this evening you will come to a village in which stand two inns opposite to one another. One of them is lighted up brightly, and all goes on merrily within, but do not go into it; go rather into the other, even though it seems a bad one." "How can such a silly beast give wise advice?" thought the King's son, and he pulled the trigger. But he missed the Fox, who stretched out his tail and ran quickly into the wood.

So he pursued his way, and by evening came to the village where the two inns were; in one they were singing and dancing; the other had a poor, miserable look. "I should be a fool, indeed," he thought, "if I were to go into the shabby tavern, and pass by the good one." So he went into the cheerful one, lived there in riot and revel, and forgot the bird and his father, and all good counsels.

When some time had passed, and the eldest son for month after month did not come back home, the second set out, wishing to find the Golden Bird. The Fox met him as he had met the eldest, and gave him the good advice of which he took no heed. He came to the two inns, and his brother was standing at the window of the one from which came the music, and called out to him. He could not resist, but went inside and lived only for pleasure.

Again some time passed, and then the King's youngest son wanted to set off and try his luck, but his father would not allow it. "It is of no use," said he, "he will find the Golden Bird still less than his brothers, and if a mishap were to befall him he knows not how to help himself; he is a little wanting at the best." But at last, as he had no peace, he let him go.

Again the Fox was sitting outside the wood, and begged for his life, and offered his good advice. The youth was good-natured, and said, "Be easy, little Fox, I will do you no harm." "You shall not repent it," answered the Fox; "and that you may get on more quickly, get up behind on my tail." And scarcely had he seated himself when the Fox began to run, and away he went over stock and stone till his hair whistled in the wind. When they came to the village the youth got off; he followed the good advice, and without looking round turned into the little inn, where he spent the night quietly.

The next morning, as soon as he got into the open country, there sat the Fox already, and said, "I will tell you further what you have to do. Go on quite straight, and at last you will come to a castle, in front of which a whole regiment of soldiers is lying, but do not trouble yourself about them, for they will all be asleep and snoring. Go through the midst of them straight into the castle, and go through all the rooms, till at last you will come to a chamber where a Golden Bird is hanging in a wooden cage. Close by, there stands an empty gold cage for show, but beware of taking the bird out of the common cage and putting it into the fine one, or it may go badly with you." With these words the Fox again stretched out his tail, and the King's son seated himself upon it, and away he went over stock and stone till his hair whistled in the wind.

When he came to the castle he found everything as the Fox had said. The King's son went into the chamber where the Golden Bird was shut up in a wooden cage, whilst a golden one stood hard by; and the three golden apples lay about the room. "But," thought he, "it would be absurd if I were to leave the beautiful bird in the common and ugly cage," so he opened the door, laid hold of it, and put it into the golden cage. But at the same moment the bird uttered a shrill cry. The soldiers awoke, rushed in, and took him off to prison. The next morning he was taken before a court of justice, and as he confessed everything, was sentenced to death.

The King, however, said that he would grant him his life on one condition—namely, if he brought him the Golden Horse which ran faster than the wind; and in that case he should receive, over and above, as a reward, the Golden Bird.

The King's son set off, but he sighed and was sorrowful, for how was he to find the Golden Horse? But all at once he saw his old friend the Fox sitting on the road. "Look you," said the Fox, "this has happened because you did not give heed to me. However, be of good courage. I will give you my help, and tell you how to get to the Golden Horse. You must go straight on, and you will come to a castle, where in the stable stands the horse. The grooms will be lying in front of the stable; but they will be asleep and snoring, and you can quietly lead out the Golden Horse. But of one thing you must take heed; put on him the common saddle of wood and leather, and not the golden one, which hangs close by, else it will go ill with you." Then the Fox stretched out his tail, the King's son seated himself upon it, and away he went over stock and stone until his hair whistled in the wind.

Everything happened just as the Fox had said; the prince came to the stable in which the Golden Horse was standing, but just as he was going to put the common saddle upon him, he thought, "It will be a shame to such a beautiful beast, if I do not give him the good saddle which belongs to him by right." But scarcely had the golden saddle touched the horse than he began to neigh loudly. The grooms awoke, seized the youth, and threw him into prison. The next morning he was sentenced by the court to death; but the King promised to grant him his life, and the Golden Horse as well, if he could bring back the beautiful princess from the Golden Castle.

With a heavy heart the youth set out; yet luckily for him he soon found the trusty Fox. "I ought only to leave you to your ill-luck," said the Fox, "but I pity you, and will help you once more out of your trouble. This road takes you straight to the Golden Castle, you will reach it by eventide; and at night when everything is quiet the beautiful princess goes to the bathing-house to bathe. When she enters it, run up to her and give her a kiss, then she will follow you, and you can take her away with you; only do not allow her to take leave of her parents first, or it will go ill with you."

Then the Fox stretched out his tail, the King's son seated himself upon it, and away the Fox went, over stock and stone, till his hair whistled in the wind.

When he reached the Golden Castle it was just as the Fox had said. He waited until midnight, when everything lay in deep sleep, and the beautiful princess was going to the bathing-house. Then he sprang out and gave her a kiss. She said that she would like to go with him, but she asked him pitifully, and with tears, to allow her first to take leave of her parents. At first he withstood her prayer, but when she wept more and more, and fell at his feet, he at last gave in. But no sooner had the maiden reached the bedside of her father than he and all the rest in the castle awoke, and the youth was laid hold of and put into prison.

The next morning the King said to him, "Your life is forfeited, and you can only find mercy if you take away the hill which stands in front of my windows, and prevents my seeing beyond it; and you must finish it all within eight days. If you do that you shall have my daughter as your reward."

The King's son began, and dug and shovelled without leaving off, but when after seven days he saw how little he had done, and how all his work was as good as nothing, he fell into great sorrow and gave up all hope. But on the evening of the seventh day the Fox appeared and said, 'You do not deserve that I should take any trouble about you; but just go away and lie down to sleep, and I will do the work for you."

The next morning when he awoke and looked out of the window the hill had gone. The youth ran, full of joy, to the King, and told him that the task was fulfilled, and whether he liked it or not, the King had to hold to his word and give him his daughter.

So the two set forth together, and it was not long before the trusty Fox came up with them. "You have certainly got what is best," said he, "but the Golden Horse also belongs to the maiden of the Golden Castle." "How shall I get it?" asked the youth. "That I will tell you," answered the Fox; "first take the beautiful maiden to the King who sent you to the Golden Castle. There will be unheard-of rejoicing;

they will gladly give you the Golden Horse, and will bring it out to you. Mount it as soon as possible, and offer your hand to all in farewell; last of all to the beautiful maiden. And as soon as you have taken her hand swing her up on to the horse, and gallop away, and no one will be able to bring you back, for the horse runs faster than the wind."

All was carried out successfully, and the King's son carried off the beautiful princess on the Golden Horse.

The Fox did not remain behind, and he said to the youth, "Now I will help you to get the Golden Bird. When you come near to the castle where the Golden Bird is to be found, let the maiden get down, and I will take her into my care. Then ride with the Golden Horse into the castle-yard; there will be great rejoicing at the sight, and they will bring out the Golden Bird for you. As soon as you have the cage in your hand gallop back to us, and take the maiden away again."

When the plan had succeeded, and the King's son was about to ride home with his treasures, the Fox said, "Now you shall reward me for my help." "What do you require for it?" asked the youth. "When you get into the wood yonder, shoot me dead, and chop off my head and feet."

"That would be fine gratitude," said the King's son. "I cannot possibly do that for you."

The Fox said, "If you will not do it I must leave you, but before I go away I will give you a piece of good advice. Be careful about two things. Buy no gallows'-flesh, and do not sit at the edge of any well." And then he ran into the wood.

The youth thought, "That is a wonderful beast, he has strange whims; who is going to buy gallows'-flesh? and the desire to sit at the edge of a well has never yet seized me."

He rode on with the beautiful maiden, and his road took him again through the village in which his two brothers had remained. There was a great stir and noise, and, when he asked what was going on, he was told that two men were going to be hanged. As he came nearer to the place he saw that they were his brothers, who had been playing all kinds of wicked pranks, and had squandered all their wealth. He inquired whether they could not be set free. "If you will pay for them," answered the people; "but why should you waste your money on wicked men, and buy them free." He did not think twice about it, but paid for them, and when they were set free they all went on their way together.

They came to the wood where the Fox had first met them, as it was cool and pleasant within it, whilst the sun shone hotly, the two brothers said, "Let us rest a little by the well, and eat and drink." He agreed, and whilst they were talking he forgot himself, and sat down upon the edge of the well without foreboding any evil. But the two brothers threw him backwards into the well, took the maiden, the Horse, and the Bird, and went home to their father. "Here we bring you not only the Golden Bird," said they; "we have won the Golden Horse also, and the maiden from the Golden Castle." Then was there great joy; but the Horse would not eat, the Bird would not sing, and the maiden sat and wept.

But the youngest brother was not dead. By good fortune the well was dry, and he fell upon soft moss without being hurt, but he could not get out again. Even in this strait the faithful Fox did not leave him: it came and leapt down to him, and upbraided him for having forgotten its advice. "But yet I cannot give it up so," he said; "I will help you up again into daylight." He bade him grasp his tail and keep tight hold of it; and then he pulled him up.

"You are not out of all danger yet," said the Fox. "Your brothers were not sure of your death, and have surrounded the wood with watchers, who are to kill you if you let yourself be seen." But a poor man was sitting upon the road, with whom the youth changed clothes, and in this way he got to the King's palace.

No one knew him, but the Bird began to sing, the Horse began to eat, and the beautiful maiden left off weeping. The King, astonished, asked, "What does this mean?" Then the maiden said, "I do not know, but I have been so sorrowful and now I am so happy! I feel as if my true bridegroom had come." She told him all that had happened, although the other brothers had threatened her with death if she were to betray anything.

The King commanded that all people who were in his castle should be brought before him; and amongst them came the youth in his ragged clothes; but the maiden knew him at once and fell upon his neck. The wicked brothers were seized and put to death, but he was married to the beautiful maiden and declared heir to the King.

But how did it fare with the poor Fox? Long afterwards the King's son was once again walking in the wood, when the Fox met him and said, "You have everything now that you can wish for, but there is never an end to my misery, and yet it is in your power to free me," and again he asked him with tears to shoot him dead and chop off his head and feet. So he did it, and scarcely was it done when the Fox was changed into a man, and was no other than the brother of the beautiful princess, who at last was freed from the magic charm which had been laid upon him. And now nothing more was wanting to their happiness as long as they lived.

THE LITTLE PEASANT

THERE WAS a certain village wherein no one lived but really rich peasants, and just one poor one, whom they called the little peasant. He had not even so much as a cow, and still less money to buy one, and yet he and his wife did so wish to have one. One day he said to her, "Hark you, I have a good thought, there is our gossip the carpenter, he shall make us a wooden calf, and paint it brown, so that it look like any other, and in time it will certainly get big and be a cow." The woman also liked the idea, and their gossip the carpenter cut and planed the calf, and painted it as it ought to be, and made it with its head hanging down as if it were eating.

Next morning when the cows were being driven out, the little peasant called the cow-herd and said, "Look, I have a little calf there, but it is still small and has still to be carried." The cow-herd said, "All right, and took it in his arms and carried it to the pasture, and set it among the grass." The little calf always remained standing like one which was eating, and the cow-herd said, "It will soon run alone, just look how it eats already!" At night when he was going to drive the herd home again, he said to the calf, "If thou canst stand there and eat thy fill, thou canst also go on thy four legs; I don't care to drag thee home again in my arms." But the little peasant stood at his door, and waited for his little calf, and when the cow-herd drove the cows through the village, and the calf was missing, he inquired where it was. The cow-herd answered, "It is still standing out there eating. It would not stop and come with us." But the little peasant said, "Oh, but I must have my beast back again." Then they went back to the meadow together, but some one had stolen the calf, and it was gone. The cow-herd said, "It must have run away." The peasant, however, said, "Don't tell me that," and led the cow-herd before the mayor, who for his carelessness condemned him to give the peasant a cow for the calf which had run away.

And now the little peasant and his wife had the cow for which they had so long wished, and they were heartily glad, but they had no food for it, and could give it nothing to eat, so it soon had to be killed. They salted the flesh, and the peasant went into the town and wanted to sell the skin there, so that he might buy a new calf with the proceeds. On the way he passed by a mill, and there sat a raven with broken wings, and out of pity he took him and wrapped him in the skin. As, however, the weather grew so bad and there was a storm of rain and wind, he could go no farther, and turned back to the mill and begged for shelter. The miller's wife was alone in the house, and said to the peasant, "Lay thyself on the straw there," and gave him a slice of bread with cheese on it. The peasant ate it, and lay down with his skin beside him, and the woman thought, "He is tired and has gone to sleep." In the meantime came the parson; the miller's wife received him well, and said, "My husband is out, so we will have a feast." The peasant listened, and when he heard about feasting he was vexed that he had been forced to make shift with a slice of bread with cheese on it. Then the woman served up four different things, roast meat, salad, cakes, and wine.

Just as they were about to sit down and eat, there was a knocking outside. The woman said, "Oh, heavens! It is my husband!" She quickly hid the roast meat inside the tiled stove, the wine under the pillow, the salad on the bed, the cakes under it, and the parson in the cupboard in the entrance. Then she opened the door for her husband, and said, "Thank heaven, thou art back again! There is such a storm, it looks as if the world were coming to an end." The miller saw the peasant lying on the straw, and asked, "What is that fellow doing there?" "Ah," said the wife, "the poor knave came in the storm and rain, and begged for shelter, so I gave him a bit of bread and cheese, and showed him where the straw was." The man said, "I have no objection, but be quick and get me something to eat." The woman said, "But I have nothing but bread and cheese." "I am contented with anything," replied the husband, "so far as I am concerned, bread and cheese will do," and looked at the peasant and said, "Come and eat some more with me." The peasant did not require to be invited twice, but got up and ate. After this the miller saw the skin in which the raven was, lying on the ground, and asked, "What hast thou there?" The peasant answered, "I have a soothsayer inside it." "Can he foretell anything to me?" said the miller. "Why not?" answered the peasant, "but he only says four things, and the fifth he keeps to himself." The miller was curious, and said, "Let him foretell something for once." Then the peasant pinched the raven's head, so that he croaked and made a noise like krr, krr. The miller said, "What did he say?" The peasant answered, "In the first place, he says that there is some wine hidden under the pillow." "Bless me!" cried the miller, and went there and found the wine. "Now go on," said he. The peasant made the raven croak again, and said, "In the second place, he says that there is some roast meat in the tiled stove." "Upon my word!" cried the miller, and went thither, and found the roast meat. The peasant made the raven prophesy still more, and said, "Thirdly, he says that there is some salad on the bed." "That would be a fine thing!" cried the miller, and went there and found the salad. At last the peasant pinched the raven once more till he croaked, and said, "Fourthly, he says that there are some cakes under the bed." "That would be a fine thing!" cried the miller, and looked there, and found the cakes.

And now the two sat down to the table together, but the miller's wife was frightened to death, and went to bed and took all the keys with her. The miller would have liked much to know the fifth, but the little peasant said, "First, we will quickly eat the four things, for the fifth is something bad." So they ate, and after that they bargained how much the miller was to give for the fifth prophesy, until they agreed on three hundred thalers. Then the peasant once more pinched the raven's head till he croaked loudly. The miller asked, "What did he say?" The peasant replied, "He says that the Devil is hiding outside there in the cupboard in the entrance." The miller said, "The Devil must go out," and opened the house-door; then the woman was forced to give up the keys, and the peasant unlocked the cupboard. The parson ran out as fast as he could, and the miller said, "It was true; I saw the black rascal with my own eyes." The peasant, however, made off next morning by daybreak with the three hundred thalers.

At home the small peasant gradually launched out; he built a beautiful house, and the peasants said, "The small peasant has certainly been to the place where golden snow falls, and people carry the gold home in shovels." Then the small peasant was brought before the Mayor, and bidden to say from whence his wealth came. He answered, "I sold my cow's skin in the town, for three hundred thalers." When the peasants heard that, they too wished to enjoy this great profit, and ran home, killed all their cows, and stripped off their skins in order to sell them in the town to the greatest advantage. The Mayor, however, said, "But my servant must go first." When she came to the merchant in the town, he did not give her more than two thalers for a skin, and when the others came, he did not give them so much, and said, "What can I do with all these skins?"

Then the peasants were vexed that the small peasant should have thus overreached them, wanted to take vengeance on him, and accused him of this treachery before the Mayor. The innocent little peasant was unanimously sentenced to death, and was to be rolled into the water, in a barrel pierced full of holes. He was led forth, and a priest was brought who was to say a mass for his soul. The others were all obliged to retire to a distance, and when the peasant looked at the priest, he recognized the man who had been with the miller's wife. He said to him, "I set you free from the cupboard, set me free from the barrel." At this same moment up came, with a flock of sheep, the very shepherd who as the peasant knew had long been wishing to be Mayor, so he cried with all his might, "No, I will not do it; if the whole world insists on it, I will not do it!" The shepherd hearing that, came up to him, and asked, "What art thou about? What is it that thou wilt not do?" The peasant said, "They want to make me Mayor, if I will but put myself in the barrel, but I will not do it." The shepherd said, "If nothing more than that is needful in order to be Mayor, I would get into the barrel at once." The peasant said, "If thou wilt get in, thou wilt be Mayor." The shepherd was willing, and got in, and the peasant shut the top down on him; then he took the shepherd's flock for himself, and drove it away. The parson went to the crowd, and declared that the mass had been said. Then they came and rolled the barrel towards the water. When the barrel began to roll, the shepherd cried, "I am quite willing to be Mayor." They believed no otherwise than that it was the peasant who was saying this, and answered, "That is what we intend, but first thou shalt look about thee a little down below there," and they rolled the barrel down into the water.

After that the peasants went home, and as they were entering the village, the small peasant also came quietly in, driving a flock of sheep and looking quite contented. Then the peasants were astonished, and said, "Peasant, from whence comest thou? Hast thou come out of the water?" "Yes, truly," replied the peasant, "I sank deep, deep down, until at last I got to the bottom; I pushed the bottom out of the barrel, and crept out, and there were pretty meadows on which a number of lambs were feeding, and from thence I brought this flock away with me." Said the peasants, "Are there any more there?" "Oh, yes," said he, "more than I could do anything with." Then the peasants made up their minds that they too would fetch some sheep for themselves, a flock apiece, but the Mayor said, "I come first." So they went to the water together, and just then there were some of the small fleecy clouds in the blue sky, which are called little lambs, and they were reflected in the water, whereupon the peasants cried, "We already see the sheep down below!" The Mayor pressed forward and said, "I will go down first, and look about me, and if things promise well I'll call you." So he jumped in; splash! went the water; he made a sound as if he were calling them, and the whole crowd plunged in after him as one man. Then the entire village was dead, and the small peasant, as sole heir, became a rich man.

THE QUEEN BEE

TWO KINGS' sons once went out in search of adventures, and fell into a wild, disorderly way of living, so that they never came home again. The youngest, who was called Simpleton, set out to seek his brothers, but when at length he found them they mocked him for thinking that he with his simplicity could get through the world, when they two could not make their way, and yet were so much cleverer. They all three travelled away together, and came to an ant-hill. The two elder wanted to destroy it, to see the little ants creeping about in their terror, and carrying their eggs away, but Simpleton said, "Leave the creatures in peace; I will not allow you to disturb them." Then they went onwards and came to a lake, on which a great number of ducks were swimming. The two brothers wanted to catch a couple and roast them, but Simpleton would not permit it, and said, "Leave the creatures in peace, I will not suffer you to kill them." At length they came to a bee's nest, in which there was so much honey that it ran out of the trunk of the tree where it was. The two wanted to make a fire beneath the tree, and suffocate the bees in order to take away the honey, but Simpleton again stopped them and said, "Leave the creatures in peace, I will not allow you to burn them." At length the three brothers arrived at a castle where stone horses were standing in the stables, and no human being was to be seen, and they went through all the halls until, quite at the end, they came to a door in which were three locks. In the middle of the door, however, there was a little pane, through which they could see into the room. There they saw a little grey man, who was sitting at a table. They called him, once, twice, but he did not hear; at last they called him for the third time, when he got up, opened the locks, and came out. He said nothing, however, but conducted them to a handsomely-spread table, and when they had eaten and drunk, he took each of them to a bedroom. Next morning the little grey man came to the eldest, beckoned to him, and conducted him to a stone table, on which were inscribed three tasks, by the performance of which the castle could be delivered. The first was that in the forest, beneath the moss, lay the princess's pearls, a thousand in number, which must be picked up, and if by sunset one single pearl was wanting, he who had looked for them would be turned to stone. The eldest went thither, and sought the whole day, but when it came to an end, he had only found one hundred, and what was written on the table came to pass, and he was changed into stone. Next day, the second brother undertook the adventure; it did not, however, fare much better with him than with the eldest; he did not find more than two hundred pearls, and was changed to stone. At last the turn came to Simpleton also, who sought in the moss. It was, however, so hard to find the pearls, and he got on so slowly, that he seated himself on a stone, and wept. And while he was thus sitting, the King of the ants whose life he had once saved, came with five thousand ants, and before long the little creatures had got all the pearls together, and laid them in a heap. The second task, however, was to fetch out of the lake the key of the King's daughter's bed-chamber. When Simpleton came to the lake, the ducks which he had saved, swam up to him, dived down, and brought the key out of the water. But the third task was the most difficult; from amongst the three sleeping daughters of the King was the youngest and dearest to be sought out. They, however, resembled each other exactly, and were only to be distinguished by their having eaten different sweetmeats before they fell asleep: the eldest a bit of sugar; the second a little syrup; and the youngest a spoonful of honey. Then the Queen of the bees, which Simpleton had protected from the fire, came and tasted the lips of all three, and at last she remained sitting on the mouth which had eaten honey, and thus the King's son recognized the right princess. Then the enchantment was at an end; everything was released from sleep, and those who had been turned to stone received once more their natural forms. Simpleton married the youngest and sweetest princess, and after her father's death became King, and his two brothers received the two other sisters.

THE GOLDEN GOOSE

THERE WAS a man who had three sons, the youngest of whom was called Dummling*, and was despised, mocked, and put down on every occasion.

It happened that the eldest wanted to go into the forest to hew wood, and before he went his mother gave him a beautiful sweet cake and a bottle of wine in order that he might not suffer from hunger or thirst.

When he entered the forest there met him a little grey-haired old man who bade him good-day, and said, "Do give me a piece of cake out of your pocket, and let me have a draught of your wine; I am so hungry and thirsty." But the prudent youth answered, "If I give you my cake and wine, I shall have none for myself; be off with you," and he left the little man standing and went on.

But when he began to hew down a tree, it was not long before he made a false stroke, and the axe cut him in the arm, so that he had to go home and have it bound up. And this was the little grey man's doing.

After this the second son went into the forest, and his mother gave him, like the eldest, a cake and a bottle of wine. The little old grey man met him likewise, and asked him for a piece of cake and a drink of wine. But the second son, too, said with much reason, "What I give you will be taken away from myself; be off!" and he left the little man standing and went on. His punishment, however, was not delayed; when he had made a few strokes at the tree he struck himself in the leg, so that he had to be carried home.

Then Dummling said, "Father, do let me go and cut wood." The father answered, "Your brothers have hurt themselves with it, leave it alone, you do not understand anything about it." But Dummling begged so long that at last he said, "Just go then, you will get wiser by

*Simpleton.

hurting yourself." His mother gave him a cake made with water and baked in the cinders, and with it a bottle of sour beer.

When he came to the forest the little old grey man met him likewise, and greeting him, said, "Give me a piece of your cake and a drink out of your bottle; I am so hungry and thirsty." Dummling answered, "I have only cinder-cake and sour beer; if that pleases you, we will sit down and eat." So they sat down, and when Dummling pulled out his cinder-cake, it was a fine sweet cake, and the sour beer had become good wine. So they ate and drank, and after that the little man said, "Since you have a good heart, and are willing to divide what you have, I will give you good luck. There stands an old tree, cut it down, and you will find something at the roots." Then the little man took leave of him.

Dummling went and cut down the tree, and when it fell there was a goose sitting in the roots with feathers of pure gold. He lifted her up, and taking her with him, went to an inn where he thought he would stay the night. Now the host had three daughters, who saw the goose and were curious to know what such a wonderful bird might be, and would have liked to have one of its golden feathers.

The eldest thought, "I shall soon find an opportunity of pulling out a feather," and as soon as Dummling had gone out she seized the goose by the wing, but her finger and hand remained sticking fast to it.

The second came soon afterwards, thinking only of how she might get a feather for herself, but she had scarcely touched her sister than she was held fast.

At last the third also came with the like intent, and the others screamed out, "Keep away; for goodness' sake keep away!" But she did not understand why she was to keep away. "The others are there," she thought, "I may as well be there too," and ran to them; but as soon as she had touched her sister, she remained sticking fast to her. So they had to spend the night with the goose.

The next morning Dummling took the goose under his arm and set out, without troubling himself about the three girls who were hanging on to it. They were obliged to run after him continually, now left, now right, just as he was inclined to go.

In the middle of the fields the parson met them, and when he saw the procession he said, "For shame, you good-for-nothing girls, why are you running across the fields after this young man? is that seemly?" At the same time he seized the youngest by the hand in order to pull her away, but as soon as he touched her he likewise stuck fast, and was himself obliged to run behind.

Before long the sexton came by and saw his master, the parson, running behind three girls. He was astonished at this and called out, "Hi! your reverence, whither away so quickly? do not forget that we have a christening to-day!" and running after him he took him by the sleeve, but was also held fast to it.

Whilst the five were trotting thus one behind the other, two labourers came with their hoes from the fields; the parson called out to them and begged that they would set him and the sexton free. But they had scarcely touched the sexton when they were held fast, and now there were seven of them running behind Dummling and the goose.

Soon afterwards he came to a city, where a king ruled who had a daughter who was so serious that no one could make her laugh. So he had put forth a decree that whosoever should be able to make her laugh should marry her. When Dummling heard this, he went with his goose and all her train before the King's daughter, and as soon as she saw the seven people running on and on, one behind the other, she began to laugh quite loudly, and as if she would never leave off. Thereupon Dummling asked to have her for his wife, and the wedding was celebrated. After the King's death Dummling inherited the kingdom and lived a long time contentedly with his wife.

ALLERLEIRAUH

THERE WAS once on a time a King who had a wife with golden hair, and she was so beautiful that her equal was not to be found on earth. It came to pass that she lay ill, and as she felt that she must soon die, she called the King and said, "If thou wishest to marry again after my death, take no one who is not quite as beautiful as I am, and who has not just such golden hair as I have: this thou must promise me." And after the King had promised her this she closed her eyes and died.

For a long time the King could not be comforted, and had no thought of taking another wife. At length his councillors said, "There is no help for it, the King must marry again, that we may have a Queen." And now messengers were sent about far and wide, to seek a bride who equalled the late Queen in beauty. In the whole world, however, none was to be found, and even if one had been found, still there would have been no one who had such golden hair. So the messengers came home as they went.

Now the King had a daughter, who was just as beautiful as her dead mother, and had the same golden hair. When she was grown up the King looked at her one day, and saw that in every respect she was like his late wife, and suddenly felt a violent love for her. Then he spake to his councillors, "I will marry my daughter, for she is the counterpart of my late wife, otherwise I can find no bride who resembles her." When the councillors heard that, they were shocked, and said, "God has forbidden a father to marry his daughter, no good can come from such a crime, and the kingdom will be involved in the ruin."

The daughter was still more shocked when she became aware of her father's resolution, but hoped to turn him from his design. Then she said to him, "Before I fulfil your wish, I must have three dresses, one as golden as the sun, one as silvery as the moon, and one as bright as the stars; besides this, I wish for a mantle of a thousand different kinds of fur and hair joined together, and one of every kind of animal in your kingdom must give a bit of his skin for it." But she thought,

"To get that will be quite impossible, and thus I shall divert my father from his wicked intentions." The King, however, did not give it up, and the cleverest maidens in his kingdom had to weave the three dresses, one as golden as the sun, one as silvery as the moon, and one as bright as the stars, and his huntsmen had to catch one of every kind of animal in the whole of his kingdom, and take from it a piece of its skin, and out of these was made a mantle of a thousand different kinds of fur. At length, when all was ready, the King caused the mantle to be brought, spread it out before her, and said, "The wedding shall be to-morrow."

When, therefore, the King's daughter saw that there was no longer any hope of turning her father's heart, she resolved to run away from him. In the night whilst every one was asleep, she got up, and took three different things from her treasures, a golden ring, a golden spinning-wheel, and a golden reel. The three dresses of the sun, moon, and stars she put into a nutshell, put on her mantle of all kinds of fur, and blackened her face and hands with soot. Then she commended herself to God, and went away, and walked the whole night until she reached a great forest. And as she was tired, she got into a hollow tree, and fell asleep.

The sun rose, and she slept on, and she was still sleeping when it was full day. Then it so happened that the King to whom this forest belonged, was hunting in it. When his dogs came to the tree, they snuffed, and ran barking round about it. The King said to the huntsmen, "Just see what kind of wild beast has hidden itself in there." The huntsmen obeyed his order, and when they came back they said, "A wondrous beast is lying in the hollow tree; we have never before seen one like it. Its skin is fur of a thousand different kinds, but it is lying asleep." Said the King, "See if you can catch it alive, and then fasten it to the carriage, and we will take it with us." When the huntsmen laid hold of the maiden, she awoke full of terror, and cried to them, "I am a poor child, deserted by father and mother; have pity on me, and take me with you." Then said they, "Allerleirauh, thou wilt be useful in the kitchen, come with us, and thou canst sweep up the ashes." So they put her in the carriage, and took her home to the royal palace. There they pointed out to her a closet under the stairs, where no daylight entered, and said, "Hairy animal, there canst thou live and sleep." Then she was sent into the kitchen, and there she carried wood and water, swept the hearth, plucked the fowls, picked the vegetables, raked the ashes, and did all the dirty work.

Allerleirauh lived there for a long time in great wretchedness. Alas, fair princess, what is to become of thee now! It happened, however, that one day a feast was held in the palace, and she said to the cook,

"May I go up-stairs for a while, and look on? I will place myself outside the door." The cook answered, "Yes, go, but you must be back here in half-an-hour to sweep the hearth." Then she took her oil-lamp, went into her den, put off her fur-dress, and washed the soot off her face and hands, so that her full beauty once more came to light. And she opened the nut, and took out her dress which shone like the sun, and when she had done that she went up to the festival, and every one made way for her, for no one knew her, and thought no otherwise than that she was a king's daughter. The King came to meet her, gave his hand to her, and danced with her, and thought in his heart, "My eyes have never yet seen any one so beautiful!" When the dance was over she curtsied, and when the King looked round again she had vanished, and none knew whither. The guards who stood outside the palace were called and questioned, but no one had seen her.

She had, however, run into her little den, had quickly taken off her dress, made her face and hands black again, put on the fur-mantle, and again was Allerleirauh. And now when she went into the kitchen, and was about to get to her work and sweep up the ashes, the cook said, "Leave that alone till morning, and make me the soup for the King; I, too, will go upstairs awhile, and take a look; but let no hairs fall in, or in future thou shalt have nothing to eat." So the cook went away, and Allerleirauh made the soup for the king, and made bread soup and the best she could, and when it was ready she fetched her golden ring from her little den, and put it in the bowl in which the soup was served. When the dancing was over, the King had his soup brought and ate it, and he liked it so much that it seemed to him he had never tasted better. But when he came to the bottom of the bowl, he saw a golden ring lying, and could not conceive how it could have got there. Then he ordered the cook to appear before him. The cook was terrified when he heard the order, and said to Allerleirauh, "Thou hast certainly let a hair fall into the soup, and if thou hast, thou shalt be beaten for it." When he came before the King the latter asked who had made the soup? The cook replied, "I made it." But the King said, "That is not true, for it was much better than usual, and cooked differently." He answered, "I must acknowledge that I did not make it, it was made by the rough animal." The King said, "Go and bid it come up here."

When Allerleirauh came, the King said, "Who art thou?" "I am a poor girl who no longer has any father or mother." He asked further, "Of what use art thou in my palace?" She answered, "I am good for nothing but to have boots thrown at my head." He continued, "Where didst thou get the ring which was in the soup?" She answered, "I know nothing about the ring." So the King could learn nothing, and had to send her away again.

After a while, there was another festival, and then, as before, Allerleirauh begged the cook for leave to go and look on. He answered, "Yes, but come back again in half-an-hour, and make the King the bread soup which he so much likes." Then she ran into her den, washed herself quickly, and took out of the nut the dress which was as silvery as the moon, and put it on. Then she went up and was like a princess, and the King stepped forward to meet her, and rejoiced to see her once more, and as the dance was just beginning they danced it together. But when it was at an end, she again disappeared so quickly that the King could not observe where she went. She, however, sprang into her den, and once more made herself a hairy animal, and went into the kitchen to prepare the bread soup. When the cook had gone up-stairs, she fetched the little golden spinning-wheel, and put it in the bowl so that the soup covered it. Then it was taken to the King, who ate it, and liked it as much as before, and had the cook brought, who this time likewise was forced to confess that Allerleirauh had prepared the soup. Allerleirauh again came before the King, but she answered that she was good for nothing else but to have boots thrown at her head, and that she knew nothing at all about the little golden spinning-wheel.

When, for the third time, the King held a festival, all happened just as it had done before. The cook said, "Faith rough-skin, thou art a witch, and always puttest something in the soup which makes it so good that the King likes it better than that which I cook," but as she begged so hard, he let her go up at the appointed time. And now she put on the dress which shone like the stars, and thus entered the hall. Again the King danced with the beautiful maiden, and thought that she never yet had been so beautiful. And whilst she was dancing, he contrived, without her noticing it, to slip a golden ring on her finger, and he had given orders that the dance should last a very long time. When it was ended, he wanted to hold her fast by her hands, but she tore herself loose, and sprang away so quickly through the crowd that she vanished from his sight. She ran as fast as she could into her den beneath the stairs, but as she had been too long, and had stayed more than half-an-hour she could not take off her pretty dress, but only threw over it her fur-mantle, and in her haste she did not make herself quite black, but one finger remained white. Then Allerleirauh ran into the kitchen, and cooked the bread soup for the King, and as the cook was away, put her golden reel into it. When the King found the reel at the bottom of it, he caused Allerleirauh to be summoned, and then he espied the white finger, and saw the ring which he had put on it during the dance. Then he grasped her by the hand, and held her fast, and when she wanted to release herself and run away, her fur-mantle opened a little, and the star-dress shone forth. The King clutched the mantle and tore it off. Then her golden hair shone forth, and she stood there in full splendour, and could no longer hide herself. And when she had washed the soot and ashes from her face, she was more beautiful than any-one who had ever been seen on earth. But the King said, "Thou art my dear bride, and we will never more part from each other." Thereupon the marriage was solemnized, and they lived happily until their death.

JORINDA AND JORINGEL*

THERE WAS once an old castle in the midst of a large and thick forest, and in it an old woman who was a witch dwelt all alone. In the day-time she changed herself into a cat or a screech-owl, but in the evening she took her proper shape again as a human being. She could lure wild beasts and birds to her, and then she killed and boiled and roasted them. If any one came within one hundred paces of the castle he was obliged to stand still, and could not stir from the place until she bade him be free. But whenever an innocent maiden came within this circle, she changed her into a bird, and shut her up in a wicker-work cage, and carried the cage into a room in the castle. She had about seven thousand cages of rare birds in the castle.

Now, there was once a maiden who was called Jorinda, who was fairer than all other girls. She and a handsome youth named Joringel had promised to marry each other. They were still in the days of betrothal, and their greatest happiness was being together. One day in order that they might be able to talk together in quiet they went for a walk in the forest. "Take care," said Joringel, "that you do not go too near the castle."

It was a beautiful evening; the sun shone brightly between the trunks of the trees into the dark green of the forest, and the turtle-doves sang mournfully upon the young boughs of the birch-trees.

Jorinda wept now and then: she sat down in the sunshine and was sorrowful. Joringel was sorrowful too; they were as sad as if they were about to die. Then they looked around them, and were quite at a loss, for they did not know by which way they should go home. The sun was still half above the mountain and half set.

Joringel looked through the bushes, and saw the old walls of the castle close at hand. He was horror-stricken and filled with deadly fear. Jorinda was singing—

*Jorinker, a bird of the titmouse species, Gall. Enc. It is said to be named from its cry. See Jamieson's Dict.—TR.

"My little bird, with the necklace red,
Sings sorrow, sorrow, sorrow,
He sings that the dove must soon be dead,
Sings sorrow, sor—jug, jug, jug."

Joringel looked for Jorinda. She was changed into a nightingale, and sang, "jug, jug, jug." A screech-owl with glowing eyes flew three times round about her, and three times cried, "to-whoo, to-whoo, to-whoo!"

Joringel could not move: he stood there like a stone, and could neither weep nor speak, nor move hand or foot.

The sun had now set. The owl flew into the thicket, and directly afterwards there came out of it a crooked old woman, yellow and lean, with large red eyes and a hooked nose, the point of which reached to her chin. She muttered to herself, caught the nightingale, and took it away in her hand.

Joringel could neither speak nor move from the spot; the nightingale was gone. At last the woman came back, and said in a hollow voice, "Greet thee, Zachiel. If the moon shines on the cage, Zachiel, let him loose at once." Then Joringel was freed. He fell on his knees before the woman and begged that she would give him back his Jorinda, but she said that he should never have her again, and went away. He called, he wept, he lamented, but all in vain, "Ah, what is to become of me?"

Joringel went away, and at last came to a strange village; there he kept sheep for a long time. He often walked round and round the castle, but not too near to it. At last he dreamt one night that he found a blood-red flower, in the middle of which was a beautiful large pearl; that he picked the flower and went with it to the castle, and that everything he touched with the flower was freed from enchantment; he also dreamt that by means of it he recovered his Jorinda.

In the morning, when he awoke, he began to seek over hill and dale if he could find such a flower. He sought until the ninth day, and then, early in the morning, he found the blood-red flower. In the middle of it there was a large dew-drop, as big as the finest pearl.

Day and night he journeyed with this flower to the castle. When he was within a hundred paces of it he was not held fast, but walked on to the door. Joringel was full of joy; he touched the door with the flower, and it sprang open. He walked in through the courtyard, and listened for the sound of the birds. At last he heard it. He went on and found the room from whence it came, and there the witch was feeding the birds in the seven thousand cages.

When she saw Joringel she was angry, very angry, and scolded and spat poison and gall at him, but she could not come within two paces of him. He did not take any notice of her, but went and looked at the cages with the birds; but there were many hundred nightingales, how was he to find his Jorinda again?

Just then he saw the old woman quietly take away a cage with a bird in it, and go towards the door.

Swiftly he sprang towards her, touched the cage with the flower, and also the old woman. She could now no longer bewitch any one; and Jorinda was standing there, clasping him round the neck, and she was as beautiful as ever!

HOW SIX MEN GOT ON IN THE WORLD

THERE WAS once a man who understood all kinds of arts; he served in war, and behaved well and bravely, but when the war was over he received his dismissal, and three farthings for his expenses on the way. "Stop," said he, "I shall not be content with this. If I can only meet with the right people, the King will yet have to give me all the treasure of the country." Then full of anger he went into the forest, and saw a man standing therein who had plucked up six trees as if they were blades of corn. He said to him, "Wilt thou be my servant and go with me?" "Yes," he answered, "but, first, I will take this little bundle of sticks home to my mother," and he took one of the trees, and wrapped it round the five others, lifted the bundle on his back, and carried it away. Then he returned and went with his master, who said, "We two ought to be able to get through the world very well," and when they had walked on for a short while they found a huntsman who was kneeling, had shouldered his gun, and was about to fire. The master said to him, "Huntsman, what art thou going to shoot?" He answered, "Two miles from here a fly is sitting on the branch of an oak-tree, and I want to shoot its left eye out." "Oh, come with me," said the man, "if we three are together, we certainly ought to be able to get on in the world!" The huntsman was ready, and went with him, and they came to seven windmills whose sails were turning round with great speed, and yet no wind was blowing either on the right or the left, and no leaf was stirring. Then said the man, "I know not what is driving the windmills, not a breath of air is stirring," and he went onwards with his servants, and when they had walked two miles they saw a man sitting on a tree who was shutting one nostril, and blowing out of the other. "Good gracious! what are you doing up there?" He answered, "Two miles from here are seven windmills; look, I am blowing them till they turn round." "Oh, come with me," said the man. "If we four are together, we shall carry the whole world before us!" Then the blower came down and went with him, and after a while they saw a man who was standing on one leg and had taken off the other, and laid it beside him. Then the master said, "You have arranged things very comfortably to have a rest." "I am a runner," he replied, "and to stop myself running far too fast, I have taken off one of my legs, for if I run with both, I go quicker than any bird can fly." "Oh, go with me. If we five are together, we shall carry the whole world before us." So he went with them, and it was not long before they met a man who wore a cap, but had put it quite on one ear. Then the master said to him, "Gracefully, gracefully, don't stick your cap on one ear, you look just like a tom-fool!" "I must not wear it otherwise," said he, "for if I set my hat straight, a terrible frost comes on, and all the birds in the air are frozen, and drop dead on the ground." "Oh, come with me," said the master. "If we six are together, we can carry the whole world before us."

Now the six came to a town where the King had proclaimed that whosoever ran a race with his daughter and won the victory, should be her husband, but whosoever lost it, must lose his head. Then the man presented himself and said, "I will, however, let my servant run for me." The King replied, "Then his life also must be staked, so that his head and thine are both set on the victory." When that was settled and made secure, the man buckled the other leg on the runner, and said to him, "Now be nimble, and help us to win." It was fixed that the one who was first to bring some water from a far distant well was to be the victor. The runner received a pitcher, and the King's daughter one too, and they began to run at the same time, but in an instant, when the King's daughter had got a very little way, the people who were looking on could see no more of the runner, and it was just as if the wind had whistled by. In a short time he reached the well, filled his pitcher with water, and turned back. Half-way home, however, he was overcome with fatigue, and set his pitcher down, lay down himself, and fell asleep. He had, however, made a pillow of a horse's skull which was lying on the ground, in order that he might lie uncomfortably, and soon wake up again. In the meantime the King's daughter, who could also run very well—quite as well as any ordinary mortal can—had reached the well, and was hurrying back with her pitcher full of water, and when she saw the runner lying there asleep, she was glad and said, "My enemy is delivered over into my hands," emptied his pitcher, and ran on. And now all would have been lost if by good luck the huntsman had not been standing at the top of the castle, and had not seen everything with his sharp eyes. Then said he, "The King's daughter shall still not prevail against us"; and he loaded his gun, and shot so cleverly, that he shot the horse's skull away from under the runner's head without hurting him. Then the runner awoke, leapt up, and saw that his pitcher was empty, and that the King's daughter was already far in advance. He did not lose heart, however, but ran back to the well with his pitcher, again drew some water, and was at home again, ten minutes before the King's daughter. "Behold!" said he, "I have not bestirred myself till now, it did not deserve to be called running before."

But it pained the King, and still more his daughter, that she should be carried off by a common disbanded soldier like that; so they took counsel with each other how to get rid of him and his companions. Then said the King to her, "I have thought of a way; don't be afraid, they shall not come back again." And he said to them, "You shall now make merry together, and eat and drink," and he conducted them to a room which had a floor of iron, and the doors also were of iron, and the windows were guarded with iron bars. There was a table in the room covered with delicious food, and the King said to them, "Go in, and enjoy yourselves." And when they were inside, he ordered the doors to be shut and bolted. Then he sent for the cook, and commanded him to make a fire under the room until the iron became red-hot. This the cook did, and the six who were sitting at table began to feel quite warm, and they thought the heat was caused by the food; but as it became still greater, and they wanted to get out, and found that the doors and windows were bolted, they became aware that the King must have an evil intention, and wanted to suffocate them. "He shall not succeed, however," said the one with the cap. "I will cause a frost to come, before which the fire shall be ashamed, and creep away." Then he put his cap on straight, and immediately there came such a frost that all heat disappeared, and the food on the dishes began to freeze. When an hour or two had passed by, and the King believed that they had perished in the heat, he had the doors opened to behold them himself. But when the doors were opened, all six were standing there, alive and well, and said that they should very much like to get out to warm themselves, for the very food was fast frozen to the dishes with the cold. Then, full of anger, the King went down to the cook, scolded him, and asked why he had not done what he had been ordered to do. But the cook replied, "There is heat enough there, just look yourself." Then the King saw that a fierce fire was burning under the iron room, and perceived that there was no getting the better of the six in this way.

Again the King considered how to get rid of his unpleasant guests, and caused their chief to be brought and said, "If thou wilt take gold and renounce my daughter, thou shalt have as much as thou wilt."

"Oh, yes, Lord King," he answered, "give me as much as my servant can carry, and I will not ask for your daughter."

On this the King was satisfied, and the other continued, "In fourteen days, I will come and fetch it." Thereupon he summoned together all the tailors in the whole kingdom, and they were to sit for fourteen days and sew a sack. And when it was ready, the strong one who could tear up trees had to take it on his back, and go with it to the King. Then said the King, "Who can that strong fellow be who is carrying a bundle of linen on his back that is as big as a house?" and he was alarmed and said, "What a lot of gold he can carry away!" Then he commanded a ton of gold to be brought; it took sixteen of his strongest men to carry it, but the strong one snatched it up in one hand, put it in his sack, and said, "Why don't you bring more at the same time? that hardly covers the bottom!" Then, little by little, the King caused all his treasure to be brought thither, and the strong one pushed it into the sack, and still the sack was not half full with it." "Bring more," cried he, "these few crumbs don't fill it." Then seven thousand carts with gold had to be gathered together in the whole kingdom, and the strong one thrust them and the oxen harnessed to them into his sack. "I will examine it no longer," said he, "but will just take what comes, so long as the sack is but full." When all that was inside, there was still room for a great deal more; then he said, "I will just make an end of the thing; people do sometimes tie up a sack even when it is not full." So he took it on his back, and went away with his comrades. When the King now saw how one single man was carrying away the entire wealth of the country, he became enraged, and bade his horsemen mount and pursue the six, and ordered them to take the sack away from the strong one. Two regiments speedily overtook the six, and called out, "You are prisoners, put down the sack with the gold, or you will all be cut to pieces!" "What say you?" cried the blower, "that we are prisoners! Rather than that should happen, all of you shall dance about in the air." And he closed one nostril, and with the other blew on the two regiments. Then they were driven away from each other, and carried into the blue sky over all the mountains one here, the other there. One sergeant cried for mercy; he had nine wounds, and was a brave fellow who did not deserve ill treatment. The blower stopped a little so that he came down without injury, and then the blower said to him, "Now go home to thy King, and tell him he had better send some more horsemen, and I will blow them all into the air." When the King was informed of this he said, "Let the rascals go. They have the best of it." Then the six conveyed the riches home, divided it amongst them, and lived in content until their death.

HANS IN LUCK

HANS HAD served his master for seven years, so he said to him, "Master, my time is up; now I should be glad to go back home to my mother; give me my wages." The master answered, "You have served me faithfully and honestly; as the service was so shall the reward be"; and he gave Hans a piece of gold as big as his head. Hans pulled his handkerchief out of his pocket, wrapped up the lump in it, put it on his shoulder, and set out on the way home.

As he went on, always putting one foot before the other, he saw a horseman trotting quickly and merrily by on a lively horse. "Ah!" said Hans quite loud, "what a fine thing it is to ride! There you sit as on a chair; you stumble over no stones, you save your shoes, and get on, you don't know how."

The rider, who had heard him, stopped and called out, "Hollo! Hans, why do you go on foot, then?"

"I must," answered he, "for I have this lump to carry home; it is true that it is gold, but I cannot hold my head straight for it, and it hurts my shoulder."

"I will tell you what," said the rider, "we will exchange: I will give you my horse, and you can give me your lump."

"With all my heart," said Hans, "but I can tell you, you will have to crawl along with it."

The rider got down, took the gold, and helped Hans up; then gave him the bridle tight in his hands and said, "If you want to go at a really good pace, you must click your tongue and call out, "Jup! Jup!"

Hans was heartily delighted as he sat upon the horse and rode away so bold and free. After a little while he thought that it ought to go faster, and he began to click with his tongue and call out, "Jup! Jup!" The horse put himself into a sharp trot, and before Hans knew where he was, he was thrown off and lying in a ditch which separated the field from the highway. The horse would have gone off too if it had not been stopped by a countryman, who was coming along the road and driving a cow before him.

Hans got his limbs together and stood up on his legs again, but he was vexed, and said to the countryman, "It is a poor joke, this riding, especially when one gets hold of a mare like this, that kicks and throws one off, so that one has a chance of breaking one's neck. Never again will I mount it. Now I like your cow, for one can walk quietly behind her, and have, over and above, one's milk, butter and cheese every day without fail. What would I not give to have such a cow." "Well," said the countryman, "if it would give you so much pleasure, I do not mind giving the cow for the horse." Hans agreed with the greatest delight; the countryman jumped upon the horse, and rode quickly away.

Hans drove his cow quietly before him, and thought over his lucky bargain. "If only I have a morsel of bread—and that can hardly fail me—I can eat butter and cheese with it as often as I like; if I am thirsty, I can milk my cow and drink the milk. Good heart, what more can I want?"

When he came to an inn he made a halt, and in his great content ate up what he had with him—his dinner and supper—and all he had, and with his last few farthings had half a glass of beer. Then he drove his cow onwards along the road to his mother's village.

As it drew nearer mid-day, the heat was more oppressive, and Hans found himself upon a moor which it took about an hour to cross. He felt it very hot and his tongue clave to the roof of his mouth with thirst. "I can find a cure for this," thought Hans; "I will milk the cow now and refresh myself with the milk." He tied her to a withered tree, and as he had no pail he put his leather cap underneath; but try as he would, not a drop of milk came. And as he set himself to work in a clumsy way, the impatient beast at last gave him such a blow on his head with its hind foot, that he fell on the ground, and for a long time could not think where he was.

By good fortune a butcher just then came along the road with a wheel-barrow, in which lay a young pig. "What sort of a trick is this?" cried he, and helped the good Hans up. Hans told him what had happened. The butcher gave him his flask and said, "Take a drink and refresh yourself. The cow will certainly give no milk, it is an old beast; at the best it is only fit for the plough, or for the butcher." "Well, well," said Hans, as he stroked his hair down on his head, "who would have thought it? Certainly it is a fine thing when one can kill a beast like that at home; what meat one has! But I do not care much for beef, it is not juicy enough for me. A young pig like that now is the thing to have it tastes quite different; and then there are the sausages!"

"Hark ye, Hans," said the butcher, "out of love for you I will exchange, and will let you have the pig for the cow." "Heaven repay you for your kindness!" said Hans as he gave up the cow, whilst the pig was unbound from the barrow, and the cord by which it was tied was put in his hand.

Hans went on, and thought to himself how everything was going just as he wished; if he did meet with any vexation it was immediately set right. Presently there joined him a lad who was carrying a fine white goose under his arm. They said good morning to each other, and Hans began to tell of his good luck, and how he had always made such good bargains. The boy told him that he was taking the goose to a christening-feast. "Just lift her," added he, and laid hold of her by the wings; "how heavy she is—she has been fattened up for the last eight weeks. Whoever has a bit of her when she is roasted will have to wipe the fat from both sides of his mouth." "Yes," said Hans, as he weighed her in one hand, "she is a good weight, but my pig is no bad one."

Meanwhile the lad looked suspiciously from one side to the other, and shook his head. "Look here," he said at length, "it may not be all right with your pig. In the village through which I passed, the Mayor himself had just had one stolen out of its sty. I fear—I fear that you have got hold of it there. They have sent out some people and it would be a bad business if they caught you with the pig; at the very least, you would be shut up in the dark hole."

The good Hans was terrified. "Goodness!" he said, "help me out of this fix; you know more about this place than I do, take my pig and leave me your goose." "I shall risk something at that game," answered the lad, "but I will not be the cause of your getting into trouble." So he took the cord in his hand, and drove away the pig quickly along a by-path.

The good Hans, free from care, went homewards with the goose under his arm. "When I think over it properly," said he to himself, "I have even gained by the exchange: first there is the good roast-meat, then the quantity of fat which will drip from it, and which will give me dripping for my bread for a quarter of a year, and lastly the beautiful white feathers; I will have my pillow stuffed with them, and then indeed I shall go to sleep without rocking. How glad my mother will be!"

As he was going through the last village, there stood a scissors-grinder with his barrow; as his wheel whirred he sang—

"I sharpen scissors and quickly grind,
My coat blows out in the wind behind."

Hans stood still and looked at him; at last he spoke to him and said, "All's well with you, as you are so merry with your grinding." "Yes," answered the scissors-grinder, "the trade has a golden foundation. A real grinder is a man who as often as he puts his hand into his pocket finds gold in it. But where did you buy that fine goose?"

"I did not buy it, but exchanged my pig for it."

"And the pig?"

"That I got for a cow."

"And the cow?"

"I took that instead of a horse."

"And the horse?"

"For that I gave a lump of gold as big as my head."

"And the gold?"

"Well, that was my wages for seven years' service."

"You have known how to look after yourself each time," said the grinder. "If you can only get on so far as to hear the money jingle in your pocket whenever you stand up, you will have made your fortune."

"How shall I manage that?" said Hans. "You must be a grinder, as I am; nothing particular is wanted for it but a grindstone, the rest finds itself. I have one here; it is certainly a little worn, but you need not give me anything for it but your goose; will you do it?"

"How can you ask?" answered Hans. "I shall be the luckiest fellow on earth; if I have money whenever I put my hand in my pocket, what need I trouble about any longer?" and he handed him the goose and received the grindstone in exchange. "Now," said the grinder, as he took up an ordinary heavy stone that lay by him, "here is a strong stone for you into the bargain; you can hammer well upon it, and straighten your old nails. Take it with you and keep it carefully."

Hans loaded himself with the stones, and went on with a contented heart; his eyes shone with joy. "I must have been born with a caul," he cried; "everything I want happens to me just as if I were a Sunday-child."

Meanwhile, as he had been on his legs since daybreak, he began to feel tired. Hunger also tormented him, for in his joy at the bargain by which he got the cow he had eaten up all his store of food at once. At last he could only go on with great trouble, and was forced to stop every minute; the stones, too, weighed him down dreadfully. Then he could not help thinking how nice it would be if he had not to carry them just then.

He crept like a snail to a well in a field, and there he thought that he would rest and refresh himself with a cool draught of water, but in order that he might not injure the stones in sitting down, he laid them carefully by his side on the edge of the well. Then he sat down on it, and was to stoop and drink, when he made a slip, pushed against the stones, and both of them fell into the water. When Hans saw them with his own eyes sinking to the bottom, he jumped for joy, and then knelt down, and with tears in his eyes thanked God for having shown him this favour also, and delivered him in so good a way, and without his having any need to reproach himself, from those heavy stones which had been the only things that troubled him.

"There is no man under the sun so fortunate as I," he cried out. With a light heart and free from every burden he now ran on until he was with his mother at home.

THE GOOSE-GIRL

THERE WAS once upon a time an old Queen whose husband had been dead for many years, and she had a beautiful daughter. When the princess grew up she was betrothed to a prince who lived at a great distance. When the time came for her to be married, and she had to journey forth into the distant kingdom, the aged Queen packed up for her many costly vessels of silver and gold, and trinkets also of gold and silver; and cups and jewels, in short, everything which appertained to a royal dowry, for she loved her child with all her heart. She likewise sent her maid in waiting, who was to ride with her, and hand her over to the bridegroom, and each had a horse for the journey, but the horse of the King's daughter was called Falada, and could speak. So when the hour of parting had come, the aged mother went into her bedroom, took a small knife and cut her finger with it until it bled, then she held a white handkerchief to it into which she let three drops of blood fall, gave it to her daughter and said, "Dear child, preserve this carefully, it will be of service to you on your way."

So they took a sorrowful leave of each other; the princess put the piece of cloth in her bosom, mounted her horse, and then went away to her bridegroom. After she had ridden for a while she felt a burning thirst, and said to her waiting-maid, "Dismount, and take my cup which thou hast brought with thee for me, and get me some water from the stream, for I should like to drink." "If you are thirsty," said the waiting-maid, "get off your horse yourself, and lie down and drink out of the water, I don't choose to be your servant." So in her great thirst the princess alighted, bent down over the water in the stream and drank, and was not allowed to drink out of the golden cup. Then she said, "Ah, Heaven!" and the three drops of blood answered, "If thy mother knew this, her heart would break." But the King's daughter was humble, said nothing, and mounted her horse again. She rode some miles further, but the day was warm, the sun scorched her, and she was thirsty once more, and when they came to a stream of water, she again cried to her waiting-maid, "Dismount, and give me some water in my golden cup," for she had long ago forgotten the girl's ill words. But the waiting-maid said still more haughtily, "If you wish to drink, drink as you can, I don't choose to be your maid." Then in her great thirst the King's daughter alighted, bent over the flowing stream, wept and said, "Ah, Heaven!" and the drops of blood again replied, "If thy mother knew this, her heart would break." And as she was thus drinking and leaning right over the stream, the handkerchief with the three drops of blood fell out of her bosom, and floated away with the water without her observing it, so great was her trouble. The waiting-maid, however, had seen it, and she rejoiced to think that she had now power over the bride, for since the princess had lost the drops of blood, she had become weak and powerless. So now when she wanted to mount her horse again, the one that was called Falada, the waiting-maid said, "Falada is more suitable for me, and my nag will do for thee" and the princess had to be content with that. Then the waiting-maid, with many hard words, bade the princess exchange her royal apparel for her own shabby clothes; and at length she was compelled to swear by the clear sky above her, that she would not say one word of this to any one at the royal court, and if she had not taken this oath she would have been killed on the spot. But Falada saw all this, and observed it well.

The waiting-maid now mounted Falada, and the true bride the bad horse, and thus they travelled onwards, until at length they entered the royal palace. There were great rejoicings over her arrival, and the prince sprang forward to meet her, lifted the waiting-maid from her horse, and thought she was his consort. She was conducted upstairs, but the real princess was left standing below. Then the old King looked out of the window and saw her standing in the courtyard, and how dainty and delicate and beautiful she was, and instantly went to the royal apartment, and asked the bride about the girl she had with her who was standing down below in the courtyard, and who she was? "I picked her up on my way for a companion; give the girl something to work at, that she may not stand idle." But the old King had no work for her, and knew of none, so he said, "I have a little boy who tends the geese, she may help him." The boy was called Conrad, and the true bride had to help him to tend the geese. Soon afterwards the false bride said to the young King, "Dearest husband, I beg you to do me a favour." He answered, "I will do so most willingly." "Then send for the knacker, and cut off the head of the horse on which I rode here, for it vexed me on the way." In reality, she was afraid that the horse might tell how she had behaved to the King's daughter. Then she succeeded in making the King promise that it should be done, and the faithful Falada was to die; this came to the ears of the real princess, and she secretly promised to pay the knacker a piece of gold if he would perform a small service for her. There was a great dark-looking gateway in the town, through which morning and evening she had to pass with the geese: would he be so good as to nail up Falada's head on it, so that she might see him again, more than once. The knacker's man promised to do that, and cut off the head, and nailed it fast beneath the dark gateway.

Early in the morning, when she and Conrad drove out their flock beneath this gateway, she said in passing,

"Falada, Falada, hanging high . . ."

Then the head answered,

"Princess, Princess, passing by.
Alas, alas! If thy mother knew it,
Sadly, sadly her heart would rue it."

Then they went still further out of the town, and drove their geese into the country. And when they had come to the meadow, she sat down and unbound her hair which was like pure gold, and Conrad saw it and delighted in its brightness, and wanted to pluck out a few hairs. Then she said,

"Blow, breezes, blow!
Let Conrad's hat go!
Blow, breezes blow!
Let him after it go
O'er hills, dales and rocks
Away be it whirled
Till the silvery locks
Are all combed and curled."

And there came such a violent wind that it blew Conrad's hat far away across country, and he was forced to run after it. When he came back she had finished combing her hair and was putting it up again, and he could not get any of it. Then Conrad was angry, and would not speak to her, and thus they watched the geese until the evening, and then they went home.

Next day when they were driving the geese out through the dark gateway, the maiden said,

"Falada, Falada, hanging high . . ."

Falada answered,

"Princess, Princess, passing by.

Alas, alas! If thy mother knew it,
Sadly, sadly her heart would rue it."

And she sat down again in the field and began to comb out her hair, and Conrad ran and tried to clutch it, so she said in haste,

"Blow, breezes, blow!
Let Conrad's hat go!
Blow, breezes blow!
Let him after it go
O'er hills, dales and rocks
Away be it whirled
Till the silvery locks
Are all combed and curled."

Then the wind blew, and blew his little hat off his head and far away, and Conrad was forced to run after it, and when he came back, her hair had been put up a long time, and he could get none of it, and so they looked after their geese till evening came.

But in the evening after they had got home, Conrad went to the old King, and said, "I won't tend the geese with that girl any longer!" "Why not?" inquired the aged King. "Oh, because she vexes me the whole day long." Then the aged King commanded him to relate what it was that she did to him. And Conrad said, "In the morning when we pass beneath the dark gateway with the flock, there is a sorry horse's head on the wall, and she says to it,

"Falada, Falada, hanging high . . ."

And the head replies,

"Princess, Princess, passing by.
Alas, alas! If thy mother knew it,
Sadly, sadly her heart would rue it."

And Conrad went on to relate what happened on the goose pasture, and how when there he had to chase his hat.

The aged King commanded him to drive his flock out again next day, and as soon as morning came, he placed himself behind the dark gateway, and heard how the maiden spoke to the head of Falada, and then he too went into the country, and hid himself in the thicket in the meadow. There he soon saw with his own eyes the goose-girl and the goose-boy bringing their flock, and how after a while she sat down and unplaited her hair, which shone with radiance. And soon she said,

"Blow, breezes, blow!
Let Conrad's hat go!

Blow, breezes blow!
Let him after it go
O'er hills, dales and rocks
Away be it whirled
Till the silvery locks
Are all combed and curled."

Then came a blast of wind and carried off Conrad's hat, so that he had to run far away, while the maiden quietly went on combing and plaiting her hair, all of which the King observed. Then, quite unseen, he went away, and when the goose-girl came home in the evening, he called her aside, and asked why she did all these things. "I may not tell you that, and I dare not lament my sorrows to any human being, for I have sworn not to do so by the heaven which is above me; if I had not done that, I should have lost my life." He urged her and left her no peace, but he could draw nothing from her. Then said he, "If thou wilt not tell me anything, tell thy sorrows to the iron-stove there," and he went away. Then she crept into the iron-stove, and began to weep and lament, and emptied her whole heart, and said, "Here am I deserted by the whole world, and yet I am a King's daughter, and a false waiting-maid has by force brought me to such a pass that I have been compelled to put off my royal apparel, and she has taken my place with my bridegroom, and I have to perform menial service as a goose-girl. If my mother did but know that, her heart would break."

The aged King, however, was standing outside by the pipe of the stove, and was listening to what she said, and heard it. Then he came back again, and bade her come out of the stove. And royal garments were placed on her, and it was marvellous how beautiful she was! The aged King summoned his son, and revealed to him that he had got the false bride who was only a waiting-maid, but that the true one was standing there, as the sometime goose-girl. The young King rejoiced with all his heart when he saw her beauty and youth, and a great feast was made ready to which all the people and all good friends were invited. At the head of the table sat the bridegroom with the King's daughter at one side of him, and the waiting-maid on the other, but the waiting-maid was blinded, and did not recognize the princess in her dazzling array. When they had eaten and drunk, and were merry, the aged King asked the waiting-maid as a riddle, what a person deserved who had behaved in such and such a way to her master, and at the same time related the whole story, and asked what sentence such an one merited? Then the false bride said, "She deserves no better fate than to be stripped entirely naked, and put in a barrel which is studded inside with pointed nails, and two white horses should be harnessed to it, which will drag her along through one street after another, till she is dead." "It is thou," said the aged King, "and thou hast pronounced thine own sentence, and thus shall it be done unto thee." And when the sentence had been carried out, the young King married his true bride, and both of them reigned over their kingdom in peace and happiness.

SNOW-WHITE AND ROSE-RED

THERE WAS once a poor widow who lived in a lonely cottage. In front of the cottage was a garden wherein stood two rose trees, one of which bore white and the other red roses. She had two children who were like the two rose trees, and one was called Snow-white, and the other Rose-red. They were as good and happy, as busy and cheerful as ever two children in the world were, only Snow-white was more quiet and gentle than Rose-red. Rose-red liked better to run about in the meadows and fields seeking flowers and catching butterflies; but Snow-white sat at home with her mother, and helped her with her housework, or read to her when there was nothing to do.

The two children were so fond of each another that they always held each other by the hand when they went out together, and when Snow-white said, "We will not leave each other," Rose-red answered, "Never so long as we live," and their mother would add, "What one has she must share with the other."

They often ran about the forest alone and gathered red berries, and no beasts did them any harm, but came close to them trustfully. The little hare would eat a cabbage leaf out of their hands, the roe grazed by their side, the stag leapt merrily by them, and the birds sat still upon the boughs, and sang whatever they knew.

No mishap overtook them; if they had stayed too late in the forest, and night came on, they laid themselves down near one another upon the moss, and slept until morning came, and their mother knew this and had no distress on their account.

Once when they had spent the night in the wood and the dawn had roused them, they saw a beautiful child in a shining white dress sitting near their bed. He got up and looked quite kindly at them, but said nothing and went away into the forest. And when they looked round they found that they had been sleeping quite close to a precipice, and would certainly have fallen into it in the darkness if they had gone only a few paces further. And their mother told them that it must have been the angel who watches over good children.

Snow-white and Rose-red kept their mother's little cottage so neat that it was a pleasure to look inside it. In the summer Rose-red took care of the house, and every morning laid a wreath of flowers by her mother's bed before she awoke, in which was a rose from each tree. In the winter Snow-white lit the fire and hung the kettle on the hob. The kettle was of copper and shone like gold, so brightly was it polished. In the evening, when the snowflakes fell, the mother said, "Go, Snow-white, and bolt the door," and then they sat round the hearth, and the mother took her spectacles and read aloud out of a large book, and the two girls listened as they sat and spun. And close by them lay a lamb upon the floor, and behind them upon a perch sat a white dove with its head hidden beneath its wings.

One evening, as they were thus sitting comfortably together, some one knocked at the door as if he wished to be let in. The mother said, "Quick, Rose-red, open the door, it must be a traveller who is seeking shelter." Rose-red went and pushed back the bolt, thinking that it was a poor man, but it was not; it was a bear that stretched his broad, black head within the door.

Rose-red screamed and sprang back, the lamb bleated, the dove fluttered, and Snow-white hid herself behind her mother's bed. But the bear began to speak and said, "Do not be afraid, I will do you no harm! I am half-frozen, and only want to warm myself a little beside you."

"Poor bear," said the mother, "lie down by the fire, only take care that you do not burn your coat." Then she cried, "Snow-white, Rose-red, come out, the bear will do you no harm, he means well." So they both came out, and by and by the lamb and dove came nearer, and were not afraid of him. The bear said, "Here, children, knock the snow out of my coat a little"; so they brought the broom and swept the bear's hide clean; and he stretched himself by the fire and growled contentedly and comfortably. It was not long before they grew quite at home, and played tricks with their clumsy guest. They tugged his hair with their hands, put their feet upon his back and rolled him about, or they took a hazel switch and beat him, and when he growled they laughed. But the bear took it all in good part; only when they were too rough he called out, "Leave me alive, children,

"Leave me alive, children,
Snowy-white, Rosy-red,
Will you beat your lover dead?"

When it was bedtime, and the others went to bed, the mother said to the bear, "You can lie there by the hearth, and then you will be safe from the cold and the bad weather." As soon as day dawned the two children let him out, and he trotted across the snow into the forest.

Henceforth the bear came every evening at the same time, laid himself down by the hearth, and let the children amuse themselves with him as much as they liked; and they got so used to him that the doors were never fastened until their black friend had arrived.

When spring had come and all outside was green, the bear said one morning to Snow-white, "Now I must go away, and cannot come back for the whole summer." "Where are you going, then, dear bear?" asked Snow-white. "I must go into the forest and guard my treasures from the wicked dwarfs. In the winter, when the earth is frozen hard, they are obliged to stay below and cannot work their way through; but now, when the sun has thawed and warmed the earth, they break through it, and come out to pry and steal; and what once gets into their hands, and in their caves, does not easily see daylight again."

Snow-white was quite sorry that he was going away, and as she unbolted the door for him, and the bear was hurrying out, he caught against the bolt and a piece of his hairy coat was torn off, and it seemed to Snow-white as if she had seen gold shining through it, but she was not sure. The bear ran away quickly, and was soon out of sight behind the trees.

A short time afterwards the mother sent her children into the forest to get firewood. There they found a big tree which lay felled on the ground, and close by the trunk something was jumping backwards and forwards in the grass, but they could not make out what it was. When they came nearer they saw a dwarf with an old withered face and a snow-white beard a yard long. The end of the beard was caught in a crevice of the tree, and the little fellow was jumping backwards and forwards like a dog tied to a rope, and did not know what to do.

He glared at the girls with his fiery red eyes and cried, "Why do you stand there? Can you not come here and help me?" "What are you about there, little man?" asked Rose-red. "You stupid, prying goose!" answered the dwarf; "I was going to split the tree to get a little wood for cooking. The little bit of food that one of us wants gets burnt up directly with thick logs; we do not swallow so much as you coarse, greedy folk. I had just driven the wedge safely in, and everything was going as I wished; but the wretched wood was too smooth and suddenly sprang asunder, and the tree closed so quickly that I could not pull out my beautiful white beard; so now it is tight in and I cannot get away, and the silly, sleek, milk-faced things laugh! Ugh! how odious you are!"

The children tried very hard, but they could not pull the beard out—it was caught too fast. "I will run and fetch some one," said

Rose-red. "You senseless goose!" snarled the dwarf; "why should you fetch some one? You are already two too many for me; can you not think of something better?" "Don't be impatient," said Snow-white, "I will help you," and she pulled her scissors out of her pocket, and cut off the end of the beard.

As soon as the dwarf felt himself free he laid hold of a bag which lay amongst the roots of the tree, and which was full of gold, and lifted it up, grumbling to himself, "Uncouth people, to cut off a piece of my fine beard. Bad luck to you!" and then he swung the bag upon his back, and went off without even once looking at the children.

Some time after that Snow-white and Rose-red went to catch a dish of fish. As they came near the brook they saw something like a large grasshopper jumping towards the water, as if it were going to leap in. They ran to it and found it was the dwarf. "Where are you going?" said Rose-red; "you surely don't want to go into the water?" "I am not such a fool!" cried the dwarf; "don't you see that the accursed fish wants to pull me in?" The little man had been sitting there fishing, and unluckily the wind had twisted his beard with the fishing line; just then a big fish bit, and the feeble creature had not strength to pull it out; the fish kept the upper hand and pulled the dwarf towards him. He held on to all the reeds and rushes, but it was of little good, he was forced to follow the movements of the fish, and was in urgent danger of being dragged into the water.

The girls came just in time; they held him fast and tried to free his beard from the line, but all in vain, beard and line were entangled fast together. Nothing was left but to bring out the scissors and cut the beard, whereby a small part of it was lost. When the dwarf saw that he screamed out, "Is that civil, you toadstool, to disfigure one's face? Was it not enough to clip off the end of my beard? Now you have cut off the best part of it. I cannot let myself be seen by my people. I wish you had been made to run the soles off your shoes!" Then he took out a sack of pearls which lay in the rushes, and without saying a word more he dragged it away and disappeared behind a stone.

It happened that soon afterwards the mother sent the two children to the town to buy needles and thread, and laces and ribbons. The road led them across a heath upon which huge pieces of rock lay strewn here and there. Now they noticed a large bird hovering in the air, flying slowly round and round above them; it sank lower and lower, and at last settled near a rock not far off. Directly afterwards they heard a loud, piteous cry. They ran up and saw with horror that the eagle had seized their old acquaintance the dwarf, and was going to carry him off.

The children, full of pity, at once took tight hold of the little man, and pulled against the eagle so long that at last he let his booty go. As soon as the dwarf had recovered from his first fright he cried with his shrill voice, "Could you not have done it more carefully! You dragged at my brown coat so that it is all torn and full of holes, you helpless clumsy creatures!" Then he took up a sack full of precious stones, and slipped away again under the rock into his hole. The girls, who by this time were used to his thanklessness, went on their way and did their business in the town.

As they crossed the heath again on their way home they surprised the dwarf, who had emptied out his bag of precious stones in a clean spot, and had not thought that anyone would come there so late. The evening sun shone upon the brilliant stones; they glittered and sparkled with all colors so beautifully that the children stood still and looked at them. "Why do you stand gaping there?" cried the dwarf, and his ashen-gray face became copper-red with rage. He was going on with his bad words when a loud growling was heard, and a black bear came trotting towards them out of the forest. The dwarf sprang up in a fright, but he could not get to his cave, for the bear was already close. Then in the dread of his heart he cried, "Dear Mr. Bear, spare me, I will give you all my treasures; look at the beautiful jewels lying there! Grant me my life; what do you want with such a slender little fellow as I? You would not feel me between your teeth. Come, take these two wicked girls, they are tender morsels for you, fat as young quails; for mercy's sake eat them!" The bear took no heed of his words, but gave the wicked creature a single blow with his paw, and he did not move again.

The girls had run away, but the bear called to them, "Snow-white and Rose-red, do not be afraid; wait, I will come with you." Then they knew his voice and waited, and when he came up to them suddenly his bearskin fell off, and he stood there a handsome man, clothed all in gold. "I am a King's son," he said, "and I was bewitched by that wicked dwarf, who had stolen my treasures; I have had to run about the forest as a savage bear until I was freed by his death. Now he has got his well-deserved punishment."

Snow-white was married to him, and Rose-red to his brother, and they divided between them the great treasure which the dwarf had gathered together in his cave. The old mother lived peacefully and happily with her children for many years. She took the two rose trees with her, and they stood before her window, and every year bore the most beautiful roses, white and red.

THE MASTER-THIEF

One day an old man and his wife were sitting in front of a miserable house resting a while from their work. Suddenly a splendid carriage with four black horses came driving up, and a richly-dressed man descended from it. The peasant stood up, went to the great man, and asked what he wanted, and in what way he could be useful to him? The stranger stretched out his hand to the old man, and said, "I want nothing but to enjoy for once a country dish; cook me some potatoes, in the way you always have them, and then I will sit down at your table and eat them with pleasure." The peasant smiled and said, "You are a count or a prince, or perhaps even a duke; noble gentlemen often have such fancies, but you shall have your wish." The wife went into the kitchen, and began to wash and rub the potatoes, and to make them into balls, as they are eaten by the country-folks. Whilst she was busy with this work, the peasant said to the stranger, "Come into my garden with me for a while, I have still something to do there." He had dug some holes in the garden, and now wanted to plant some trees in them. "Have you no children," asked the stranger, "who could help you with your work?" "No," answered the peasant, "I had a son, it is true, but it is long since he went out into the world. He was a ne'er-do-well; sharp, and knowing, but he would learn nothing and was full of bad tricks, at last he ran away from me, and since then I have heard nothing of him."

The old man took a young tree, put it in a hole, drove in a post beside it, and when he had shovelled in some earth and had trampled it firmly down, he tied the stem of the tree above, below, and in the middle, fast to the post by a rope of straw. "But tell me," said the stranger, "why you don't tie that crooked knotted tree, which is lying in the corner there, bent down almost to the ground, to a post also that it may grow straight, as well as these?" The old man smiled and said, "Sir, you speak according to your knowledge, it is easy to see that you are not familiar with gardening. That tree there is old, and mis-shapen, no one can make it straight now. Trees must be trained while they are young." "That is how it was with your son," said the stranger, "if you had trained him while he was still young, he would not have run away; now he too must have grown hard and mis-shapen." "Truly it is a long time since he went away," replied the old man, "he must have changed." "Would you know him again if he were to come to you?" asked the stranger. "Hardly by his face," replied the peasant, "but he has a mark about him, a birth-mark on his shoulder, that looks like a bean." When he had said that the stranger pulled off his coat, bared his shoulder, and showed the peasant the bean. "Well-a-day!" cried the old man, "Thou art really my son!" and love for his child stirred in his heart. "But," he added, "how canst thou be my son, thou hast become a great lord and livest in wealth and luxury? How hast thou contrived to do that?" "Ah, father," answered the son, "the young tree was bound to no post and has grown crooked, now it is too old, it will never be straight again. How have I got all that? I have become a thief, but do not be alarmed, I am a master-thief. For me there are neither locks nor bolts, whatsoever I desire is mine. Do not imagine that I steal like a common thief, I only take some of the superfluity of the rich. Poor people are safe, I would rather give to them than take anything from them. It is the same with anything which I can have without trouble, cunning and dexterity, I never touch it." "Alas, my son," said the father, "it still does not please me, a thief is still a thief, I tell thee it will end badly." He took him to his mother, and when she heard that was her son, she wept for joy, but when he told her that he had become a master-thief, two streams flowed down over her face. At length she said, "Even if he has become a thief, he is still my son, and my eyes have beheld him once more." They sat down to table, and once again he ate with his parents the wretched food which he had not eaten for so long. The father said, "If our Lord, the count up there in the castle, learns who thou art, and what trade thou followest, he will not take thee in his arms and cradle thee in them as he did when he held thee at the font, but will cause thee to swing from a halter." "Be easy, father, he will do me no harm, for I understand my trade. I will go to him myself this very day." When evening drew near, the master-thief seated himself in his carriage, and drove to the castle. The count received him civilly, for he took him for a distinguished man. When, however, the stranger made himself known, the count turned pale and was quite silent for some time. At length he said, "Thou art my godson, and on that account mercy shall take the place of justice, and I will deal leniently with thee. Since thou pridest thyself on being a master-thief, I will put thy art to the proof, but if thou dost not stand the test, thou must marry the rope-maker's daughter, and the croaking of the raven must be thy music on the occasion." "Lord count," answered the master-thief, "Think of three things, as difficult as you like, and if I do not perform your tasks, do with me what you will." The count reflected for some minutes, and then said, "Well, then, in the first place, thou shalt steal the horse I keep for my own riding, out of the stable; in the next, thou shalt steal the sheet from beneath the bodies of my wife and myself when we are asleep, without our observing it, and the wedding-ring of my wife as well; thirdly and lastly, thou shalt steal away out of the church, the parson and clerk. Mark what I am saying, for thy life depends on it."

The master-thief went to the nearest town; there he bought the clothes of an old peasant woman, and put them on. Then he stained his face brown, and painted wrinkles on it as well, so that no one could have recognized him. Then he filled a small cask with old Hungary wine in which was mixed a powerful sleeping-drink. He put the cask in a basket, which he took on his back, and walked with slow and tottering steps to the count's castle. It was already dark when he arrived. He sat down on a stone in the court-yard and began to cough, like an asthmatic old woman, and to rub his hands as if he were cold. In front of the door of the stable some soldiers were lying round a fire; one of them observed the woman, and called out to her, "Come nearer, old mother, and warm thyself beside us. After all, thou hast no bed for the night, and must take one where thou canst find it." The old woman tottered up to them, begged them to lift the basket from her back, and sat down beside them at the fire. "What hast thou got in thy little cask, old lady?" asked one. "A good mouthful of wine," she answered. "I live by trade, for money and fair words I am quite ready to let you have a glass." "Let us have it here, then," said the soldier, and when he had tasted one glass he said, "When wine is good, I like another glass," and had another poured out for himself, and the rest followed his example. "Hallo, comrades," cried one of them to those who were in the stable, "here is an old goody who has wine that is as old as herself; take a draught, it will warm your stomachs far better than our fire." The old woman carried her cask into the stable. One of the soldiers had seated himself on the saddled riding-horse, another held its bridle in his hand, a third had laid hold of its tail. She poured out as much as they wanted until the spring ran dry. It was not long before the bridle fell from the hand of the one, and he fell down and began to snore, the other left hold of the tail, lay down and snored still louder. The one who was sitting in the saddle, did remain sitting, but bent his head almost down to the horse's neck, and slept and blew with his mouth like the bellows of a forge. The soldiers outside had already been asleep for a long time, and were lying on the ground motionless, as if dead. When the master-thief saw that he had succeeded, he gave the first a rope in his hand instead of the bridle, and the other who had been holding the tail, a wisp of straw, but what was he to do with the one who was sitting on the horse's back? He did not want to throw him down, for he might have awakened and have uttered a cry. He had a good idea, he unbuckled the girths of the saddle, tied a couple of ropes which were hanging to a ring on the wall fast to the saddle, and drew the sleeping rider up into the air on it, then he twisted the rope round the posts, and made it fast. He soon unloosed the horse from the chain, but if he had ridden over the stony pavement of the yard they would have heard the noise in the castle. So he wrapped the horse's hoofs in old rags, led him carefully out, leapt upon him, and galloped off.

When day broke, the master galloped to the castle on the stolen horse. The count had just got up, and was looking out of the window. "Good morning, Sir Count," he cried to him, "here is the horse, which I have got safely out of the stable! Just look, how beautifully your soldiers are lying there sleeping; and if you will but go into the stable, you will see how comfortable your watchers have made it for themselves." The count could not help laughing, then he said, "For once thou hast succeeded, but things won't go so well the second time, and I warn thee that if thou comest before me as a thief, I will handle thee as I would a thief." When the countess went to bed that night, she closed her hand with the wedding-ring tightly together, and the count said, "All the doors are locked and bolted, I will keep awake and wait for the thief, but if he gets in by the window, I will shoot him." The master-thief, however, went in the dark to the gallows, cut a poor sinner who was hanging there down from the halter, and carried him on his back to the castle. Then he set a ladder up to the bedroom, put the dead body on his shoulders, and began to climb up. When he had got so high that the head of the dead man showed at the window, the count, who was watching in his bed, fired a pistol at him, and immediately the master let the poor sinner fall down, and hid himself in one corner. The night was sufficiently lighted by the moon, for the master to see distinctly how the count got out of the window on to the ladder, came down, carried the dead body into the garden, and began to dig a hole in which to lay it. "Now," thought the thief, "the favourable moment has come," stole nimbly out of his corner, and climbed up the ladder straight into the countess's bedroom. "Dear wife," he began in the count's voice, "the thief is dead, but, after all, he is my godson, and has been more of a scape-grace than a villain. I will not put him to open shame; besides, I am sorry for the parents. I will bury him myself before daybreak, in the garden that the thing may not be known, so give me the sheet, I will wrap up the body in it, and bury him under a tree and no one will know." The countess gave him the sheet. "I tell you what," continued the thief, "I have a fit of magnanimity on me, give me the ring too—the unhappy man risked his life for it, so he may take it with him into his grave." She would not gainsay the count, and although she did it unwillingly she drew the ring from her finger, and gave it to him. The thief made off with both these things, and reached home safely before the count in the garden had finished his work of burying.

What a long face the count made when the master came next morning, and brought him the sheet and the ring. "Art thou a wizard?" said he, "Who has fetched thee out of the grave in which I myself laid thee, and brought thee to life again?" "You did not bury me," said the thief, "but the poor sinner on the gallows," and he told him exactly how everything had happened, and the count was forced to own to him that he was a clever, crafty thief. "But thou hast not reached the end yet," he added, "thou hast still to perform the third task, and if thou dost not succeed in that, all is of no use." The master smiled and returned no answer.

When night had fallen he went with a long sack on his back, a bundle under his arms, and a lantern in his hand to the village-church. After this he put on a long black garment that looked like a monk's cowl, and stuck a gray beard on his chin. When at last he was quite unrecognizable, he took the sack and the lighted lantern, went into the church, and ascended the pulpit. The clock in the tower was just striking twelve; when the last stroke had sounded, he cried with a loud and piercing voice, "Hearken, sinful men, the end of all things has come! The last day is at hand! Hearken! Hearken! Whosoever wishes to go to heaven with me must creep into the sack. I am Peter, who opens and shuts the gate of heaven. Into the sack! The world is ending!" The cry echoed through the whole village. The parson and clerk who lived nearest to the church, heard it first, and when they saw the lights which were moving about the churchyard, they observed that something unusual was going on, and went into the church. They listened to the sermon for a while, and then the clerk nudged the parson and said, "It would not be amiss if we were to use the opportunity together, and before the dawning of the last day, find an easy way of getting to heaven." "To tell the truth," answered the parson, "that is what I myself have been thinking, so if you are inclined, we will set out on our way." "Yes," answered the clerk, "but you, the pastor, have the precedence, I will follow." So the parson went first, and ascended the pulpit where the master opened his sack. The parson crept in first, and then the clerk. The master immediately tied up the sack tightly, seized it by the middle, and dragged it down the pulpit-steps, and whenever the heads of the two fools bumped against the steps, he cried, "We are going over the mountains." Then he drew them through the village in the same way, and when they were passing through puddles, he cried, "Now we are going through wet clouds." And when at last he was dragging them up the steps of the castle, he cried, "Now we are on the steps of heaven, and will soon be in the outer court." When he had got to the top, he pushed the sack into the pigeon-house, and when the pigeons fluttered about, he said, "Hark how glad the angels are, and how they are flapping their wings!" Then he bolted the door upon them, and went away.

Next morning he went to the count, and told him that he had performed the third task also, and had carried the parson and clerk out of the church. "Where hast thou left them?" asked the lord. "They are lying upstairs in a sack in the pigeon-house, and imagine that they are in heaven." The count went up himself, and convinced himself that the master had told the truth. When he had delivered the parson and clerk from their captivity, he said, "Thou art an arch-thief, and hast won thy wager. For once thou escapest with a whole skin, but see that thou leavest my land, for if ever thou settest foot on it again, thou shalt not escape punishment." The master-thief took leave of his parents, once more went forth into the wide world, and no one has ever heard of him since.

DOVER · THRIFT · EDITIONS

FICTION

FLATLAND: A ROMANCE OF MANY DIMENSIONS, Edwin A. Abbott. 96pp. 0-486-27263-X

SHORT STORIES, Louisa May Alcott. 64pp. 0-486-29063-8

WINESBURG, OHIO, Sherwood Anderson. 160pp. 0-486-28269-4

PERSUASION, Jane Austen. 224pp. 0-486-29555-9

PRIDE AND PREJUDICE, Jane Austen. 272pp. 0-486-28473-5

SENSE AND SENSIBILITY, Jane Austen. 272pp. 0-486-29049-2

LOOKING BACKWARD, Edward Bellamy. 160pp. 0-486-29038-7

BEOWULF, Beowulf (trans. by R. K. Gordon). 64pp. 0-486-27264-8

CIVIL WAR STORIES, Ambrose Bierce. 128pp. 0-486-28038-1

WUTHERING HEIGHTS, Emily Brontë. 256pp. 0-486-29256-8

THE THIRTY-NINE STEPS, John Buchan. 96pp. 0-486-28201-5

TARZAN OF THE APES, Edgar Rice Burroughs. 224pp. (Not available in Europe or United Kingdom.) 0-486-29570-2

ALICE'S ADVENTURES IN WONDERLAND, Lewis Carroll. 96pp. 0-486-27543-4

THROUGH THE LOOKING-GLASS, Lewis Carroll. 128pp. 0-486-40878-7

MY ÁNTONIA, Willa Cather. 176pp. 0-486-28240-6

O PIONEERS!, Willa Cather. 128pp. 0-486-27785-2

FIVE GREAT SHORT STORIES, Anton Chekhov. 96pp. 0-486-26463-7

TALES OF CONJURE AND THE COLOR LINE, Charles Waddell Chesnutt. 128pp. 0-486-40426-9

FAVORITE FATHER BROWN STORIES, G. K. Chesterton. 96pp. 0-486-27545-0

THE AWAKENING, Kate Chopin. 128pp. 0-486-27786-0

A PAIR OF SILK STOCKINGS AND OTHER STORIES, Kate Chopin. 64pp. 0-486-29264-9

HEART OF DARKNESS, Joseph Conrad. 80pp. 0-486-26464-5

LORD JIM, Joseph Conrad. 256pp. 0-486-40650-4

THE SECRET SHARER AND OTHER STORIES, Joseph Conrad. 128pp. 0-486-27546-9

THE "LITTLE REGIMENT" AND OTHER CIVIL WAR STORIES, Stephen Crane. 80pp. 0-486-29557-5

THE OPEN BOAT AND OTHER STORIES, Stephen Crane. 128pp. 0-486-27547-7

THE RED BADGE OF COURAGE, Stephen Crane. 112pp. 0-486-26465-3

MOLL FLANDERS, Daniel Defoe. 256pp. 0-486-29093-X

ROBINSON CRUSOE, Daniel Defoe. 288pp. 0-486-40427-7

A CHRISTMAS CAROL, Charles Dickens. 80pp. 0-486-26865-9

THE CRICKET ON THE HEARTH AND OTHER CHRISTMAS STORIES, Charles Dickens. 128pp. 0-486-28039-X

A TALE OF TWO CITIES, Charles Dickens. 304pp. 0-486-40651-2

THE DOUBLE, Fyodor Dostoyevsky. 128pp. 0-486-29572-9

THE GAMBLER, Fyodor Dostoyevsky. 112pp. 0-486-29081-6

NOTES FROM THE UNDERGROUND, Fyodor Dostoyevsky. 96pp. 0-486-27053-X

THE ADVENTURE OF THE DANCING MEN AND OTHER STORIES, Sir Arthur Conan Doyle. 80pp. 0-486-29558-3

THE HOUND OF THE BASKERVILLES, Arthur Conan Doyle. 128pp. 0-486-28214-7

THE LOST WORLD, Arthur Conan Doyle. 176pp. 0-486-40060-3

DOVER · THRIFT · EDITIONS

FICTION

THE QUEEN OF SPADES AND OTHER STORIES, Alexander Pushkin. 128pp. 0-486-28054-3
THE STORY OF AN AFRICAN FARM, Olive Schreiner. 256pp. 0-486-40165-0
FRANKENSTEIN, Mary Shelley. 176pp. 0-486-28211-2
THE JUNGLE, Upton Sinclair. 320pp. (Available in U.S. only.) 0-486-41923-1
THREE LIVES, Gertrude Stein. 176pp. (Available in U.S. only.) 0-486-28059-4
THE BODY SNATCHER AND OTHER TALES, Robert Louis Stevenson. 80pp. 0-486-41924-X
THE STRANGE CASE OF DR. JEKYLL AND MR. HYDE, Robert Louis Stevenson. 64pp. 0-486-26688-5
TREASURE ISLAND, Robert Louis Stevenson. 160pp. 0-486-27559-0
GULLIVER'S TRAVELS, Jonathan Swift. 240pp. 0-486-29273-8
THE KREUTZER SONATA AND OTHER SHORT STORIES, Leo Tolstoy. 144pp. 0-486-27805-0
THE WARDEN, Anthony Trollope. 176pp. 0-486-40076-X
FATHERS AND SONS, Ivan Turgenev. 176pp. 0-486-0073-5
ADVENTURES OF HUCKLEBERRY FINN, Mark Twain. 224pp. 0-486-28061-6
THE ADVENTURES OF TOM SAWYER, Mark Twain. 192pp. 0-486-40077-8
THE MYSTERIOUS STRANGER AND OTHER STORIES, Mark Twain. 128pp. 0-486-27069-6
HUMOROUS STORIES AND SKETCHES, Mark Twain. 80pp. 0-486-29279-7
AROUND THE WORLD IN EIGHTY DAYS, Jules Verne. 160pp. 0-486-41111-7
CANDIDE, Voltaire (François-Marie Arouet). 112pp. 0-486-26689-3
GREAT SHORT STORIES BY AMERICAN WOMEN, Candace Ward (ed.). 192pp. 0-486-28776-9
"THE COUNTRY OF THE BLIND" AND OTHER SCIENCE-FICTION STORIES, H. G. Wells. 160pp. (Not available in Europe or United Kingdom.) 0-486-29569-9
THE ISLAND OF DR. MOREAU, H. G. Wells. 112pp. (Not available in Europe or United Kingdom.) 0-486-29027-1
THE INVISIBLE MAN, H. G. Wells. 112pp. (Not available in Europe or United Kingdom.) 0-486-27071-8
THE TIME MACHINE, H. G. Wells. 80pp. (Not available in Europe or United Kingdom.) 0-486-28472-7
THE WAR OF THE WORLDS, H. G. Wells. 160pp. (Not available in Europe or United Kingdom.) 0-486-29506-0
ETHAN FROME, Edith Wharton. 96pp. 0-486-26690-7
SHORT STORIES, Edith Wharton. 128pp. 0-486-28235-X
THE AGE OF INNOCENCE, Edith Wharton. 288pp. 0-486-29803-5
THE PICTURE OF DORIAN GRAY, Oscar Wilde. 192pp. 0-486-27807-7
JACOB'S ROOM, Virginia Woolf. 144pp. (Not available in Europe or United Kingdom.) 0-486-40109-X
MONDAY OR TUESDAY: Eight Stories, Virginia Woolf. 64pp. (Not available in Europe or United Kingdom.) 0-486-29453-6

NONFICTION

POETICS, Aristotle. 64pp. 0-486-29577-X
POLITICS, Aristotle. 368pp. 0-486-41424-8
NICOMACHEAN ETHICS, Aristotle. 256pp. 0-486-40096-4
MEDITATIONS, Marcus Aurelius. 128pp. 0-486-29823-X
THE LAND OF LITTLE RAIN, Mary Austin. 96pp. 0-486-29037-9
THE DEVIL'S DICTIONARY, Ambrose Bierce. 144pp. 0-486-27542-6
THE ANALECTS, Confucius. 128pp. 0-486-28484-0
CONFESSIONS OF AN ENGLISH OPIUM EATER, Thomas De Quincey. 80pp. 0-486-28742-4
THE SOULS OF BLACK FOLK, W. E. B. Du Bois. 176pp. 0-486-28041-1

DOVER · THRIFT · EDITIONS

PLAYS

LIFE IS A DREAM, Pedro Calderón de la Barca. 96pp. 0-486-42124-4
H. M. S. PINAFORE, William Schwenck Gilbert. 64pp. 0-486-41114-1
THE MIKADO, William Schwenck Gilbert. 64pp. 0-486-27268-0
SHE STOOPS TO CONQUER, Oliver Goldsmith. 80pp. 0-486-26867-5
THE LOWER DEPTHS, Maxim Gorky. 80pp. 0-486-41115-X
A DOLL'S HOUSE, Henrik Ibsen. 80pp. 0-486-27062-9
GHOSTS, Henrik Ibsen. 64pp. 0-486-29852-3
HEDDA GABLER, Henrik Ibsen. 80pp. 0-486-26469-6
PEER GYNT, Henrik Ibsen. 144pp. 0-486-42686-6
THE WILD DUCK, Henrik Ibsen. 96pp. 0-486-41116-8
VOLPONE, Ben Jonson. 112pp. 0-486-28049-7
DR. FAUSTUS, Christopher Marlowe. 64pp. 0-486-28208-2
TAMBURLAINE, Christopher Marlowe. 128pp. 0-486-42125-2
THE IMAGINARY INVALID, Molière. 96pp. 0-486-43789-2
THE MISANTHROPE, Molière. 64pp. 0-486-27065-3
RIGHT YOU ARE, IF YOU THINK YOU ARE, Luigi Pirandello. 64pp. (Not available in Europe or United Kingdom.) 0-486-29576-1
SIX CHARACTERS IN SEARCH OF AN AUTHOR, Luigi Pirandello. 64pp. (Not available in Europe or United Kingdom.) 0-486-29992-9
PHÈDRE, Jean Racine. 64pp. 0-486-41927-4
HANDS AROUND, Arthur Schnitzler. 64pp. 0-486-28724-6
ANTONY AND CLEOPATRA, William Shakespeare. 128pp. 0-486-40062-X
AS YOU LIKE IT, William Shakespeare. 80pp. 0-486-40432-3
HAMLET, William Shakespeare. 128pp. 0-486-27278-8
HENRY IV, William Shakespeare. 96pp. 0-486-29584-2
JULIUS CAESAR, William Shakespeare. 80pp. 0-486-26876-4
KING LEAR, William Shakespeare. 112pp. 0-486-28058-6
LOVE'S LABOUR'S LOST, William Shakespeare. 64pp. 0-486-41929-0
MACBETH, William Shakespeare. 96pp. 0-486-27802-6
MEASURE FOR MEASURE, William Shakespeare. 96pp. 0-486-40889-2
THE MERCHANT OF VENICE, William Shakespeare. 96pp. 0-486-28492-1
A MIDSUMMER NIGHT'S DREAM, William Shakespeare. 80pp. 0-486-27067-X
MUCH ADO ABOUT NOTHING, William Shakespeare. 80pp. 0-486-28272-4
OTHELLO, William Shakespeare. 112pp. 0-486-29097-2
RICHARD III, William Shakespeare. 112pp. 0-486-28747-5
ROMEO AND JULIET, William Shakespeare. 96pp. 0-486-27557-4
THE TAMING OF THE SHREW, William Shakespeare. 96pp. 0-486-29765-9
THE TEMPEST, William Shakespeare. 96pp. 0-486-40658-X
TWELFTH NIGHT; OR, WHAT YOU WILL, William Shakespeare. 80pp. 0-486-29290-8
ARMS AND THE MAN, George Bernard Shaw. 80pp. (Not available in Europe or United Kingdom.) 0-486-26476-9
HEARTBREAK HOUSE, George Bernard Shaw. 128pp. (Not available in Europe or United Kingdom.) 0-486-29291-6
PYGMALION, George Bernard Shaw. 96pp. (Available in U.S. only.) 0-486-28222-8
THE RIVALS, Richard Brinsley Sheridan. 96pp. 0-486-40433-1
THE SCHOOL FOR SCANDAL, Richard Brinsley Sheridan. 96pp. 0-486-26687-7
ANTIGONE, Sophocles. 64pp. 0-486-27804-2
OEDIPUS AT COLONUS, Sophocles. 64pp. 0-486-40659-8
OEDIPUS REX, Sophocles. 64pp. 0-486-26877-2

DOVER · THRIFT · EDITIONS

PLAYS

ELECTRA, Sophocles. 64pp. 0-486-28482-4

MISS JULIE, August Strindberg. 64pp. 0-486-27281-8

THE PLAYBOY OF THE WESTERN WORLD AND RIDERS TO THE SEA, J. M. Synge. 80pp. 0-486-27562-0

THE DUCHESS OF MALFI, John Webster. 96pp. 0-486-40660-1

THE IMPORTANCE OF BEING EARNEST, Oscar Wilde. 64pp. 0-486-26478-5

LADY WINDERMERE'S FAN, Oscar Wilde. 64pp. 0-486-40078-6

BOXED SETS

FAVORITE JANE AUSTEN NOVELS: *Pride and Prejudice*, *Sense and Sensibility* and *Persuasion* (Complete and Unabridged), Jane Austen. 800pp. 0-486-29748-9

BEST WORKS OF MARK TWAIN: Four Books, Dover. 624pp. 0-486-40226-6

EIGHT GREAT GREEK TRAGEDIES: Six Books, Dover. 480pp. 0-486-40203-7

FIVE GREAT ENGLISH ROMANTIC POETS, Dover. 496pp. 0-486-27893-X

GREAT AFRICAN-AMERICAN WRITERS: Seven Books, Dover. 704pp. 0-486-29995-3

GREAT WOMEN POETS: 4 Complete Books, Dover. 256pp. (Available in U.S. only.) 0-486-28388-7

MASTERPIECES OF RUSSIAN LITERATURE: Seven Books, Dover. 880pp. 0-486-40665-2

SIX GREAT AMERICAN POETS: Poems by Poe, Dickinson, Whitman, Longfellow, Frost, and Millay, Dover. 512pp. (Available in U.S. only.) 0-486-27425-X

FAVORITE NOVELS AND STORIES: Four Complete Books, Jack London. 568pp. 0-486-42216-X

FIVE GREAT SCIENCE FICTION NOVELS, H. G. Wells. 640pp. 0-486-43978-X

FIVE GREAT PLAYS OF SHAKESPEARE, Dover. 496pp. 0-486-27892-1

TWELVE PLAYS BY SHAKESPEARE, William Shakespeare. 1,173pp. 0-486-44336-1